The Dead Sh

Booklocker.com, Inc.
2002

The Dead Shall Inherit The Earth

Vince Churchill

To everyone who believed in me.

Prologue

He pressed the gun to his face, a feeble attempt to ease the throbbing ache of his closed, swollen eye. The weapon's cool metal dispensed little relief. A variety of wounds stung and ached, staining his skin and his tattered uniform with blood. His body had curled into the shape of a question mark in the middle of the floor, his one good eye staring at the locked cabin door, his functioning hand clutching the force pistol in a white-knuckle grip. His eye shifted and he noticed the pistol was trembling. His other gnarled set of fingers were pressed into his chest as if the contact close to his heart would some how draw away the pain and mend the ravaged flesh and shattered bone. As he examined the useless wreck of his right hand, he hissed his pain and anguish. There was no time to reflect on the beating he had taken at the hands of his infected crewmates. Hell, even if he was able to survive the current situation, odds were he was infected too. But first things first---he needed to get to his computer. The way this mission had played out, any message he left would sound like a suicide note. And whatever he decided to write, he'd address it to his brother.

Christopher Gale squirmed across the floor until he was at the foot of his bed, clenching his teeth to keep from crying out. Pushing through the agonizing bursts of pain from what felt like shards of broken glass where his ribs were, he propped himself to a slumped, half-seated position. As he caught his breath, he realized how much punishment he had endured. His white Star Corp officer's uniform was ripped and ragged, splattered in a variety of both wet and dry bloodstains. The majority of the blood was his, but there were contributions from many parties. Knife slashes crisscrossed his upper body, most of the cuts superficial. It hadn't been until they had held him down and poured liquor on him that the wounds had really screamed out. His left eye was totally closed, dark and swollen like a ripe tomato. Its aching throb matched the beat of his heart, and he prayed there wasn't permanent damage to his eye. He was having trouble breathing through his nose, which was still oozing thick, black blood. He sniffled and a sharp, fresh pain sliced up into his skull. He couldn't help but laugh, though it manifested itself as a painful cough. Better not do that again, he

vii

thought. Groaning, he wasn't sure which wound had caused it. He'd sit for a couple more minutes, then work his way over to the computer. He lifted his head and glanced at his desk. The way his ribs were feeling, it might as well be miles away. He took a moment and let his good eye close, allowing recent events to wash over his mind.

His ship, the Star Corp cruiser Merlin, had received encrypted orders from earth's World Government to proceed with all available speed and caution to Avaric, an outworld earth colony set up as a mineral/resource planet. Though initial details were minimal, it was clear there was some type of biological outbreak endangering the colony. More information was made available to the ranking officers aboard when they had arrived and established an orbit.

The situation was determined as a Level Two outbreak stemming from a yet unidentified viral source. Their mission orders were simple: transport the surviving research team and their equipment back to earth and keep them quarantined. The research team was to continue to spearhead the medical containment of the outbreak from the Merlin. Also detailed was that the Merlin, until other Star Corp vessels could be re-routed, was to establish a "no fly zone" for all spacecraft attempting to leave the colony. Any vessel ignoring the planetary quarantine was to be destroyed before leaving orbital space. Officers had balked, wondering out loud why ships were to be shot down during a Level Two alert. The authorization for martial law, under the World Government charter, was reserved for Level Three situations, such as declared war and medical outbreaks of potentially devastating magnitudes. The Merlin's commanding officer, Captain Hopkins, had responded with a communiqué for verification of the level status of the mission, and moments later the orders were verified by both the Secretary of World Defense and the Commissioner of World Health and Safety at the New York headquarters.

The mission was set into motion, a portion of the hanger bay/hold area established as temporary lab space. But the mission was a disaster from the start. Officers had been initially advised that the research team had numbered thirty, with two members of the team infected. When the Merlin arrived three days later, the colony was in chaos. The local council and civil security force were at the point of announcing their own martial law with a sunset to sunrise curfew. And more alarmingly, nearly a third of the research team was infected with the unidentified agent. The first two researchers infected were now dead, carried onto the ship in black body bags. A brooding, fearful anxiety vibrated throughout the Merlin crew. In an attempt to quell suspicion and simmering fear, Dr. Stan Connors, the head of the colony research group, released a statement to the Merlin officers. The memo stated that they were on the verge of discovering the exact nature of the viral agent, which would put them on a fast track to an antidote. They had fashioned a test for infection and he confirmed that the remaining members in his unit were healthy and uninfected. He had hoped to have good news regarding the outbreak within 48 to 72 hours...

Christopher took a deep breath, easing it out slowly, a flare of pain and anger surging through his body. His mind fought the pain, refusing to let it master him. Instead, his thoughts continued replaying the recent chain of events.

Dr. Connors had lied and the Merlin officers should have been more cautious. Connors and his team, in their own desperation to escape the colony, contaminated the Merlin despite the safety precautions. In less than 24 hours, numerous Merlin crewmen began to develop the flu-like early symptoms that lead from delusional high fevers to a comatose state. The extreme fever would literally boil the victim's brain, causing madness and violent psychosis. The weaker of those infected died during this period, but the stronger of the carriers awoke from their comas and attempted to act out violent impulses to themselves and others.

Christopher thought about his attempt to stop a young female ensign from flaying her own arm with a cutlery knife. He had gagged at the sight of what she had done to herself. One arm had been flayed; flaps of bloody skin hanging like a torn sleeve from a pale white blouse. She had started on her other arm, the blade skinning the flesh of her forearm with grotesque ease. She was in a feverish trance, mumbling under her breath, trembling. Her short brown hair was plastered to her sweat slicked face and her eyes were red rimmed and badly bloodshot. Christopher had winced at both the mutilation and her mad, rambling gibberish. He tried to wrestle the knife from her, reluctant to touch the raw, glistening wound of her arm. Unfortunately, by hesitating in his contact with her, he was punished with a few slashes in the process. Most of the cuts were shallow, but a couple would need stitches to avoid ugly scars. It took all his strength to disarm her, and he heard the crack of her wrist bone in the process. Screaming like a banshee, she acted like a mother whose child had been snatched from her arms. As the brief struggle ended, without thinking, he slapped her across the face. For a moment her eyes cleared, the veil of madness lifting. She blinked several times, straining to focus, perhaps struggling to understand, if just for an instant, what was happening to her. But then the fever clouded her mind like a blood soaked fog, and Christopher watched as her expression changed back from stunned, idle-minded confusion to bloodthirsty madness. From what he could see, whatever humanity left inside her had been completely eaten away. She roared, her body trembling. He backed away as she clawed her sweat-slicked face, gouging deep, bloody grooves. When her nails reached her lower lip, Christopher twisted away from the sight, staggering as her tormented shriek pierced the air. Something wet and sticky glanced off the back of his neck, and he barked out a curse, wiping at it, disgusted. He hadn't stopped to look at what it was or even if it had come from her.

Moments later he was knocked to the floor, blindsided by a crazed, naked man he recognized from the Merlin's medical staff. The man had carved several crosses on his arms and upper torso, some still fresh and blooding. Christopher caught a look at the crude slices as the man, rolling on top of him, began to flail punches. The naked man was like an animal, wild-eyed and slobbering at the mouth, mumbling something about 'for the love of Christ' over and over, as if reciting the lyrics to a song. As he struggled with the man, Christopher realized the lunatic had managed to carve crosses on his face, the one on his forehead looking more like an X than a T. Suddenly, someone else started kicking Christopher, battering his midsection as he fought in vain to get the man off him. He was suddenly splashed with liquor, his nose catching the familiar scent of scotch as his wounds screamed with the contact. Even with the pain-fed surge in strength, Christopher could not dislodge his attacker. Whatever delusion the Cross Man was caught up in, his madness gave him strength far beyond his slight, sunken-chest build. Christopher strained to keep the man at bay, growing desperate to escape to the safety of his cabin. Then, feeling as though it was only a matter of time before the Cross Man overwhelmed him, his mind forgot Star Corp rules and regulations. He no longer thought about maintaining himself as an officer and a gentleman. He ceased to be First Lieutenant Christopher Samuel Gale, commissioned and decorated officer in the Star Corporation Military Division. He was now just a man desperate to survive, and his mind began to reject all the training he'd received over the years. The Corp never prepared him for a possibility as unbelievable and morally corrupt as the hellish chaos around him. As he stared up into the crazed, blood red eyes, his instincts took over. His hand frantically sought and found the force pistol strapped along his right thigh. Without another thought, he jammed the pistol under the chin of his attacker and cried out in rage and grief as the man's head exploded in a shower of bony shards, brain and blood. He pushed himself away from the body, his attention on his still twitching attacker. Christopher then became aware of the Cross Man's splattered blood on his face. Using his sleeve, he smeared it around more than wiping it off, cursing in frustration and disgust. Just as he started to push himself to his feet, he received a stunning kick to the face, the crunch of his nose just another sound mixing into the symphony of death and violence playing at a deafening level all around him. Staggering to his feet, head still ringing, he stumbled toward the safety of his cabin.

During his retreat he was forced to struggle through a large melee completely blocking a major corridor artery. Attempting to dodge his way through, he tripped and fell hard to the floor. Momentarily shaken, his arm was pinned to the floor and his hand crushed by a series of vicious blows from the butt of a force rifle. He cried out, and as quick as the attack began it ended. His vision blurred by hot tears of pain, he dragged himself, half crawling, from the hellish battle around him.

Some time later he found himself slumped just outside his cabin and he managed to unlock his door and pull himself inside. He tried to use his wrist communicator, but there was no response. It might have been broken during his earlier fall, or when his hand was smashed, but with the current situation, someone might have disabled the communications network. If he was going to survive, he'd have to do it alone...And here he was, half beaten to death, the dizzying pain in his midsection maybe more than just smashed ribs, the sand in his hourglass of life steadily draining away. If he was going to do something, anything, this was the time. Sitting still wasn't going to help him. It was time to get moving.

Christopher needed to reach a senior officer to see if any steps had been implemented to regain order. He glanced across the room at his workstation and the built-in flat screen computer. As he reached out his gun hand to pull himself toward the desk, the cabin light dimmed once, then twice, then faded out completely. Anxiously his eyes moved about the now darkened room, his mind becoming aware that the only light was from his computer screen saver. His head turned toward the locked door. He could hear muffled voices in the corridor, perhaps coming in the direction of his cabin. Yes, they were definitely getting closer. A feeling of dread took root in the pit of his stomach as he continued to work his body painfully toward the computer.

As he reached for the desk's edge to pull himself up, his fear was realized as voices and movement came from just outside his quarters. He bit his tongue to keep quiet, using his arm to balance as he pushed to his feet. His ribs kept him doubled at the waist, but there was no time to waste. He activated his computer, pausing to gather his thoughts.

There was a soft, dainty knock at his door, accompanied by a quiet evil giggle. The giggle stopped as if a switch had been flipped off, and Christopher couldn't help but stare across at the shadowed door. As he turned back to the computer, his eyes flickered to the photo holograph displayed on his nightstand. He took a moment and looked at the picture of himself with his older brother Jefferson. Christopher thought about what his brother would do if he were here, and he couldn't stop the grin that tugged at the corner of his mouth. He looked down at his gun. He knew that if Jefferson thought he was hell bound, he'd take out as many of the enemy as he could. But it was too difficult to think of his infected crew as his enemies. His real adversary was that damned virus, and it had him outnumbered, billions to one. As another series of soft rapping sounded, Christopher used his good hand to start typing.

Two minutes later he tried to ignore the pounding and threatening shrieks outside his door, concentrating on the two fingers working the keyboard. He was out of time and he knew that his life could now be measured in seconds. With a pair of final jabs he saved the brief message, wincing at the jagged agony his damaged ribs caused. Sudden dead silence outside his door caused him to grab up his pistol.

Christopher was caught staring into the shadows when the explosion tore the door from its slide frame. Instinctively he tossed himself toward the bed, pain erupting from his bad hand and ribs as he struck the floor. Without thinking he was firing his weapon as deranged crewman flowed, whooping and screaming, through the smoky darkness. He actually shot two or three of them as they were momentarily disoriented, searching for the wounded officer. But it only took one brutal kick to his midsection for him to forget he even had a gun in his hand. A second kick made him clench into an agonized ball.

Someone tore the gun from his hand and then he was kicked a third time in the small of his back. He cried out, his body arching with the continued assault. Even with his one good eye open, he was blinded by tiny red and silver flashes, pain exploding in a sparkling brilliance that would have been breathtakingly beautiful had it not signaled the approach of his death.

Strong fingers snatched his head up by the hair. Blinking away the colors, he focused on the face of a man whose eyes were as feral as any wounded animal in the wild. The man's other hand welded a knife, his bloodstained fingers curled through the metal eyelets of the hilt. Christopher watched as a solitary drop of blood fell from the blade's edge to the floor. The rich crimson reminded him of the rose he had given to his mom last Mother's Day. She had hugged him so tight, tears in her eyes about the rose and his absence during a lengthy, deep space tour of duty. Her hair had smelled of---

He grunted as he was lifted slightly higher, his scalp screaming in protest. Pain forced the last thought of his mother out of his mind. The man leaned in close as if he were going to kiss him. His captor might have been handsome before the virus had ravaged his body, but it was hard to tell. His skin was pulled taunt to the muscle and bone, a symptom of those affected. Most of the surviving victims looked like the man he was face to face with: extreme bloodshot eyes staring out from an unnaturally tight skin mask. The vampire-like eyes alone would have held Christopher's attention until the grotesque necklace swung away from the man's chest. Christopher moaned in disbelief, closing his eye at the sight of the crudely severed ears strung one after another. There must have been a dozen of the things, ragged and bloody. The sight was beyond anything that his mind and stomach could cope with. Something deep inside him shattered into a thousand pieces. He retched, but nothing came up, and his injured ribs tightened like razor wire. But the sight of the ears disconnected him from his ravaged body. For the first time in hours, Christopher Gale felt no pain at all.

"You tell me where the antidote for the bug is and I'll do you quick." The man whispered the words to Christopher though he could feel the smattering of spit flying from the angry man's mouth. The Ear Man's breath was as hot as a desert wind and smelled of blood and a sour stomach. Christopher could only stare at the ears, a tear welling up in his good eye. Slowly, he was able to pull his attention away from the obscenities, and look into the faces surrounding him. The Ear Man's eyes darted around at the others, his mouth splitting into a malignant smile. The infected men and women crowded around Christopher, held in check only by the presence of the Ear Man. Most were carrying knives or broken pieces of furniture and seemed ready to descend upon him like locusts. One woman, dark blood smeared over her naked torso, was staring into Christopher's eyes with an intensity that caused him to swallow. The nipples of her bare breasts were taut, and an image so vivid struck him with such power he almost cried out and begged for his life. The way she was staring at his eyes wasn't from some unleashed primal lust. She craved his eyes, like some others in the pack wanted to break his bones, or others wanted to taste his hot blood straight from his veins. She wanted his eyes, whether to pop in her mouth and munch like grapes or just to put in her pocket like a rabbit's foot. Or maybe she just wanted to feel them ooze between her fingers when she crushed them in her fist.

The Ear Man finally turned his attention back to Christopher with a grin that would have looked perfect on a snake. "Maybe you didn't hear me, sir." He cackled at his own joke, only sparse laughter joining in. The knife blade slid closer, becoming blurry in Christopher's limited sight.

Christopher's last act as an officer and a gentleman was to spit into the man's leering face.

An instant later the Ear Man's knife blurred, slicing the officer's throat from ear to ear. Blood sprayed the air like a fountain. Christopher hardly struggled as his life drained away. The Ear Man tossed the dying officer aside and waved a hand absently in the air. His crazed followers fell on top of the bleeding, dying man like a ravenous pack of wolves, ripping and hacking, wallowing in the bloody heap of remains that quickly could no longer be recognized as human.

Christopher Gale was well beyond suffering when the various trophies were taken from his body. The Ear Man casually added to his collection, using his knife to slice and puncture. Then he laced up the newest additions, dangling the bloody necklace in front of himself, the pieces of flesh twirling slightly. He admired the severed ears like an owner of priceless art, a mad glee in his eye. It was nearly a minute later that he hung his hunting trophies back around his neck. He could feel the strength of his many victims flowing like fire through his veins. He drifted out of the cabin, the other deranged crew people straggling behind. The Ear Man turned down the hallway, the flickering ceiling lights causing an eerie strobe effect, making the sight of their movements jittery and strange. He headed toward the suite of the ship's captain with the same cancerous smile plastered on his face, content to continue the search for the antidote, and so much more fun...

She cried.

Face tear-streaked, her emerald eyes stared at nothing. Dark circles hung below those eyes, and her complexion was sickly pale. She lay on the crisp white sheets, hugging herself into a tight, fetal ball. Her eyes took in none of the stark white interior of her room, as clean and sterile as its color. The room had only a single bed, a small dresser, and the built-in toilet and sink. Only the shiny metal sink and her rose red hair weren't white. Her white hospital gown and slippers completed the lack of color, and with the twin suns shining unchecked through the double pane window, the room was almost blinding. The stabbing pain in her chest had gradually eased to just a tightness, but with every beat her heart ached. She had come out of her shock unable to get beyond what she had found at her family's home. Just the thought made her stomach clench like a fist. It was still too fresh. She tried to push away the black thoughts and close her eyes, searching for some memory to help her escape the nightmare of her life. But even with her eyes closed, the specter of death taunted and teased her. And like a dam suddenly grown weak then collapsing, the ugly memories washed through her. It was almost as overwhelming as the day she stood screaming in her parent's home...

She stood motionless in a doorway off the main corridor that led to the hospital's loading dock, staring blankly as motorized carts, loaded with plastic shrouded bodies, rolled by her. The drivers of the carts, like her, looked like space walkers in their self-contained biohazard suits, hardly seeming human anymore. She looked into their face shields as they went by, but they all focused straight ahead, expressionless, concentrating on the unsavory business at hand. The carts were not designed to maneuver within hospital corridors, but there was no other way to move the dead out of the hospital more efficiently. They were headed for the medical center's swimming pool, which had been converted into a large liquid crematorium. Standard outbreak procedures deemed acid to be the most efficient and thorough method of disposal. Along the way she was stopped several times, teams of bio-suited men moving from room to room and floor to floor loading bodies. She was numb and exhausted from a double 12-hour shift. With an epidemic of such proportions, the medical staff was overwhelmed. Some of the staff hadn't left the hospital since the outbreak. The laboratory technicians had the continuous burden of research and testing to keep them temporarily housed in the medical center, but plenty of doctors and nurses felt the hospital was the safest place to be. She had been determined to get out and visit her family, giving herself a break from the stress, chaos and suffering. The outbreak's devastating effects had repercussions far beyond what she had studied at university.

Communication to the outskirts of the colony had been disrupted almost two days ago, so she hadn't been able to just check in with her family. Martial law had been declared shortly after the outbreak, so she expected to be stopped several times along the way. She had her hospital I.D. hung around her neck for ready examination. Her mind froze for a moment, recent events surging, forcing her sincere acknowledgement. She had witnessed such an overwhelming amount of pain and suffering that part of her had simply shut down, no longer capable of absorbing any more misery.

Her boyfriend Richard had been a member of the security team at the government bio-research facility when the outbreak occurred. They had been seeing each other casually for a couple of months, and had slept together. He was easygoing with a boyish smile, his skin deeply tanned from hiking in the desert outlands. He was athletic with slim hips and lean muscles, and he snorted when he laughed. Tammara sighed, staring as she watched the men drop another body onto the growing pile on the cart. The men seemed more like garbage collectors than hospital orderlies or police. There was nothing delicate or gentle about the handling of the bodies. The workers simply grabbed and tossed, occasionally arranging the pile to avoid bodies sliding off during transport. She suddenly realized Richard had received the same treatment as the rest of these poor souls. She hadn't even been there to help prepare his body, or just to say goodbye. There were no funerals, no last rites given, though she had seen someone in a bio-suit out by the acid. Perhaps that had been a priest. She stared hard into the pile of corpses, but the plastic prevented her from clearly seeing the faces. The outbreak had changed colonists she had seen regularly at the trading post or the theatre or at the recreation center into infectious waste, wrapped not in plastic, but human skin.

Richard had been one of the earliest victims, and over the two days he was studied, she watched her lover evolve into a crazed animal. The doctors couldn't control his mercurial fever, and, after a period of violent psychosis, his brain finally stopped functioning. He died in isolation, restrained in an empty padded cell in the psych ward, drooling and snapping like a rabid dog. His death had been a relief. Tammara still had trouble believing it had even been him near the end. The doctors explained to her that once Richard had emerged from the brief fever induced coma, he was probably never conscious of any of his actions, the constant high temperature having caused severe brain damage. As a medical professional, the explanation was matter-a-fact and very acceptable. As a woman, it was very difficult to deal with the fact that the man who had made heartfelt, passionate love to you just days before was now spewing vile profanity and making such obscene movements that it disgusted you to look at him. During one visit she had caught him masturbating with such ferocity she thought he might injure himself. Walking away she couldn't tell if his cries were of pleasure or agony. And despite what the doctors had told her, the one thought she could not dismiss was if he was thinking of her while he did it.

Feeling a tear roll down her cheek, she knew she had to get away before she ended up in Richard's old room. When the last of the carts passed, she followed them outside, thankful her suit would keep the stench at bay. Soon death would become a second skin she would never be able to shed.

The gentle touch on her cheek jolted her, her eyes bursting open, wide and frightened. Her sudden reaction caused the startled nurse to stumble back. Chest heaving, Tammara frantically searched the hospital room, fear blinding her. As her sight returned she was able to focus on the nurse. She relaxed, her body easing back to the bed. Tammara barely recognized the comforting whispers of her friend Lydia but didn't flinch away when her hair has softly stroked. She closed her eyes again, using the quiet tones of her friend as a comforting blanket, soon falling into a restless, gray half-sleep.

PHASE 1

The World Government was in a precarious situation. Naturally, Avaric was immediately quarantined after the outbreak on the Merlin. But a very real problem remained: what to do with the colony survivors and the remaining deceased? Cremation pits were being used on the colony but there were bodies that were being salvaged for autopsies and research. Star Corp was delaying the assignment of more vessels because of the unacceptably high risk of viral transmission and infection. Star Corp already had a trio of battle cruisers patrolling the space around the planet, though the ships were at a maximum distance to ensure crew safety while still maintaining control of Avaric airspace. Orders had already been given to the colony that any attempts to leave the planet would be met with immediate termination force. There had been confirmation of five small crafts destroyed within 24 hours of the order. All had passenger loads far beyond the specs of their ships, and all the vessels ignored the war cruiser warnings and the opportunity to return to the planet. A missionary priest assigned to Avaric had piloted one of the ships. The craft carried himself and 47 children between the ages of 7 months and 12 years old. The press was given no details on that matter and the government had every intention of keeping that tragedy "an internal matter".

Overwhelming opposition prevented the government from dispatching another ship to have direct contact with the colony. Discussions of using robotic instruments and disposal androids had been shelved when details were leaked to powerful human rights organizations. Their contention was that the Avaric colony, once a vital mineral resource base for Earth, now deserved attention and assistance from the real human beings they once helped to support. The only action agreed upon so far was the conversion of an Earth orbiting space station into a research laboratory to deal with the virus and prepare for a possible future outbreak on Earth. It was also agreed that no Avaric colonists were to be allowed back on Earth for a period of one year, or until the organism had been isolated, researched and a cure had been found. And like the colonists on Avaric, there was still the issue of what to do with the Merlin and her crew of nearly 500.

Official communication with the ship had ceased over 3 days before, though reports noted some type of antiquated, makeshift code had been received from the Merlin for nearly a day after mainline ship communication had failed. It was rumored to have been Morse code, repeating a simple SOS signal over and over until it too stopped. The top authorities of Star Corp was now referring to the Merlin as a dead ship, but resisted having it destroyed because of the research data aboard.

1

The colony received supplies in automated cargo shuttles programmed for one-way transfers while the government seemed to be getting no closer to a solid plan of action.

The people of Earth demanded that the Avaric disaster be handled at once. Families of colonists publicly denounced the World Government as cowards and tyrants. Lawsuits were being threatened. And somehow the issue of the plague devastating Earth was becoming secondary amidst all the sympathetic uproar.

The people cried out for the government to do its duty to the colony.

The government was paralyzed with no clear, acceptable course of action.

It was a time ripe for heroes.

Eleven days after the Avaric disaster, mid-way through a sunny Friday morning, a World Government limo transport parked outside a small, inconspicuous industrial complex. The moment the transport stopped moving, the driver sprang out and scurried around the lengthy black vehicle to open the rear passenger side door. The occupant wasted no time in getting out. The gentleman was tall and gaunt, his black suit hanging from his bony frame. In his eighties, World Government Representative Conrad Whittington had the weathered face of a lifelong cowboy, deep lines around his eyes and mouth. His chalk white hair was thin and straight pulled back into a short ponytail. The paleness of his hair was exaggerated against the red, ruddy skin of his face, which seemed not to burn or tan from the sun.

He moved with quick, steady strides, entering the building well ahead of his assigned personal protector, whose massive muscular bulk made exiting the transport difficult. Whittington heard his bodyguard call out to him, demanding him to wait, but the elderly Texan ignored the plea, a mischievous grin tugging at his lips. As he strode across the main floor lobby, Whittington was looking forward to meeting the man who just might hand him the World Government Presidency in the next election. He smiled with the thought, proud of the plan he had engineered to resolve the Avaric crisis and launch his campaign with the title of Avaric's savior.

With an elevator waiting for him, he did not wait for the huge, lumbering man cursing on the outside walkway. It was currently not a good time to be a member of the World Government, all high-ranking Government officials having been assigned protection if they didn't have it already. Fringe fanatical groups were always in search of ways to promote their crazy causes, and several representatives had been threatened. Whittington actually preferred the comfort of the small laser holstered under his suit coat to the trained ape stumbling around behind him. For God's sake---if his bodyguard couldn't keep up with an eighty-year-old man, what good was he?

The elevator took him smoothly to the top floor, the sixth, and after stepping out of the lift, he found himself in another world. It was as if he had stepped into the middle of dense, tropical forest.

There were no visible walls, ceiling or floor. He was standing in thick, emerald green grass, surrounded by lush green vegetation. There was just enough light piercing the jungle growth to show him a path, but not enough to easily read a book.

He took one very hesitant step forward.

As he did so the jungle seemed to come alive, strange smells and exotic animal sounds smothering him. His eyes darted back and forth, suddenly nervous, already having forgotten he had just been in an elevator. From the bushes to his left, he imagined rather than saw something slithering toward him, something that sensed his warm, soft flesh as meat. He thought about the laser holstered under his jacket, but when a soft, dangerous hiss reached his ears, he found himself paralyzed. The muscles of his arm would not respond to his mental command to draw his weapon. He could only stare wide-eyed into the thick growth, expecting a beast to spring out at him, venom dripping from its fangs as it lunged with blinding speed at his throat...

"Please follow the path, Mr. Whittington." The feather soft voice startled him so much he jumped, and then flushed, realizing someone must have been observing his silly antics. But even as he followed the path, he couldn't help but be impressed by the realistic environ. It certainly had him going.

It only took him several paces to see a clearing ahead, and he increased his pace to reach it and put the jungle behind him. In the clearing the atmosphere lightened, though the actual decor changed little.

There were actually globe lights hanging just below the vegetation covered ceiling, and to his right a very attractive woman sat behind an impressive chrome and glass desk. It was impossible for him not to notice her long, shapely legs, and reluctantly he forced himself to meet her eyes. Whittington was not disappointed. The receptionist was an exotic beauty, obviously statuesque despite sitting. She had a stunning Eurasian look, with a smooth, creamy complexion and slightly almond shaped eyes. Her hair was thick and wavy, the color of molasses, pulled back into a ponytail whose length fell well down her back. He would have loved to have seen that beautiful hair fanned out over a satin pillow... She was dressed in a black skirt and a light colored, silky blouse, her small, firm breasts pressed slightly under the soft material. As his eyes settled on hers, he flashed his well rehearsed politician's smile.

"Representative Conrad Whittington with an appointment to see Jefferson Gale."

Her eyes sparkled as her smile lit up the room. She pressed a button on her desk and spoke, her eyes never leaving the man. "Jefferson, Mr.Whittington is here." A man's voice replied, but Whittington couldn't tell where it originated.

"Show him in, Maggie." She nodded, turning as she rose from her chair. Whittington enjoyed the moment, but was startled to see a nasty scar running from just behind her left ear down her shoulder. The scar disappeared under the collar of her blouse and immediately Whittington wondered how far it extended. From what he could see, the scar's impression in her skin looked as though she had been attacked by something with a tentacle. And then, as he took a step to follow, a thought struck him: why in heaven hadn't she had the scar removed? She walked to the right of her desk a few steps, then a section of the jungle parted, granting entrance to a spacious office. As he smiled and stepped past her, she whispered, "Some soldiers don't want their scars removed." The statement startled him, but he recovered quickly enough to give her the tiniest nod. At that moment he had never wanted to see a woman unclothed more than he wanted to see her.

Whittington stepped into a large, plant filled, but more normal looking office, his shoes leaving grass for dark, thick carpeting. The entire rear wall of the office was Plexiglas offering a beautiful view of the San Gabriel Mountains. Two steps inside, the doors closed with a soft hiss, and he watched Jefferson Gale get to his feet. The Representative couldn't take his eyes off the black man's arms. Head freshly shaved, Gale was dressed casually in denims and a tight short-sleeved black shirt, looking every bit the super soldier described in the files Whittington and his staff had researched. When Gale used his arms to push himself to his feet, the veins running over the top of Gale's massive biceps looked like big worms resting just under the skin. There was a distinct tattoo on each of his muscular arms, and Whittington recognized the symbols from the military. On his right arm, starting at the space just inside his thumb, a vivid, black inked strand of barbed wire crept up the light brown skin of his arm. The creation was so realistic Whittington flinched, almost expecting blood to flow. It circled Gale's forearm and bicep like a living thing, disappearing under the form fitting black shirt. The other tattoo was a single word drawn in gothic style. In bold blood red, it read KILLER. Along his left forearm was a long, badly healed scar, the new skin pale and soft looking. As he stepped around the desk, Whittington reached his hand out in greeting, forcing his eyes to meet those of the ex-Star Corp Commander. He was again momentarily startled as he looked into shark black eyes, and he had to fight to keep eye contact. He had never been so intimidated. From the moment he stepped off the elevator, he had felt like he was trespassing on sacred, ancient burial ground or unknown enemy territory. He could feel his nerves rolling and twisting his stomach. Gale's handshake was dry and firm, and Whittington was grateful that the ex-soldier didn't squeeze too hard. Most of the macho, ex-military types seemed to take sadistic pleasure in grinding the hand bones of other, non-military men. It was a display of physical superiority Gale, for obvious reasons, didn't bother with.

"Nice to meet you, Representative Whittington. I think I heard your name once or twice when I was in the Corp. Make yourself comfortable." Even with that simple statement, Gale projected himself as a man who was used to giving orders. Whittington, despite his anxiety, knew he had chosen the right man. Gale offered either of the two chairs in front of his tidy oak desk.

"Thank you, Mr. Gale. May I call you Jefferson?"

Gale moved back around the desk, sitting and putting his legs up on the desk's edge. He smiled. "Sure." Whittington took a moment and looked around the office, which, though far from the jungle surroundings of the outer office, had a significant amount of exotic foliage. Some of it looked a bit too exotic. Gale must have noticed. "Don't worry Representative, I had all the plant life cleared through either Star Corp or Planetary customs. I have paperwork on file for everything I've brought back from missions."

Whittington fake smile relaxed and his natural smile began to peek through. "Your jungle environ is very realistic."

Gale nodded, wearing his own tiny smile. "Maggie liked the jungle from a salvage mission we went on a while back, so we recreated it. And it's great for hiding our sensors and security." Whittington felt Gale's eyes boring into him, and it made him feel more than a little uncomfortable. "For instance, we're aware of the small laser you're packing, and the hardware on your bodyguard. I normally don't allow weapons in our offices, but with your current situation, we excused it."

Whittington's eyes dropped away from Gale's for a moment, glancing over the broad desk. "So, what would you like to discuss with me?" Whittington cleared his throat, returning his gaze to Gale. Before he could speak, the deep growling voice of his bodyguard could be heard from the outer lobby. Gale lowered his feet to the floor and stood, his eyes appearing to stare through the closed doorway. He glanced at Whittington.

"Your bodyguard?" Gale asked quietly.

5

Sighing, Whittington nodded. "Yes, it's Albert. Please allow me to handle this." He got to his feet.

Gale's voice was barely a whisper.

"Door open."

The doorway opened and before Whittington could take a step, his hulking protector stormed in. Albert's face was red, and his breathing was heavy. His glare was so focused on Whittington he didn't seem to notice Gale. Maggie, obviously upset, had followed the bodyguard into the office, her full attention locked on Albert. Whittington's eyes slid from Albert to Maggie and the Representative could feel the tension in the room, the kind of energy that made the fine, baby hairs on the back of his neck stand up. The situation was ripe for violence, and surprisingly, Whittington sensed it as strongly from Maggie as he did from Albert.

Albert stepped right up to Whittington, dwarfing the politician by sheer mass. Unnaturally wide and thickly built, Albert stood over two meters high. His photo would have been appropriate in the dictionary next to the word intimidation. His scarlet, moon shaped face inches from Whittington's, the bodyguard bellowed.

"Jesus Christ, sir! I wish you would allow me to do my fracking job!"

Whittington stared back into the man's eyes, the politician's jaw muscles flexing under the skin. He did not step back one centimeter.

"Albert, you're dismissed. You can wait for me down at the transport."

The brute stood his ground looking like he wanted to spit into his client's face. "Those aren't my orders, sir." Albert spoke the word 'sir' like he was looking at a steaming heap of shit with whipped cream on top. With that, Gale moved from around the desk.

"Excuse me. Albert?" For the first time, the bodyguard looked fully at Gale, and his eyes flashed both recognition and malice. Looking directly into his face, a corner of Gale's mouth started to smile but stopped. "I know you. From a free-form fighting tournament in the Corp" Gale took another step forward. "I beat you in the finals. You got hacked off and accidentally hit the referee when you went after the judges." Gale allowed himself to smile for an instant, then let the smile slip away. "But you were all human then, right?"

Maggie was still staring at Albert and she spoke up before the bodyguard could answer. "Should I take out the garbage, Jefferson?" Albert turned slowly to face her, his mouth split into an ugly grin. It was as if he didn't know how to smile and this was practice. He needed more.

"Oh, I wish you would tussle with me, lady. I always enjoy a woman who likes a little pain with her pleasure." Despite the taunt, Maggie continued to be focused and ready, shifting herself to a side stance to give Albert a tougher target.

Gale took another step forward, nodding toward his coordinator. "He's been tampered with, Maggie." Gale looked into Albert's eyes. "What is it---Gorilla?"

Albert looked at Gale, amused. "Good guess. Rottweiler." He nodded at Gale. "By the looks of your arms I would say you have some ape in you, brownie."

Gale stared at Albert for a moment, then glanced at Maggie. Gale looked her full in the eyes. "I know you could, but I'll take care of this." Maggie hesitated, then returned to her desk, the doors closing behind her. Gale's eyes then bored into the mutant's. "This is private property, and if Mr. Whittington doesn't want you here, I'll have to ask you to leave." Gale's expression was unreadable, as was his tone. Albert glared, stepping past the Representative. His motions reminded Whittington of a monster bull eyeing a matador.

"This is none of your fucking business, brownie. Don't make me prove how bad my bite is." His jaws flexed and he gave Gale a glimpse of his upper and lower incisors. At his back, Whittington raised his voice.

"Do as I've ordered, Albert."

In a mocking tone, though his expression was blank, Gale spoke. "Yes Albert, do as you're *ordered*." Gale smiled warmly, like he was looking at a baby. "You're being a very bad doggie." Albert smiled, his mouth crowded with teeth that belonged more to a shark than a dog. He was either too aggressive or just too stupid not to take the bait.

"You sure you don't want your secretary to take care of me?"

Gale stared into the bodyguard's eyes. "Oh, I'm sure there's a long list of women you've built your reputation on, Albert. But trust me, you don't want her. She'll fight back. Hard." Gale moved a step closer. "Not like your daughter, who couldn't stop you from bouncing on her night after night." Albert's face burst into a darker shade of scarlet, fury making his body tremble. Albert literally sprayed spit as he responded.

"That was a fuckin' lie that bitch made up during the divorce. I never touched my little girl!"

Gale replied coolly with a simple question. "So... how did your twelve year old get pregnant?" The taunting question hung in the air like the putrid perfume from an open sewer. Albert's whole body shook like a volcano ready to erupt. His nostrils flared, the veins in his neck strained under the skin, his eyes narrowed to slits. Chest heaving, he shrugged out of his suit coat, Albert's eyes burning with boundless hate.

"All right, hero. I'm gonna do you like every stray that could pick up your momma's scent." The bodyguard lumbered forward, his thick fingers balling into meaty fists, jaws snapping. Gale couldn't stop a smile from spreading over his face. Whittington stumbled out of the way quickly. Albert actually looked like a bull preparing to charge, his muscles coiling and bunching, straining his white dress shirt. And with surprising agility, Albert attacked.

Gale's eyes never left Albert's. Gale stepped forward into the man's quick, powerful punch. The blow slid over his left shoulder, and in a blurred motion, Gale grabbed the wrist with his left hand, then hooked his right arm under Albert's extended one. In the instant just before Gale completed his movement, a flash of astonishment and fear passed through Albert's eyes. With a sharp jerk, Gale broke the man's arm at the elbow, the crack of the bone like a gunshot. Before he could even cry out, Gale gracefully sidestepped and delivered a crunching side kick into Albert's knee, toppling the massive bodyguard like a domino, his arm flopping. Albert hit the ground hard, instinctively attempting to break his fall with his snapped arm. A second bone, his wrist, snapped on impact with the floor. Albert hit the carpet shrieking like an unfed baby. Gale's footwork danced him behind the downed man, and Gale looked like he was inspecting a nasty stain on the rug. The soft hiss of the doorway caused him to half look over his shoulder at a satisfied looking Maggie.

"You always have all the fun," she grinned, eyeing the defeated chaperone.

"Call a medi-transport for Albert."

"One's already on the way."

Whittington's mouth was hanging slightly open. The Representative's eyes were on his bodyguard, who was in obvious pain. His eyes slowly rolled up to Gale. Gale returned casually to his seat behind the desk. The ex-Star Corp Commander's demeanor hadn't appeared to change. "No wonder you pack a laser with protection that limp. Maggie could have handled him---no problem." Whittington's mouth started to move, but Gale cut him off. "Don't be fooled by Maggie's appearance. She is currently training with me for martial art Ph.D. testing. And her legs are as deadly as they look, believe me." Whittington looked back down at the whimpering hulk, Albert's arm bent at a grotesque angle. Shattered bone was straining under the now bloody cloth of his shirt. Whittington couldn't imagine the pain Albert was experiencing, but after another couple of moments, he looked away from his bodyguard, no longer caring. He had business to take care of. Gale looked over his desk at the big man. "Are you sure the government didn't want something bad to happen to you?" Albert looked up at Gale with watery, pain-filled eyes, his lips moving in silent curses. Gale shook his head, partly in disgust and partly in warning. The genetically enhanced protector lowered his eyes, gritting his teeth and grunting against the waves of pain washing through him.

Whittington resettled himself in his chair, still in awe of Gale's brutal skills. He had been briefed on Gale's combat proficiency, but he was still impressed, considering Gale had left active duty over three years ago. Gale had made Albert Tragin, an ex-Secret Service operative and highly regarded personal protector look like a drunken accountant. Whittington looked back down at his bodyguard for a long moment, bending from his chair to quietly console his ex-protector. After a few moments, Gale's voice broke the quiet of the room. "Is this visit concerning Avaric?" Without turning to face him, Whittington gave the barest of nods.

After the medical-transport left with Albert, Whittington, feeling anxious, couldn't resist asking what was on his mind. "Did you have to hurt him so badly?"

Gale's shark eyes stared into the older man's.

"Yes." Gale's flat line voice revealed little emotion. If anything, he sounded a little bored. Whittington didn't answer, hoping for more of an answer, forcing Gale to elaborate. "Men like Albert have very long memories. When he's healing up and going through rehab, I don't want him even thinking about payback. Hopefully I hurt him bad enough that he'll think long and hard about making any trouble for me or Maggie." The Representative still felt uneasy. "If he had gotten his hands on me, he would have hurt me just as badly, if not worse." Whittington blinked quickly a couple of times, the last statement getting through. He slowly nodded his agreement.

"You're right. He might have beaten you to death. Since his enhancement, Albert's strength is superhuman." The worry drained from Whittington, and in a few moments he had relaxed enough to issue a little smile. "I apologize, Mr. Gale. I think I was just taken aback by the, uh, situation. And I certainly apologize for Albert's rude actions."

Gale nodded his acceptance, an uneasy silence hanging in the air while Whittington gathered his thoughts. Gale finally prompted him. "There was some urgent business you wanted to discuss...?"

Whittington cleared his throat. "Well, I'm sure that you're well informed about the Avaric situation."

Gale continued to stare into Whittington's eyes. "Just what I've seen on the televiewer." Gale's answer caught him a bit off guard.

"Hmmm, well I'm sure you're aware of the government's precarious position concerning the colony. Extremist groups are using Avaric to promote their anti-government agendas, and the media is having a field day." Gale seemed ready to smile, but didn't. "The government has to take immediate action, and that's why I'm here. I have casually discussed a plan of action with some of my fellow representatives, and there is a possibility that the World Government could offer you and your paramilitary corporation a very lucrative contract, not including specialized equipment and ship modifications the government would provide for you..."

"For us," Gale interrupted, "to go to Avaric for you." Whittington nodded. It looked like Gale tried to fight back a grin, but failed, the eerie one appearing causing a cold shiver to crawl up Whittington's spine. Jefferson Gale was turning out to be as odd as the research had indicated. Gale suddenly turned toward a large tropical plant behind his desk, his attention diverted as if the plant had spoken to him. The Omni Incorporated CEO spoke softly, admiring the plant in a way that didn't ease the representative's discomfort. "A very intriguing offer, Mr. Whittington. Get me some specifics, and I'll call a staff meeting tomorrow. Does that work for you?" Whittington didn't try to fight back his smile. He was happy with the response and pleased this meeting was ending. He bounced to his feet, removing a brown envelope from a jacket pocket. He took a step and passed it to Gale.

"That's fine. Here are the preliminary mission objectives and parameters. The financial package will be in the range of probably 20 million credits with normal negotiable flexibility." Whittington took a step back, hesitating before continuing to speak. "I'd also like to pass on my condolences regarding your brother Christopher, I..."

Gale was on his feet and facing the representative in the blink of an eye. "What? What about Chris?"

Seeing the dead serious look on Gale's face, Whittington realized Gale really hadn't been informed about the Avaric situation. And this was not a position Whittington wanted to find himself in. He took a deep breath before explaining. "Your brother was serving on the Merlin, which was the first ship assigned to the colony. The outbreak spread to the ship shortly after their arrival. There has been no communication from the Merlin for days, and Star Corp has designated the ship and entire crew dead in space."

Gale stared at the man, the veins in his neck straining. He started to speak, but his head sagged to his chest before the words became sound. Whittington, looking both saddened and uncomfortable, sought to finish the bad news. "The colony has confirmed that no shuttles landed on the planet after the Merlin's arrival, and no communication has been received. We've curtained off the planet, and long range scans show there is still minimum power, but the ship is in a slowly decaying orbit that eventually will send it crashing to the planet."

Whittington glanced down for a moment, and when he looked up, Gale was staring him in the eye.

"But you have no confirmation that the entire crew is dead, correct? There might be crew holed up on board waiting to get rescued, or maybe some escaped on shuttles and didn't go to the planet. Maybe they headed for open space..."

Whittington shrugged, doing his best to avoid theorizing hypothetical situations. "It's possible there might be survivors, but highly unlikely. There has been absolutely no communication from the ship for days. If someone had escaped by shuttle, even if they steered clear of Avaric, we'd have heard word by now, from them or some other ship spotting them. And with the data we received from the lab and hospital at the colony, both the infection and fatality percentages were running extremely high. With the closed environment on the ship, an outbreak would have devastating results." Whittington's gaze didn't waver, and he hardly flinched when Gale began slamming his fist down onto the desk. Maggie burst into the room, moving directly to Gale. She glanced at Whittington, then quietly whispered to Gale, gently steering his arms away from the desk. Distraught, Gale blurted out his brother's name, slumping to a knee, pulling Maggie down with him. She hugged him to her, and he crushed her against him, his strong arms squeezing a gasp from her. She just let him hang on, glancing up again at Whittington. The representative nodded respectfully, then turned and quietly left, Jefferson Gale's quiet sobs echoing off his back. Once he stepped outside the building, Whittington's mortician smile replaced his politically practiced concerned expression, a look he had perfected over the years. Whittington was even more confident Gale and his Omni Incorporated crew would accept the assignment because of the bad news he had passed on. Gale was not the kind of man that would dismiss an opportunity to play hero, and he certainly wasn't about to leave his brother, dead or miraculously still alive, drifting out in space. Whittington clapped his hands together as he ducked into the rear of his transport. Whittington had read all their background files, and was fully aware of each team member's superlative military record. Jefferson Gale and his Omni team were not to be underestimated by any means, but even a super soldier like Gale was still only a man. Flesh and blood. Mortal. And that meant he could be killed like any other man.

The plans of the aspiring next President of Earth were falling into place.

Later in the afternoon, the doors to Gale's office slid apart and Maggie entered, her face lit with her usual smile. Gale, who had been looking dreamily out into the blue sky, turned to face his corporate assistant. Maggie DeLina was

11

a beautiful woman. She was tall, nearly six foot, with a slim, tawny body. Her muscles were taut and lean, yet she retained total femininity. Her smile was contagious, and like most men, he couldn't resist it. She stepped in front of his desk, her eye contact strong and direct.

"I've been able to reach everyone about tomorrow's meeting, and we're set. I've got Kurt and Lauren on the line now. They're still in Rio. Kurt wants to speak with you." Gale's smile evaporated, and his expression hardened. He sucked in a deep breath through his nose, then let it out slowly. Without breaking their eye contact, Gale activated his desktop view screen and spoke.

"Gale." There was a pause, light static in the connection.

"Jefferson? This is Kurt. What's going on with this emergency meeting?" Gale eyes slid from Maggie's down to the screen, which showed a muscular, bare chested man lying casually on a free-form lounger. Kurt was well built, with short wavy brown hair. A tiny silver Saint Christopher medal hung around his neck. It was Kurt's good luck charm. Lauren was not in the immediate view.

"Where's Lauren?" Gale's tone was flat.

"She's enjoying the spa. What's up?" Gale's black eyes bore into the screen.

"Kurt, trust me. Be here tomorrow." Gale's voice had an underlying tone of irritation. "Did Maggie tell you the time?" Kurt propped himself up in the lounger, his expression a mixture of frustration, anger and curiosity.

"Yeah, she told me the damn time, but wha-"

"See you tomorrow, Kurt," Gale cut in. He broke off the connection. Looking back up at Maggie, he could see her smile had disappeared. She paused before deciding to speak, concern creeping into her tone.

"I know you want to keep the subject of the meeting under wraps, but do you really think its necessary pulling Kurt and Lauren off a vacation halfway around the world? I can't believe that you couldn't have been a bit more understanding. Couldn't we just conference them in?" Maggie seemed to struggle to keep her eyes locked on his. There were times when Gale's eyes appeared bottomless, and this was one of them. After a stretch of unanswered silence, she spoke again. "Jefferson, you're the best boss I've ever had. You have always been there for me, and the others. But I'm worried. You've changed. You haven't been the same since Pandora." Gale chuckled without the slightest bit of good humor.

"Yeah, I was really there for everyone when they needed me. I'm sure if Ted, Ursala or Grace were here, they might have a different opinion." He stared hard at Maggie for a moment more, then turned his chair to enjoy the view. He couldn't stop the venomous sarcasm invading his voice. "But, damn, they aren't here 'cause they're dead. Gee, sorry about that."

Gale could feel Maggie's eyes burning his back, and in a moment she stepped between him and the huge picture window. Her face was a mask of anger and frustration.

"I'm not even going to go through all the frap about guilt and responsibility. You aren't the only one who needed help to get through what happened there. We lost three close friends on that mission, Jefferson. And they all died horrible, senseless deaths. There's nothing we can do about it now, and there was nothing you could have done about it then." She leaned in close. He could smell the fragrance she wore, the mint of her breath, the cleanliness of her hair. And he knew better than for even a moment to let his eyes flicker away from her angry stare to glimpse her hardened nipples pressing through the thin material of her blouse. Gale took her seriously. "Grace is gone, Jefferson. She's been gone for over a year. No matter how much you punish yourself, she is never coming back. You have to find a way to get past what happened." The only response he gave was a blink or two. "Damn you, Jefferson! You're a soldier. You've been to war. People die. Get over it!" Maggie screamed, her face turning a light shade of scarlet. They stared at each other in silence, Gale reaching up and softly running his fingertips over the scar on her neck.

"I'll get over it when everyone else does." His fingers traced the scar under the collar of her blouse to just above her heart. Her eyes didn't leave his, even as they moistened. "Go home Maggie. I'll lock up." Somehow, she mustered up a smile, covering his hand with hers. She leaned and kissed him on the cheek, and he let his eyes close for a moment, letting the sensation of her soft, full lips warm his soul. Slowly, she pulled away from him. For an instant it felt as if they were making love and he was forced to withdraw from her. As she walked silently from his office, Gale felt his chest tighten, not sure it was his missing Grace or discovering something else.

He pushed the thought aside, closing his eyes and trying to revive the already lost feeling of Maggie's kiss.

Tammara laid on her hospital bed, her knees hugged to her chest, staring out the window into the harsh glare of Avaric's twin suns, her mind drifting, the sedative in her bloodstream easing. As her mind cleared, her thoughts returned to the shock that had her sedated and under observation in the small psychiatric wing of the hospital. Gazing out, the memories seeped back. She tried to push

13

them away, but it was like trying to fight fog. In her mind the horror began, and even when she squeezed her eyes closed, she saw it anyway...

Tammara had only passed a handful of vehicles on the twelve-mile trip out to her parents house, and like herself, all the drivers were clad in protective suits. She had decided to keep hers on for the visit until she could check her family for any preliminary symptoms. And she knew that the constant contact with the victims put her at a much higher risk for infection than her isolated family. So she'd wear the suit around them until a reliable test could be established.

The twin suns were at their usual blinding strength, and unfortunately she had been in such a hurry leaving the hospital she hadn't put on her sunglasses before securing her helmet. She had to fight the suns' intense blue-white shine the whole way, on a few occasions cupping her hand over her face shield to see the road clearly.

It was strange driving through the colony. The city looked abandoned, people having just picked up and walked away, stepping out of their lives like they'd shed work clothes at the end of a day. The truth caused her to shiver. Some colonists were barricaded in their homes, hoping to wait out the epidemic, praying for a cure. Many others had headed for the vast desert west of the colony counting on the extreme temperatures and the fresh air to give them a better chance at survival. In reality, the colony appeared like a graveyard because it had become one. There were no signs of normal colony life. The few citizens she saw weren't regular people. They were bio-suited security men, armed and patrolling for psychotic viral carriers. It occurred to her she had not seen a person outside the hospital not wearing a bio-suit for days. And as she neared the family home, she realized that she hadn't seen a dog or cat, living or dead, anywhere along the way. Though that might have happened countless times before, the lack of any semblance of normalcy magnified every odd detail, adding to the lifeless, ominous atmosphere.

Near her family home, she had stopped at a nearly deserted supplier to pick up some food, and wasn't even asked for her credit disk. Her face shield muffled her thank you, and the clerk just smiled wearily and waved her through the checkout to the exit. Her eyes dropped to her items, and she hurried out, his early symptoms obvious to her. As far as she could tell, she was the only customer in the store, and she could feel the weight of his feverish stare. Did he even realize he was dying? Had the virus already begun to cook his brain? The man had been extremely pale and was sweating profusely, which meant the fever was at work. Tammara could only hope the young man didn't suffer too long. But they all did.

She drove; the few people she saw scurrying from shelter to shelter as if the virus was a roving pack of wild animals. Just a couple of blocks from the house, she was halted by an armed Avaric security man, some activity in the middle of the road a short distance away. She displayed her hospital ID, looking past the security at what was going on. In the middle of what just days before had been a quiet neighborhood on the edge of the colony, a security team, weapons drawn, had surrounded a crawling woman. Tammara watched the woman, wrapped in a dirty house robe, her head hanging to almost scrape the pavement, her movements shaky. The woman also held a large kitchen knife in a white knuckled fist. Tammara listened as one of the security team members ordered her to drop the knife, but the woman wasn't responding, continuing to move slowly on her hands and knees. She finally raised her head, and Tammara could see her contorted features. Caused by extreme pain or a psychotic episode, her teeth were clenched, bloody spit drooling from her chin to the ground. As she gathered herself to try and stand, the security members backed away, raising their high-powered rifles in anticipation. The woman seemed completely focused on the security person who had spoken, trembling as she raised the knife over her head. The infected woman shrieked, darting forward, suicidal in her murderous intent. She seemed oblivious to being surrounded. The security team opened fired before her third step, the countless rounds of exploding projectiles tossing her body around like a kite in a heavy wind, bloody chunks of her scattering like leaves. Strangely, she never let go of the knife. What was left of her flopped to the ground, the knife still clutched in a death grip. The security team closed in, quickly kicking at her hand until the knife skidded away. The one who had spoken raised a closed fist to the man who had halted Tammara, and he in turn stepped back and waved her through, his face sullen behind the face shield. She couldn't help but stare as she drove by, the bloody corpse staring blankly into the blazing sky, blood everywhere. A few faces dotted the windows of the neighboring houses, but no one emerged from their homes, too shocked, too fearful. Sickened by the violence, necessary or not, she tried to concentrate on seeing her family. Humans were really just advanced animals; monkeys with big brains. Those who believed in a biblical evil knew that the dark side of man and chaos worked hand in hand. She tightened her grip on the steering and struggled to remember a prayer from her childhood. She couldn't recall the beginning, but the phrase that came to her was, 'I pray the Lord my soul to keep.' It was all she could pry from her memory; she'd have ask her mom how it went when she got home.

15

Tammara remembered pulling up in the drive of the large ranch style dwelling, exhausted but relieved. She sat in her vehicle for a long moment, deciding whether or not to disengage the helmet. She decided to take it off. The whole bio-suit appearance was going to upset them anyway, especially her folks. As she got out of the transport, helmet in hand, she unzipped a pocket on the jumper and pulled out her electronic door opener, activating it as she moved toward the house. She pushed the front door and walked in, calling out to her younger brother to get the groceries from her transport. She immediately noticed the shadowy gloom of the house's interior as she stepped into the oven-like heat. It was too hot in the house, even if they had lost the power to run the air conditioning and the lights. Something else struck her odd. There was an unnerving silence answering her entrance. She stopped a few steps into the house, a cold tingle caressing her spine. Without taking another step, she called out again. Silence hung in the air, and a sense of dread washed over her. She slowly turned and took in her surroundings. The entranceway, the living room and the dining room all looked normal with no sign of violence or disturbance. Feeling the shadows reaching out for her, she took a cautious step toward the living room light switch, suddenly conscious of being quiet. Her foot made a soft squishing sound with her second step, and she froze. One of her baby sister's messes, she recalled thinking as she bent down in the gloom, setting her helmet on the floor, curious to see what the puddle was. But as her eyes couldn't immediately identify what she had guessed, she reluctantly reached her gloved fingers to the dark substance. It was sort of thick---was it syrup?---with a slick, smooth feel between her fingers. Slowly, she raised her fingertips to eye level as she stood, focusing hard. There just wasn't enough light to make out the substance, though the next thought that had rushed to her mind caused a horrible dread to stab her insides. She had stumbled to turn on a light, fear making her rushed and clumsy. With a press of a pad, the living room lights came on, and her eyes widened in shock. Slack faced, she looked dumbly at the blood on her glove, her eyes sliding down to the floor. The large puddle, partially dried, was easily the size of a man's chest. A broad smear angled away from the stain toward the closed-off study as if someone had been dragged there. Trembling, her mind racing through countless horrible thoughts in an instant, Tammara franticly wiped her glove on the leg of her bio-suit, moving cautiously on her toes toward the closed double door entrance to her father's study. Her heart was pounding as she checked the display on her electronic opener.

SECURED. USE CODE FOR ENTRY.

She cursed under her breath, not wanting to do what she knew she had to. And that's when she had decided not to go into the room, but instead to contact Avaric security. Her mind flashed to the woman gunned down in the street just minutes ago, but she shook off the thought and made the call, then quietly eased herself outside to wait for their arrival. As she waited in her transport with the doors locked, she stared at the front door of the house, trying in vain not to think the worse.

It didn't take long for the security unit to arrive. Wearing protective ash gray uniforms, four men, three large and muscular and one average sized, spilled quickly from the large 4x4 transport. All four were heavily armed, two of them carrying very impressive rifles. Oxygen fed helmets covered their faces, but when she looked hard into their face shields, she was able to see their eyes. The smallest of the four stepped up to her transport window, and Tammara realized the unit commander was a woman, her blue eyes vivid behind the plastic alloy shield. The three other members moved to the front door but didn't enter, awaiting orders.

Tammara lowered her window, blurting out everything she knew in one breath. The unit commander nodded, then asked her to remain in her transport until they could assess the situation. Tammara nodded, tears blurring her vision as she handed over the door opener and told the lead security person the code to her father's study. The unit commander signaled her team, and they entered one at a time, several seconds between men, the unit commander staying just outside the front door. Tammara could see the woman's lips moving in her helmet, directing the operation. After a couple of minutes, the team leader looked up and over at Tammara, making eye contact for just an instant before joining the others inside. The moments stretched out into a full minute and beyond as she waited to know what had been discovered inside.

Then one of the team burst out of the house, stumbling to his knees in the front lawn. He jerked off his helmet, vomiting violently the moment his face was clear. He fell to all fours, his shoulders heaving as his body continued to expel food. Tammara felt her own stomach jerk, and she fumbled until she unlocked her door and stepped out, moving to help him. She knelt next to the man, his head still down. He looked up at her, wiping at his mouth with his sleeve. He used a hand to clutch at her shoulder, his voice gurgling slightly.

"You don't want to go in there, miss. Wait for Lieutenant Briggs to come back out." The man's head sagged down again, trembling. Tammara's eyes danced between the open front door and the security man, her ears filled with her own heartbeat. She took a deep breath, let it out slowly, then dashed for the door, catching the man off-guard, easily breaking away from his clutching grasp.

Tammara moved quickly into the house, past a startled security team member who was stepping out of the living room. She went straight into the now open study where the lieutenant was examining the bodies. The remaining member of the team was just inside the office doing his best not to look squarely at the desk. Tammara was three steps into the office when her brain registered what she saw, and she could not stop the scream that exploded from her lungs. She couldn't stop her hands flying to cover her face to block the sight, to take the scene from her, to make it not real. But she was still screaming when she uncovered her eyes. Both her parents were still there. Blood everywhere. Dead.

Buzzing flies danced around her mother, who was sprawled on her father's broad, dark wood desk. Her mid section had been ripped open, organs spilled out onto the desk, intestines hanging, dangling to a sloppy pile on the floor. The expression frozen on her mother's face was a mix of startling shock and pain. Her once sparkling brown eyes were now coated in a milky film, her mouth stretched wide in a silent scream. Plump green flies were using the sweet mouth that used to kiss her goodnight as both airstrip and alternative entrance to her insides.

The officer by the door reached for her, urging her to leave the room, his voice sounding slow and distant. Tamara had stepped away from him, her attention shifting to her father, whose body was on the floor, twisted grotesquely from the final painful stage of the infection. She had begun to sob as her mind rejected what was before her. His face and claw-like hands were caked thick with blood, a piece of human flesh hung from his mouth like a dried second tongue. The room had begun to spin at that point, and she reached back for the door, the muscles of her legs failing. She remembered falling but not hitting the floor, the voices around her sounding distorted and far away.

She later bolted to consciousness, screaming and shaking in the rear of a medi-transport, lying across from the bagged bodies of her entire family. At the hospital she was informed of the discovery of her much younger brother and sister, both dead. Authorities had already confirmed the children's identities from family pictures taken from the house, so she would not have to see their bodies, which were in a similar state as her mother's. The thought of her father cannibalizing the family caused her to vomit on the medic, her stomach heaving long after there was anything left to eject. They sedated her and put her in a private room in the psych ward, which kept her out of the frenzied, overflowed general hospital areas. One of her close friends checked in on her from time to time, bringing medical staff food and helping her keep clean...

This time when the memories faded, she cried softly, hugging herself so tight, rocking her body to hurry away the bad thoughts. Her eyes fluttered open and she yelped at the searing sunlight, turning her head away from the window. She felt herself needing to go to the restroom, her insides heavy and thick. She didn't want to leave the bed, to get up, but she did, shuffling to the small water room, her tears drying on her face.

Gale shivered, the cool, early morning breeze wrapping itself around him like the embrace of a wanton lover, passing through his clothes and caressing his skin.

He was at the head of the grave, standing next to the minister. The mourners were many---family and Omni crewmembers forming the closest ring around the open grave. The day had a disinterested grayness; the light wind tossing dead leaves around Gale's feet. It seemed like the minister had been speaking for hours, and Gale hadn't comprehended a single word of the eulogy. He coughed, covering his mouth with a trembling hand. Gale stared into the Plexiglas coffin, drowning in the sight of his dead fiancée's remains. He knew that time was slipping away from him and he was desperate to use every moment to be able to look at her before she was committed to the ground.

Though he saw the paleness of her skin, flawless and creamy, he couldn't forget the image of her the last few moments of her life. Splattered in red. Torn, ugly flesh. The limp, broken doll lifelessness. There had been no last words between them, no dying gasp of his name, no declaration of their love. When he had finally reached her lying so still, she had already been taken from him. Her body had fed a mindless, hellish mutation of plant and animal that had attacked her without mercy, no different than any predator hunting prey. It had not been selective, yet her life had been the only one extinguished.

The memory seemed so unreal now. There had been no war, and the mission they were on had been completed. There had been no perception of danger at all. Her life had simply been taken. As simple as it had been to document, it remained impossible for his heart and mind to accept. Tears ran unchecked down his face, and he began to sob. She still seemed so alive, just lying there resting in the clear burial tube. Her cloud white hair gleamed with plasti-spray, and Gale strained to make out her form under the simple white gown her mother had picked out for her. A part of him wanted to scream out that they were making a mistake---couldn't they see that she was just resting?

But the sane part of his mind just let himself blubber out of control as the final words were spoken.

He vaguely acknowledged the hushed sentiments of family and friends, though he clearly felt the hug of Maggie and her simple "I'm so sorry" whisper. Still in a grief-stricken daze, his eyes focused on the pair of unshaven men in greasy, filthy overalls standing a few graves away. An older, balding man in a black overcoat---was that the funeral home director? --- walked over to them, speaking with the men for a moment before continuing on. Gale watched them look over the gathering, waiting until most of the people had drifted back toward their transports before moving forward to complete their work. One of the men, a short, Hispanic looking man with a bushy mustache and a grubby baseball cap, walked to the opposite end of the grave, crossing himself in the Catholic tradition before sinking his shovel into a dark, rich mound of dirt. The other, a rotund, dark skinned Black man, looked down into the grave, nudging at his work mate, a malignant grin teasing his lips. Gale felt a spark of anger flare deep inside himself, and he took a step toward them, his hands balling into fists. The Hispanic man moved his head slightly toward Gale, and the shameful expression on the Black man's face slid off instantly, and he gave Gale a solemn, almost fearful nod of sympathy and apology before his shovel quickly joined in.

Off to the side he noticed Grace's mother still there, head down in thought, perhaps prayer. She, like Grace, was a petite woman, and she was head to toe in black. Her face was hidden from view by a black hood and shawl, drawn tight to her by the cool weather. She seemed to sense his attention, the hood lifting and turning toward him. Gale wiped at his tear-streaked face as she took a cautious step around the hole. A force seemed to tug at him, and he took an awkward step toward her. As he took another step, he felt a coldness seep inside him. Grace's mother was moving strangely, almost lurching as she continued toward him. He could feel himself trembling as she stopped an arm's length away. The wind suddenly picked up, and the sky darkened for a major storm, clouds rushing by in the sky as if on fast-forward. Strangely, the gravediggers were now gone, nowhere in sight. In fact there was no one around at all as Gale scanned his surroundings. The strong wind was making him squint, and he used a hand to shield his eyes. Strangely, Grace's mother stood strong and motionless in a wind that now threatened his balance. Gale focused, realizing that none of the woman's clothing was even moving, and Gale's eyes could not penetrate the darkness inside her hood. Slowly, and as graceful as if she had been underwater, Gale watched her frail, almost skeletal hand drift up to her hood. The movement seemed to take minutes instead of a moment, and as he stared into the black void where her face should have been, he felt his heart stop beating. The howling wind drowned out the whispers of warning in his mind, and he began to blubber in fear as her hand lingered, ready to pull the hood away. Gale only knew that he didn't want to see what was under it. He knew in his heart that he didn't have the strength to withstand the evil that lived in that darkness. The evil preparing to take his soul to hell...

He felt all his strength drain out into the ground, and he couldn't understand how he was still able to stand. His bladder and bowel released in a hot, searing flush. His mind was teetering on the razor's edge of total insanity, a madness so complete that there could be no return to this reality in a hundred lifetimes.

Her withered hand slowly pulled back the hood, Gale screaming more in anticipation than by what was actually revealed. It was Grace that appeared before him, her beauty untouched by death. Her delicious mouth curved into the smile she would wear when he woke up mornings and found her watching him. It was the same smile that would appear on her face when they talked about their future. It was the same smile she was beaming less than an hour before her death, when her soft lips brushed his ear and whispered that she was carrying his baby...

A giggle like a mentally disturbed child came out of Grace's mouth but the voice wasn't hers. It was deeper and blacker and timelessly old, with an underlying tone so foul a wave of nausea doubled him over. As the apparition stood cackling, the howling wind muted his call for help. Cautiously, Gale's eyes slid from the Grace-thing into the shadowy grave. But it was no longer an empty pit. The grave now appeared to be filled with dark, thickening blood, and his brother Christopher was thrashing and struggling to keep his head above the surface. The bloody liquid seemed to be acting like quicksand, the contents of the grave sucking hungrily at his body. Gale stood rigid, like a wooden soldier, watching helplessly, agonizing as his younger brother fought to reach out to him. Gale was allowed to fall to his knees, fresh tears streaking his face. Just a few feet away, his brother fought a losing battle.

"Jeff, help me! Please---just reach out. You can do it. Please." Gale could only watch, his own cries carried away silently by the wind.

Christopher slipped under the surface for a moment, then burst back out, his face now more angry than frightened. "You lying coward! The big war hero pissing and shitting his pants, too scared to try and save his own brother." The eyes of his brother glowed a hellish red, but Gale couldn't look away. "How does it feel to prosper off the death of others?" The two brothers stared at each other for a long moment, then Christopher's mouth split into a lunatic's smile, and he went under the red liquid, Gale somehow knew it was for the last time. Still on his knees, a heavy rumbling of thunder introduced the cloudburst. Rain crashed into Gale, stinging his face raw with the sudden force. He was instantly soaked, running a hand over his face to wipe both tears and rain away. Holding a trembling hand before his face, he saw the rain was not water but blood, and he stared down at himself. His whole body shook as he slumped to the wet ground, the banshee winds taunting him like hellish laughter, his own cries joining in, creating a symphony of mind shattering madness...

Jefferson Gale bolted to a sitting position, gulping for air as if emerging from a deep pool. Hot, musty sweat plastered the sheet to his muscular torso, his chest heaving from the nightmare. It had been a startling new variation of the recurring nightmare that had tormented him since the Pandora assignment. Gale rattled his head, trying to shake the images so branded into his mind. He stared blankly into the swirling, shadowy darkness of his bedroom, his heart hammering. The image of his brother drowning in a blood-filled grave was not going to leave him for a long time. Sitting in the dark, he couldn't help but think there was a chance his brother was still alive. A couple of minutes passed before the terror and disorientation faded, and he relaxed enough to lie back against his sweat soaked pillow. He lay there, blanketed with a nauseating dread, breathing deeply through his nose as if he were in the weight room. If there was a chance that Christopher was alive, there was only one option. He wiped the sweat from his face, trying to concentrate on slowing his heart rate. After several minutes, he gingerly peeled the wet sheet away and rolled out of bed, the hot, thick stench of urine assaulting him. Like a frightened little boy he had pissed the bed again, the third time in the last month. Cursing fiercely, he stripped off the wet shorts on the way to the water room.

The cleansing sting of the steamy, hot shower temporarily took his mind away from his intention to go to Avaric, the plague colony. Alone, if necessary.

The conference room across the lobby from Jefferson's office was near capacity. Gale had remained at his desk as Omni personnel had flowed into the meeting area. It was a few minutes past the hour and Kurt and Lauren still hadn't arrived. Staring momentarily out his window, he made a mental note, then moved to join the others.

After Gale entered he whispered, "Door close," then took his seat at the head of the table. The small talk quickly died as he looked from person to person. This gathering would never be mistaken for members of the global financial market. Too many scars, tattoos, and fashion errors... Seated around the large rectangular mahogany table was a collection of mercenaries, ex-soldiers and wannabe adventurers that made up the personnel of Omni Incorporated. There were three men and three women, roughly between the ages of mid-twenties to late thirties, all eager for the details of their next dangerous foray into deep space. Especially the details regarding the individual shares to be earned. The unofficial motto of Omni Inc. was 'take the high risk, live the high life.' Of course, the bottom line was always to survive, and several prior Omni operatives hadn't.

Finally, with deliberate slowness, Gale spoke.

"I'm glad everyone could make it today." His voice was monotone. There were small, restless movements around the room, but Gale ignored them, preferring to take his time.

"Last minute secret hush-hush meeting," a voice grumbled to his left. "This better be good, man." Gale looked at the man evenly. An ex-Star Corp field operative, Torbeck Gii was of Asian descent, a husky man of average height with a very pale complexion. The left side of his face was severely pockmarked, dozens of tiny dimpled burn scars the result of a desert battlefield explosion. White-hot granules of sand had torn into his flesh, leaving him blind in his left eye. He had declined a tech eye replacement, settling for the basic skin seal job he had received at the field hospital and the basic eye patch he covered it with. He had on a red patch today to match his overalls. The man looked up, his expression a mixture of boredom and frustration, and met the gaze of Gale. "What's with all the covert frap? I thought we were out of the army." Torbeck Gii's eyes danced around the table. If Gii was expecting support, it didn't materialize. Gii's eye flickered back to Gale's hard stare, then found the table and stared at it like he'd never seen wood before. Torbeck let out a big sigh while Gale continued.

"I've called this meeting to discuss a possible assignment to the Avaric colony and a minimum twenty million credit contract with the World Government." Gale explained, his voice a little sharper.

"20 million credits!" Gii burst out, his single eye growing big. There was mumbling and more settling in movement around the table. Gale wasn't sure if it was more because of the location of the mission or the amount of the contract.

"Avaric? The plague colony all over the media?" Helena Timmingson questioned. Gale looked over at the woman, quickly pushing away the sarcasm seeping into his response.

"The one and only, Helena." He watched the muscular woman wag her head in disbelief. Helena Timmingson was unofficially the strongest woman, pound for pound, in the history of the Star Corporation military division. From a distance, Helena's brown crewcut and symmetrically muscular physique made her easily confused as a short man, but upon closer inspection, there was no way to mistake her for anything but a woman. For a world class weight lifter, she was as graceful and feminine as a classic ballerina, but she was packaged with broad, strong shoulders, thick, muscular thighs, and stubby fingered hands made more for construction than sewing. Helena also had the sweetest, angelic face, framed by the crew cut she had maintained since leaving the military two years ago. She had large, chocolate brown doe eyes, and twin dimples appeared every time she smiled. A sun lover and a gym rat, she would routinely stand next to Jefferson and place her arm against his in comparison and smile, saying something like, "I'm catching up," or "have you been slacking off?" Of all the Omni personnel, Helena was probably Jefferson's favorite. She had put together a great career as a multi-functional field operative, and had carried over her professional focus and drive to Omni Incorporated. Like Gale, Helena had gone into Star Corp military operations looking for a direction to take her life in, and she had not only found her place, but excelled well beyond expectations. Helena was sitting away from the conference table, and Gale watched her sheer stocking covered legs flex as she re-crossed them. The hem of the short, pastel colored summer dress inched up her muscular thighs, and Gale's eyes caught the movement. Helena unsuccessfully fought back a grin. She might as well as said, "caught you" out loud. Gale chuckled to himself. A grown man caught playing sexual peek-a-boo with one of his employees.

"Any details?" The voice belonged to T.T. Jones, the medical authority for the team. He was a tall but fleshy, balding man in his forties contracted into the Star Corp when military action during the Mandroid Wars of 2088 had severely depleted doctors and nursing staffs. Dozens of hospitals had been targeted by the enemy during that conflict with hundreds of doctors and nurses killed. Humans discovered that machines, even partially human, weren't capable of mercy, or bound by the unwritten laws of warfare. Thadius Thomas Jones had survived the wholesale slaughter, more than quadrupling his civilian pay. He made no bones about not being a soldier, but he was a damn good field doctor and had enjoyed the rush of frontline field hospital duty.

"Actually," Gale explained, "this meeting was just for general discussion on the possibility of a mission there."

"Uh, not that it's a major factor," Gii began, licking his lips as he glanced around at the others, causing some chuckles. "But I'd like to hear about the proposed credit share breakdown." Gii chuckled, rubbing absently at his eye patch. "I always like hearing what my life is worth on the open market."

"You got change for a credit?" Pace Kimbro, the Omni engineer/technician teased with a grin. His wife Julie, the team pilot, jabbed him in the ribs playfully. Gale almost grinned at the banter, but before he could continue, a voice barked from the other side of the conference room doors.

"Door open! Frap!" The doors were barely apart when Patrickson stormed in, throwing his luggage against the wall. Lauren walked in behind him, quietly setting her bags down and moving to an empty chair. She looked hot and sweaty, her long, straight strawberry blonde hair pulled back in a ponytail. Her black shorts and tank top exposed a lot of sun-baked skin. Her petite size belied her outspoken, no nonsense personality. Standing inches behind Gale, Kurt growled. "Well, we made it, Jefferson. Hope you're satisfied." Gale rose and turned slowly until they were face-to-face and close enough to identify each other's lunches. The smell of Kurt's breath mint lingered.

"Why don't you take a seat? Catch your breath." Gale's tone was even, but ominous. The air in the room seemed to be draining out, and there was a moment of no sound or movement in the room. Suddenly Kurt smiled and kissed Gale on the cheek, the room bursting into laughter. Kurt bowed and blew kisses. The mood in the room lightened immeasurably, but no one saw the anger that flashed through Gale's eyes as the laughter bounced off his back. As the moment passed, Gale reseated himself, his jaw muscle slightly clenched.

Small talk around the table settled and Gale answered Gii's question. "Shares breakdown to about 1.6 million per member if we execute the contract at full crew." There were gasps and movement from around the table. "That would leave about five million for ship and equipment upgrades, the retirement fund, etc. And those are just guesswork numbers. This isn't a real figure to work with yet." Patrickson, who had sat next to Jones, listened as Jones whispered a quick catch-up. Patrickson's face paled and he couldn't stop himself from blurting out.

"The mission is to fucking Avaric! The plague colony? Are you out of your fucking mind, Jefferson?" Patrickson looked at Gale with comical surprise. "You're kidding right? It's a fucking joke, right?" Jones coughed loudly, a poorly disguised warning that Patrickson ignored. Gale stared at Kurt, Jefferson's jaw clenching tighter.

With great restraint, Gale whispered, "You don't have to go."

The room went dead silent. Stunned, Patrickson's lips moved, but no sound came out.

Sweeping his gaze around the table, Gale continued. "Another issue that needs to be addressed is the possible dissolving of Omni Incorporated at the completion of this mission. I've decided to return to smaller contracts working strictly one-man assignments. So, if we take the offer, this will be our last mission together." The room was like a graveyard at midnight, the news shocking everyone. Some looked to Maggie, who was as surprised as the others.

"Uh, this is all pretty sudden, isn't it?" Jones asked.

Gale almost smiled, and it sent a chill up the doctor's spine. "Everyone here knows I've had my fill of this business. It's time for me to move on."

"What the fuck are you talking about?" Patrickson spoke out. "We've worked our asses off to get to the position we're in. How can you do this?"

Gale looked at him, and this time he did smile. "We? We? Last time I looked, Omni Inc. was **my** company. Gosh, I'm really sorry Kurt, but now you'll have to go out and find a real job." Anger contorted Patrickson's face as he burst to his feet, tipping his chair over.

"What the fuck is wrong with you? You haven't been human in months!"

"And you haven't been sober." Jones popped to his feet to be sure to stay between the two. Gale looked at Lauren, who returned his gaze with an intensity only hatred could fuel. "How many cocktails did he have on the air carrier? Did he have a nip in the cab on the way from the airport?"

"What's the matter superman? You lose your x-ray vision?" Kurt snarled. "I'm standing right here. Why don't you ask me how much I drank today? Yesterday? I'll tell ya." Gale's black eyes slid up and over to Kurt and the two men held a cold stare. Torbeck eyed the table, slowly wagging his head, torn between the danger and the pay off. He raised his head and spoke, looking at no one in particular.

"I guess there's no need to talk about the chances of catching the plague." The room stayed quiet until Gale spoke, reluctantly taking his eyes from Kurt's.

"I don't have any concrete information yet. I told Representative Whittington I'd get back to him right away if we were interested."

"What do you think, Jefferson?" Maggie questioned.

"Well," he sighed, his face relaxing. He paused long enough to make eye contact with everyone except Kurt and Lauren. "I think we could all use the funds, and the publicity would be great for all our futures. For me, I tired of just taking assignments for the money. Those colonists need help." He took a deep breath and forced himself to say the truth in his heart. "I think we should do it for Avaric."

"That's a little melodramatic, isn't it?" Gii grinned with a light chuckle. "You aren't going to break out in God Bless Our World, are you?"

"Then don't fucking go, Gii!" Gale exploded. All other sound in the room died and the tension jumped to yet another level. This time Gii didn't wilt, his good eye staring hard into Gale's shark ones.

"Who says I'm not going? For that kind of money I'd crawl into the devil's ass. Fuck you---I just said you were laying it on a little thick, that's all."

"Get off it Gii," Helena warned. Gii locked into an 'I dare you' stare with the power lifter. Ugliness was just another comment or two away. Gale ignored the flare of tempers. It was routine among those so closely associated with danger and death.

"It sure won't be a vacation," Patrickson sighed softly to Lauren.

Gale turned his attention and anger back on Patrickson. His voice was even and low, but his body was tense. "I've already told you, you don't have to go. And if you do go, don't expect to be fucking around like you have been on the last couple of assignments!"

Jones glanced about the room, signaling a readiness as Kurt glared at the Omni CEO. Patrickson stepped around Jones, a grin stuck on his face. He stopped a few feet from Gale.

"I don't know what you're problem is, but I'm sick of it. We all are. I'm tired of pussy footing around you like some frail, abused child. You haven't been right since Grace died..." Gale was on him before Patrickson could finish. In a blur, he had grabbed Kurt, spun him and applied a chokehold. Perfected by free style wrestlers, the hold was designed to cut off the air and blood supply to the brain. Applied by an expert like Gale, it could be used as either a submission or killing technique. Gale's furious, almost feral expression didn't lend itself to thoughts of submission. Taken totally by surprise, Kurt struggled, clawing at the forearm strapped across his throat. One of the women called out, "Stop it!" but Gale wasn't sure whom it was. Everyone started to move, but Gale's glare kept them at bay as he drug Patrickson backward a few feet. Kurt continued to thrash about, panic growing on his reddening face. Gale grimaced as he applied more pressure, his black eyes freezing everyone in place. He whispered in Kurt's ear with an undertaker's tone.

"You fuckin' drunk. If I ever, ever hear you say her name again, I will give you pain beyond your imagination." Gale jerked Patrickson back with another surge of strength. Patrickson's face deepened to a dark crimson. "I will break every fucking bone in your body. I won't kill you, but you'll wish I had." Gale tossed Patrickson onto the table like a load of dirty laundry. Lauren immediately moved to him. No one else in the room seemed sure what to do. Gale's mad gaze flowed over the room. "Don't even think about putting your hands on me," Gale warned, low in his throat, his cavernous eyes skipping from Gii to Pace to Helena. Jones looked at the others, then moved to see about Kurt. Patrickson remained on the table, coughing and sputtering, staring wide-eyed at his former best friend. In the silent unease that followed, Pace and Julie Kimbro slipped quietly from the room, Pace careful to keep himself between Gale and his wife. Maggie started out of the room, hesitating at the doors. She looked at Gale, who was still staring down at Kurt. She ran her fingertips lightly over the roughened skin of her neck scar. Tears coming to her eyes, she turned and left the room. Helena moved to stand right in front of Gale, gently taking his hand, her eyes never leaving his. They stood like this for several moments as Patrickson moved shakily from the table to his feet, until finally Gale's eyes drifted down to hers. She squeezed his hand, and spoke in a feather soft voice. "Kurt didn't kill Grace. The vampire vines did."

Gale shook his head ever so slightly. "The vines attacked her. Because of Kurt I couldn't save her." Helena sighed, head dropping to her chest. She had been there when Grace had died. The mutant plants had also attacked Helena, but she had the scar damage repaired right away. It had helped her cope better with the nightmares. Helena gave his hand another squeeze, whispered goodbye, then followed Patrickson, Lauren and Gii out. Kurt was still rubbing his throat, but only Lauren returned Gale's hard stare with a venomous look of her own. At that moment she certainly was not thinking about how Gale had saved her life instead of Grace's on the Pandora mission, and in that instant Gale wished with all his heart he hadn't.

Gale started out of the conference room, realizing Jones was following him across the lobby into his office. As Gale moved around his desk to sit, Jones stopped just inside the doorway. Before he could speak, Gale did. "No lectures. I'm not in the mood." Jones stalked across the room and stepped around the desk.

"Are you losing your mind, Jefferson? Yesterday, you cripple a guy, today you nearly cancel your best friend..."

"Ex-best friend. We're not in grade school anymore."

Jones stared at Gale, who had turned his chair to gaze out at the mountains.

"You're way past scaring people, my friend. What's going on?"

Gale didn't bother to look the man. He seemed to be looking for something beyond his window view.

"They both got what they deserved. And by the way, Albert made the first move. He is an enhanced Level 1 protector for the government, which means that not only is he elite, but also has a license to kill. He wasn't fucking around and I took him down, fast and hard. Frap, even Maggie wanted a piece of him." Gale turned enough to look into Jones face. "Kurt got off easy. But he won't next time. And if he had kept up on his training, he would have gotten out of the hold. It might as well have been you, the way he was flopping around." Jones snorted, ignoring the insult. They both knew that he was as much a soldier as

28

Gale was a doctor. The extent of the doctor's exercise came from walking his German shepherd, Banshee. "I think I got Kurt's attention though." Jones shook his head, pacing away from Gale. He stopped back in front of the desk, deciding to change the subject.

"And what's this shit---shutting down the business?"

"Just bullshit 'cause I was pissed."

Jones sighed, dropping into a chair. "Is it really Grace still bothering you? It's been over a year, Jefferson. You've got to find a way to deal with it and get on with your life. Grief can be like poison, and I know you know that." Gale's expression hardened, some of that angry fire dancing behind those soulless eyes.

"Are you done? I need to contact Whittington."

Jones was dumbstruck. "Did I miss something? After your little outburst, do you think anyone is going to Avaric?"

Gale displayed a sick smile. "Oh, someone is going to Avaric, doc. I am. I can retire on 20-25 million credits. Why do you think I had the autopilot installed after the last mission? I knew the time was coming when money wasn't going to buy the team's honor, and now its here." Suddenly, the doors slid open and Maggie stepped in, her eyes red rimmed. Hands on her hips, she glared at Gale but spoke to Jones.

"He's not telling you everything, T.T. And I don't know why he didn't tell everyone at the meeting. Or was that a wrestling match?" Gale glanced down at his desk and saw the audio feed had been activated. He cursed under his breath.

Jones looked at Gale. "What's going on, Jefferson? I should have realized there was more to this than just Grace. Spill it." Gale looked away from Maggie, spinning his chair back for the outside view. He hoped his tone would be angrier, but instead it came out more tired than anything else.

"Tell 'em, Maggie. You want everyone to know so bad." Jones turned to face Maggie as she moved closer, sniffling as she sat in the other chair.

"Whittington told Jefferson that the Merlin had been the first ship involved after the outbreak, and it appears there are no survivors." Maggie glanced at Gale's back, then back at the doctor. "Jefferson's brother Christopher is a lieutenant on the Merlin."

"He might still be alive." Gale whispered, his voice hardly brimming with confidence. He continued to look outside. Jones mouth opened a little, then closed, then opened again as if to speak. He wasn't sure what to say as the information seeped beneath his thoughts. Jones reached out and squeezed Maggie's shoulder, then turned to Gale. The doctor took a deep breath, letting it out slowly.

"Why didn't you start the meeting telling us about Christopher? We'd be gearing up to leave right now."

"Because this is not just about Christopher. What about the people on the colony? What if there are survivors on the Merlin? What about the kids on Avaric? Who's gonna save them?" On the verge of rage, Gale spun back to face his friends. "In the military I earned medals and promotions for simply following orders. I lost more people under my command than I saved. I was labeled a hero for getting soldiers killed during the achievement of objectives I can't even remember. But I do remember the names and faces of most the men and women who died in my arms or in my company. And I do remember all the letters I wrote to those soldiers' families." Gale's head sagged as if it suddenly weighed a hundred pounds. "For once, just once, I'd like to make the decision to be a hero instead just getting paid to be one." No one spoke for several heartbeats. Maggie coughed up a small smile. Jones blinked slowly for a few moments before speaking.

"I must be getting old or going crazy or both when you start making moral speeches that actually mean something to me." Jones shook his head, running his hands over a head once covered in hair. "T.T. Jones, hero." He couldn't stop chuckling. "My medical school professors are going to shit themselves if they ever hear about this." Despite himself, Gale's lips almost curled into a genuine smile. Jones spoke back up. "All right, before things go too far and we start spending the credits, let's be serious for a minute. If you set a meeting with Whittington I will come and listen to the plan, but in order to be fair to the others, we have to tell them about Christopher, and they should hear the details straight from Whittington. We all need to be on the same page on this one. If we're going into a hot zone and someone doesn't follow protocol, or if somebody loses it…we all pay the maximum." Gale agreed with a single solemn nod. Talk about long odds---the nine crew members of Omni Inc. versus billions and billions of microscopic killers with one soulless objective: death. It would be no different than any other battle the crew had taken part in. But as Gale looked at Jones and Maggie, another thought immediately jumped into his mind. They would be going to war, but in all wars there were casualties...

Later that day, Jones pressed the buzzer to the residence of Kurt Patrickson and Lauren Campbell. After a few moments, Jones could detect some movement on the other side of the door, then Kurt's slightly slurred voice sounded from a speaker hidden above the door.

"Who is it?"

Jones unconsciously looked up as if the invisible speaker were a camera. "It's Jones."

The doors parted with a soft whoosh. Kurt stood in a heavy blue boxer robe, a smirk on his unshaven face and a small glass of bluish liquor in his hand. Jones stepped in, not waiting for an invitation. The doors slid closed behind him. "Did I interrupt something?" His voice sounded polite, but both men knew there was no feeling behind it. The two men were alone in the spacious living area, which was decorated with a lot of chrome and glass. Jones glanced toward the closed bedroom door, a tiny knowing smile on his face. From behind him Kurt spoke.

"Nothing that can't be restarted. What's up?" Kurt padded barefoot to the free-form couch and flopped down, careful not to spill his drink. Still standing, Jones turned in place, taking in the luxurious surroundings the Omni Inc. assignments had rewarded the couple. The Omni doctor's living arrangement was different than Kurt's but no less filled with expensive furnishings. It was no wonder when Jefferson had mentioned shutting the company down, everyone had gotten upset. Jones eventually settled his attention on Kurt.

"I think you know why I'm here." Patrickson bleary eyes stared dumbly for a moment as he took a sip of his drink, then understanding seemed to trickle into his brain, and he began to shake his head back and forth.

"Forget it, T.T. Its Jefferson's game. Leave me out of it." They held eye contact for a few seconds, each expecting the other to speak. Kurt finally relented. "For Christ's sake, he's gone over the fucking edge! Do you know what that sick son of a bitch whispered to me when he had me in that hold? He said he would cripple me if I ever mentioned Grace's name. He said he'd pull some ninja shit and start filling my plate with extra helpings of pain, T.T., but he wouldn't kill me---motherfucker wants me to suffer." Kurt rubbed his throat. "Shit---he damn near turned out my lights today. He was on me before I knew what the fuck." He wagged his head in disbelief. "I knew he had kept up his training, but you saw..."

Jones nodded. The doctor's earlier shock had been mixed with awe at the sheer speed with which Gale had moved. Gale had always been an expert fighter, but today he had shown a skill level far beyond anyone's anticipation. "And I'm sure Maggie filled you in on what happened between Jefferson and the Representative's bodyguard..."

Jones quickly spoke up. "Yeah, Maggie told me about the incident. She had wanted to fight the man herself, but Jefferson stopped her because he knew the guy had been enhanced. And we all know that when Jefferson gets in a confrontation, he lives by his golden rule: pain equals cooperation." Jones

VINCE CHURCHILL

paused, watching Kurt take a bigger sip of his drink. "Jefferson told me that he thought you were trying to show him up today, and that's why he talked about closing up the company. And he got you to react the way he wanted. But the chokehold is a whole other matter. I think we both know where all that rage is coming from." Jones' attention wandered from Kurt to an expensive piece of art mounted on the wall, and when Kurt didn't speak, he continued. "Jefferson is still not over the loss of Grace, but that's just a part of it. It's you and Lauren."

Kurt's eyebrows knitted and he cocked his head to the side as if he hadn't heard Jones correctly.

"Say what?" Jones looked at him like he was examining a patient.

"You heard me." Kurt stared in disbelief at the doctor.

"Whatever Jefferson has must be catching because you are out of your fucking mind." He slugged back the remainder of his drink and immediately moved toward the bar. "What the hell do Lauren and I have to do with Jefferson losing it?"

Jones looked at his friend, sadness in his eyes. He sounded tired when he spoke. "You really don't know what's going on with him, do you? You selfish prick."

Kurt glanced over his shoulder as he poured. "I'm the prick? I get fucking choked today and *I'm* the prick?"

Jones stared into the back of Patrickson. "Have you ever thanked Jefferson for what he did for you and Lauren?" The question hung in the air as Kurt reached for and dropped some ice into the glass. When he was done, he hesitated for just a beat before turning around. He struggled to make and keep firm eye contact with Jones.

"This is crazy. Of course I did." Kurt's tone sounded edgy, but Jones caught an underlying uncertainty.

Jones maintained his stare. "When?"

Kurt took a sip, seemingly for courage, then pointed a finger. He looked angry, but there was an emptiness to his display. Jones' question had struck an ugly chord. "You're way off," Kurt challenged, taking another sip. He turned away from his friend. He no longer had the power to meet Jones' eyes.

Jones shrugged, the tone of his reply much softer, the accusation gone, now replaced by sure knowledge. "I don't think so and neither do you. When was the last time you had a conversation with him? I haven't seen you talk to him since the mission celebration, the night before Grace died. Which, by the way, was the first time I remember you drinking heavily." Kurt kept his back to Jones, the slightest tremble passing along his frame. Jones could hear the ice clinking as Kurt raised the glass to his lips. Kurt didn't bother to reply; Jones already knew the truth. "The answer is that you have no fucking idea. On the trip back from Pandora, Jefferson never left his room and you never left Lauren's side. When we got back to Earth, Jefferson was handling funeral arrangements and the media. You immediately took Lauren away for a short cruise. You came back for the burial, then left immediately for Europe." Jones paused, waiting to see if Kurt was going to turn around. When he didn't, Jones continued. "You were gone for two months, then we took an assignment, but Jefferson didn't go. So, when exactly did you find any time to spend with your best friend?" Jones was growing angry and frustrated, and was getting tired of talking to Kurt's back. And in that moment of anger, the truth burst out. "He did save the life of your lover, at the expense of Grace's life."

The words caused Kurt to sway the tiniest bit, and he finally turned, his eyes glistening with emotion. "I tried to call him before we went to Europe, but he wouldn't answer the phone. Maggie answered once, but he was asleep. I wanted to go by but Lauren was still weak from the blood loss and the toxins." He took a breath, shaking his head. "We sent cards from Paris and London and Madrid and Rome..."

"But you never took the time to talk to him!" Jones burst, causing Kurt to flinch. "You were so caught up with Lau---"

"But she almost died!" Kurt snapped, spilling his drink as he stumbled toward Jones. Jones stared at Kurt, his anger growing stronger with each reply.

"Grace *did* die, remember? And she died while Jefferson was saving Lauren." Jones could see the confusion, guilt and frustration contorting Kurt's face. Even with all the drinking he had done, Kurt hadn't been able to erase the truth. Jones stepped within whispering distance. "In order for you to completely understand what happened to Jefferson, I'm going to break a promise to him to share something with you." Kurt did his best to stand tough, but he was failing miserably. "Grace was pregnant, Kurt." Patrickson's body twitched, and he flinched as if he had had been slapped. "The debt you owe Jefferson as a friend has gone unpaid. Think about it, Kurt. A year ago, he saved Lauren and Grace died. Have you and Lauren set a wedding date yet? Planning a family?"

Patrickson could only stand there, trembling. His free hand began to clench open and closed. Jones felt his emotions welling up, but he knew he had to finish what he started. "I'm not sure Jefferson feels like he has anything to live for. And now throw in the situation with Christopher and I think he has become very, very dangerous. And you experienced that first hand." Kurt finally moved on his own, setting his drink down on the glass and chrome coffee table. His gaze burned into the doctor.

"Wait a minute. What situation with Christopher?" Before Jones could answer, the bedroom doors opened and Lauren stepped into the room, swallowed up in a heavy, red terry cloth boxer's robe similar to Kurt's. Her long hair loose and flowing, she looked like she had been dozing. She glanced at both men as she moved to stand next to Kurt. Her eyes settled on Jones, her lips a taut, grim line.

"T.T., what are you peddling now?" Jones' eyes flickered at Lauren, thinking Kurt might speak up. He didn't, and silence stretched to an uncomfortable length. When Jones finally started to speak, Lauren cut him off. "You're here about Jefferson, aren't you?" He nodded, holding his tongue. "Did he try to hurt someone else? He's out of control. He made that clear when he attacked Kurt for no reason."

Jones eyes burned into Kurt, accusing him with his glare. Kurt let his head sag to his chest, rubbing his eyes and forehead. It didn't appear that Kurt was going to be any help, at least for the moment, so Jones sidestepped the subject. "Maggie and I have spoken with everyone, and we're seriously considering the Avaric mission." For a moment it seemed as if all the air in the room was sucked away. Both Kurt and Lauren flinched; Jones' statement was like a gunshot. Lauren's mouth dropped open a little, the breath in her lungs rushing out. Kurt's eyes went wide with surprise.

"You can't be serious, T.T." Lauren spoke.

Jones' eyes locked on hers when he spoke, but he was clearly talking to Kurt. "He was planning to go alone, and I won't allow that. And Christopher is involved now. He's on board the Star Corp ship that was initially assigned to Avaric. The Corp is officially calling the Merlin a dead ship, but there is something interfering with long-range sensors in the area that's preventing confirmation of life signs. So, there's a chance Christopher might still be alive." Kurt cursed under his breath, seeming to argue with himself. Lauren clasped her hands and brought them to her forehead, her eyes closing for a moment.

"We'd probably be better off keeping Jefferson from going. He doesn't need another chance to be a hero right now," she spoke to the floor. "But in his frame of mind, he's a dangerous to himself and everyone around him."

Jones stared hard at her, struggling in the moment with what to say or do. "Don't be ridiculous, Lauren. He had a bad day today. We all have bad days, right Kurt?" Jones eyes rolled from her down to Kurt's half empty glass. He stared at the ice-blue liquid for a moment, finally looking back up. "Grief and anger issues do not constitute mental impairment; at least not in his case. We're supposed to be his friends." Kurt wouldn't meet Jones eyes when the doctor continued. "We'd all do the same for you." Jones stood up, taking a last glance at the liquor, heading for the door. "Actually, we've been doing the same for you." When he was a step from the front door, he half-turned. "The Pandora mission screwed everyone up, and we've all handled it in different ways. Jefferson got depressed and angry. You, my friend, got drunk." Jones opened the door and walked out, looking forward to the Pacific Palisades breeze to cool him off.

The door slid closed behind him, both Lauren and Kurt staring into the air. Lauren shook her head and started back toward bedroom. When she got to the door, she glanced back. Kurt hadn't moved a muscle, his eyes locked on his drink.

"Are you coming?" Her tone was flat, yet almost accusing. He was like a statue, not speaking, not blinking. Finally, without taking his attention away from the liquor, he waved a dismissive hand in her direction, his arm dropping back at his side. Already upset, her face flushed with anger, but she kept her mouth closed, jaw muscles working under the pale skin. She turned, wishing she could slam the door behind her.

Kurt slowly squatted, his eyes staring into the liquid, searching. He searched to see something that might or might not be there. He never touched the glass.

A half an hour later, he was kneeling but still searching, and he didn't acknowledge Lauren's presence, now fully dressed and carrying luggage. If she said goodbye, Kurt didn't hear it.

The sun was sliding toward the horizon as Gale and Maggie locked up the Omni Inc. offices. Gale arrived home a couple of hours later after a pepperoni pizza dinner for one. Stars were fully visible when he unlocked the front door and stepped inside the vast, stonewalled entrance chamber. He activated the central controls, a soft light coming on in each of the main floor rooms. He moved quickly up the wide, curving staircase to the master bedroom. It was large, shadows clinging to the corners of the high ceiling. The room easily contained a king-sized sleeper, furniture, connected water room, and his home office. Most of the hillside estate's rooms were empty, and would probably remain that way. He had bought it with the intentions of getting married and having a family. A house full of kids and pets and laughter and life. But that had ended on Pandora. But he loved the house too much in its brooding, haunted house condition to sell it.

He changed into a comfortable, dull gold skin-suit, and returned to the ground floor kitchen to pour himself a cold glass of orange juice.

After a sip, he walked through the cavernous living area, ignoring the home theater system. He checked the computer system for messages, found none worth returning, then returned upstairs. Once on the second floor, he moved down the hallway away from his bedroom and stopped at the end of the shadowy corridor. It was a rich, wood paneled wall, and he whispered, "Night sky." A door-sized panel slid open, exposing a dimly lit, wrought iron spiral staircase. It only led up. He stepped in and started up, using the railing. It took him up two stories and fed into a small, stoned-walled circular room. He was at the top of the slender tower that had been sealed off from the rest of the mansion by the previous owner. When he had purchased the estate, he had the tower accessed again so he and Grace could enjoy the fantastic 'secret' view of Hollywood and Los Angeles.

He moved across the empty chamber toward the only window, a small opening closed off from the inside by solid wooden shutters. He unlatched the covers and swung them to the side, his eyes scanning past the iron bars to take in the impressive Los Angeles basin. The fantasy of Hollywood remained strong for so many people around the world, but the reality was that most of Hollywood was populated by drug dealers, addicts, perverts, flesh toys, the homeless, and the mentally lost. Hollywood was the perfect home for both predator and prey. He closed his eyes and fought the urge to become either, then let his mind wander. The images that appeared were all of Grace, still so vivid. The wedding plans, the Pandora mission. The glass in his hand began to tremble and his eyelids fluttered...

The vampire vines...

As his mind visualized that final day on Earth's primary genetic experimentation dumping ground, the images were incredibly life-like, and it was only moments before his mind had traveled back in time and space...

The mission had already claimed the lives of two crewmembers, and only a perverted sense of vengeance against the Frankenstein life forms had kept them on the planet. In fact, the assignment's contractual purposes had all been met. Members of the team wanted to take exotic plant life back to Earth, some to be placed at the empty graves of Ted McClanahan and Ursala Edwards. Torbeck Gii and Kyle Mikus, who was Maggie's lover, had escorted Grace, Lauren, Julie and Maggie to a pre-selected sight. The women focused on selecting and preparing the plant life for transport, while the men kept a wary eye out. Everyone was armed, but Gii and Kyle carried the slender metallic laser rifles slung over their shoulders. They had selected a small clearing little more than a kilometer distance, and Gale and Pace had the party under the watchful eye of the sensor-scanner when the carnivorous vines were detected. Even as they slithered out of the dense tropical overgrowth of trees, they were still registering as plants. The vines moved like eels, swaying and darting at the team from above, making a strange, high pitched whine as they attacked. Swarmed in a feeding frenzy, Grace and Lauren were the first ensnared. Gii and Kyle, standing at each end of the clearing, could barely defend themselves, much less protect any of the women. The rifles had proved useless, and everyone was trying in vain to use their handguns. Everyone's frantic struggling coupled with the vines darting, squirming attack made for near impossible targets. After a hurried stop at the equipment/weapon room, Gale and Pace, dual-edged machetes in hand, raced to the rescue. There had been no reply when Gale tried to reach Kurt in his cabin. It was early in the morning, and the crew had celebrated both the mission's end and the lives of their slain teammates the night before. Kurt had been the one that had lured McClanahan from the Corp to Omni Inc., and had been helplessly present when the flood of hungry grubs had invaded their protective suits and had eaten the two Omni members alive. At the party, Kurt had downed drinks like he was hollow, and Gale had to shoulder him back to his cabin.

They had approached the clearing at a dead run, with no time for fear or indecision, but neither had been ready for the scene they faced. They could hear the insect-like whine grow louder and louder, then suddenly they were there, at the edge of the clearing, and Gale remembered feeling stunned by the sight. Vines were everywhere, moving in a blurred frenzy around the team, the whining sound incredibly loud. Grace and Lauren were down, both women covered in writhing vines. The others were still on their feet, struggling for their lives. Gii was the closest to them, bloodied and tattered, completely surrounded by the things. Maggie was being overwhelmed, one vine attached to her neck while countless other vines sought the flesh of her arms and face. Gale had seen the laser rifle lying at Gii's feet, and he had shouted at Pace to get it and start firing into the dense growth overhead. Gale had darted toward Grace, who was the farthest away, but veered instinctively to the much closer Lauren, who was barely visible under the vines merciless attack.

As Gale dropped by Lauren's barely struggling form, he finally got a clear, close up view of a vine as it dropped in front of his face, writhing slowly, its maw dripping a clear, viscous fluid. Without thinking, Gale's gloved hand shot out and grabbed the vine, and it shrieked, high and shrill. It twisted and thrashed about like a snake, seeking to escape and attack at the same time. It was a genetic nightmare, looking from a distance like a moist, green vine the

37

width of an average man's forearm. But on closer inspection the plant-like skin concealed a thing that was part sea lamprey and part tentacle. There were small, pulsating suckers running under the entire length of the vine. The tip of the thing was nothing more than rings of small razor teeth, with a tiny, protruding maw in the center to suck in its prey's shredded, bloody flesh. And just below the tip area was a nasty looking hook claw. So, once it was securely attached, it could take its time and feed. It was disgusting to look at, and Gale's stomach had flip flopped realizing there was countless numbers of these things surrounding him and his crew, and several were attached and already feeding on Lauren. His machete sliced through air and vine, but even sliced in half, the thing was still trying to attach itself to his arm or hand, but it was too short now to squirm and clutch effectively. Gale hadn't spotted any eyes on the thing, and he hadn't been interested in taking a closer look. He went quickly to work on the ones attached to Lauren, overwhelmed by the scent of fresh blood, the sickeningly sweet musk of the dead and dying vines and the smells of the surrounding lush vegetation. He could feel the flush of the hot, humid air swirling around him, sweat running down his face.

Clearing Lauren of the vines was nasty business; his gloves were tattered and soaked with blood and goo when he was done. Her uniform was in worst shape than his gloves, and when Gale had hacked the last vine off her, her breathing was shallow and she barely looked human. She was covered from face to knees in circular, palm-sized ugly purple bruises with ragged, burrowed, blood pulsing wounds, not counting the several gashes from the hook claws he tore from her. He looked up and cried out as he checked Grace's situation. No one had been able to get to her, and not only was she completely engulfed by the vines, it looked as if the monstrosities were struggling to lift her body back into the dense vegetation overhead. Gale was still yelling franticly as he vaulted over Lauren and scrambled toward his bride-to-be. Almost to her, he lost his balance, hacking wildly at some vines, stumbling the last few meters on all fours. She was buried under the writhing things, his hearing filled with the vile sounds of sucking and chewing. He could clearly seeing one of her blue eyes amidst all the movement covering her, but it hadn't been looking at him. The crystal blue pupil was staring upward, as pretty and lifeless as a doll's eye. Something inside him wondered if she was still capable of seeing. He had been relieved that her eye hadn't looked at him, searched for him. And just that fast, a smaller vine filled that crevice and attached itself, quickly sharing in the feast. Gale couldn't recall exactly what happened next. Had he gone crazy hacking at the vines? Had he sat frozen, his own will to live shattered by the sight of her?

The next clear memory was a blur of being knocked to the thick emerald grass, his bones jarring with the contact. Air burst out of his body, sweat splashed into his eyes, his hand holding the machete was pinned to the ground by a boot, and then someone tore the machete from his grasp. He had cried out when a vine had been pulled from just below his right collarbone, and another from his left forearm. The claws had torn ragged, bloody wounds down his chest and arm. In his pain he had thrown his head to the side, and as his vision cleared he could see Jones kneeling by Grace's mutilated form. He wasn't sure whom or how many were holding him, but he fought until he was free.

He watched Jones remove the last dying vine from Grace's chest. It was still squirming as the doctor had pulled it from her, tearing back the top of her uniform, exposing one of her breasts. The vine had been attached just below her sternum, and it had left a nasty looking wound, and Gale could see how bad her flesh had been violated. He could also see her dark, hardened nipple contrasting so strongly from her pale, milky skin. He couldn't take his eyes from it, finally hearing his heartbeat, and realizing with a flinch that he was no longer fighting off the vines. In the next moment he realized that Helena had slid down next to him, gently checking his condition. As he turned toward her, Gale could see Kurt in the corner of his eye, struggling to scoop up Lauren's broken doll body, Kyle having to help him. Slowly, Gale's head swiveled and he watched Jones stand and face him for just an instant, lowering his tear filled eyes. Jones moved to help with Lauren, and Gale felt the crushing wave of truth hit him full force. He fell forward, crawling to be next to his love. A blood splattered Gii tried to keep him from her, but a screaming, threatening spew of profanity caused him to back away, hands dropping useless to his sides. Gale slid up next to her, but between his tears and all the blood, he could hardly see.

The blue eye he had glimpsed was no longer there.

He pitched himself on top of her, urging her to wake up, to get up, to open her eyes---

The remaining vines had retreated back into the trees, the ground covered in bloody, hacked tentacles, some still flexing, quivering. Eventually someone tried to pull him away from her, and Gale remembered hitting that person and blubbering another barrage of confused foul curses. He couldn't remember how long he stayed there with her, but it had been dark when he finally scooped her up, limp and lifeless, and carried her back to the base ship, stumbling his way along the rough path. Vaguely, he remembered Helena and Kyle flanking him, rifles at the ready.

At the infirmary, Gale laid Grace on an examination table, carefully placing a hanging arm against her side. Someone had said that Lauren had been revived and was going to make it, but Gale had stumbled without a word back to his cabin---Grace's cabin---and slumped to the floor crying after trying to scrub her dried blood from his hands. He hadn't emerged until five days later, a day after their return to Earth. It had been five long days of no eating, very little rest, and equal barrages of good memories and vampire vine nightmares...

Gale was still staring out into the night when movement from the edge of his vision caught his attention. He watched as Helena pressed in a code and the wrought iron gate across the driveway swung open. She jogged up the winding drive toward the front door, disappearing in and out of the shadows as motion sensors activated timer lights as she moved. When she was half way to the house he stepped back from the window, secured it, and started down the dark spiraling stairs. The front door chimed as he reached the second level, and he loped down the stairs, two at a time, never in danger of spilling his drink. As he crossed the lobby toward the door, he said, "door unlock" to give her entrance. Helena stood in the doorway, looking like a deer trying to decide if it should cross the road. Gale watched as she stepped just inside the door. Her voice was a whisper. "Can I come in?"

Gale tried to smile, but couldn't quite do it. The memories of the Pandora mission were fading but still too strong. He managed to shrug his shoulders. "Sure." She came in, the doors swinging closed behind her. Sweat ran down her face, a slick sheen covering her skin. Her expression was pained, but Gale knew it wasn't from the exercise. She was dressed in black skin suit bottoms, a short black sleeveless sweatshirt, and a pair of black runners. She crossed into the living room, finally stopping and turning, her face a mixture of emotions. Gale wasn't sure what was going to happen, but for the second time today he couldn't deny the feelings he was experiencing. He had worked with Maggie day after day, but he had somehow screened out the full extent of her physical beauty. On the other hand, he didn't see nearly as much of Helena as he would grudgingly admit he would like. At that moment he remembered hearing her voice outside his door several times on the return from Pandora, urging him to let her in, or asking if he wanted something to eat. As he stood gazing at her now, everything seemed to hit him, and he realized his blind foolishness. "Are you all right?" he asked, moving toward her. She stood still, looking a little lost. She had trouble making direct eye contact.

"I was feeling restless, so I went for a run. I ended up at the base of the foothills, and I was a little worried about you after the meeting, so I thought I'd stop by and see if you were okay." Her townhouse was a good six or seven miles away, and his place wasn't even close to her normal jogging route, so...

Her eyes were pleading, and without thinking, Gale hugged her. Her hot body melded to his and he held her tightly, feeling the remaining inner darkness disappear. The musk of her sweat was as inviting as the firm curves of her body. After a few moments they separated, a relieved smile fighting its way onto her face. He smiled back, feeling at ease. He had accepted her white lie, and he sensed something had just happened between them.

"Are you thirsty? I was going to get some more juice."

She shook her head. "No, thanks, but some water would be great." She looked around the large, lightly decorated room. "I'm going to stretch and catch my breath for a few minutes if you can stand the company."

Gale continued to smile. "Make yourself at home." She dropped to the floor in front of the couch-sized free form longer, raising her arms above her head and rotating her head, eyes closed. Gale admired her muscular beauty, her smooth dark olive skin. He remembered when she had called him to talk about fixing her scars from the vines. He had strongly urged her to do it, though when she posed the same question to him, he had committed to wearing the new scars for life, just like all the others he had received in combat. But deep down he wished he had the Pandora ones removed. The scars were a way to keep Grace close to him, which clearly was part of what hurt him so now. Grace was much closer to him now than she had been alive. 'I'll be right back. Are you sure about the water?"

She smiled up at him, her dimples in full effect. She casually slid her legs apart and leaned her chest to the floor, her arms still above her head. Without looking up she said, "I might just have a sip of your juice."

Gale nodded, thoughts swirling. When he returned, Helena was sitting in a hurdler's stretch, her hands reaching out and pulling her down, grasping her foot. He was starting to feel silly smiling so much, but he couldn't stop. She did that to him. Her eyes seemed to sparkle when he sat on the floor next to her. They looked at each other for a moment, and Gale felt a soft tug in his chest. Finally he spoke. "So, why are you really here? Did Jones put you up to checking on me?"

Helena lowered her eyes as she sat up. "Our good doctor believes I'm overly protective of you."

Gale blinked, caught off guard by the remark. He realized she was still looking at him, trying to read his expression. If she could, she was way ahead of him. He wasn't sure what he was feeling.

"Do you want me to leave?"

Gale looked into her big brown eyes, his emotions battling. Their bodies were so close he could feel the heat coming off her, and passion stirred inside him. His body was starting to respond to hers, and something passed through her eyes that told him that she knew what was happening. It was what she had wanted.

"Uh, no, it's okay. Really."

She continued to look into his eyes as she reached for his glass. When her fingers lightly brushed his, electricity surged between them. She took a sip, Gale mesmerized by a tear of sweat that moved slowly from behind her ear and trickled down her neck. Without thinking, he dabbed at it with his finger. Her eyes closed for an instant with the contact, and Gale forgot how to breathe. When he could see her eyes again, they were different. Hungry.

She offered the glass back to him, but didn't let it go when he grasped it. Unsure of what to do, he released the glass and stood up. Embarrassed, he turned away, his growing state of excitement all too obvious in his skin shorts. Only the blind could have missed it. He glanced at her, offering a hand. "Come on." She took it and was on her feet gracefully, her water magically in her hand, smiling as she followed him from the room toward the stairs. She hopped a couple of stairs in front of him, her backside swaying. Almost to the top of the stairs she looked back at him, and he didn't even try to pretend he wasn't enjoying the view. When she reached the top, she turned toward the master bedroom, pausing. Gale had stopped at the top of the stairs, his shark eyes burning a lusty hole through her. They stood looking at each other for several moments, Gale turning down the hall in the opposite direction. He took a few steps, then stopped and turned. Helena hadn't moved from her spot.

"Where you going?" Her voice was soft and low, almost a growl. Her nipples were pushing through the sweat soaked fabric of her top. Her eyes flickered to his groin, and Gale could hear her breathing. He could feel his whole body pulsing, the magnetism between them growing stronger by the minute. It took everything he had to fight the urge, feeling it blossom, filling him up. He had to force words from his mouth, watching a droplet of sweat slide into the small crease of her belly button. He wanted to fall to his knees in front of her and lick it away. He wanted to taste her so badly he was aching.

"I've got something to show you."

"Can't it wait?"

Gale almost took a step back toward her, but somehow managed not to. A tiny grin tugged at the corner of his lips. "You'll like it, trust me." He turned and started down the hall, for the first few steps wondering if she was following or not. As he stepped up to the hidden panel he felt her behind him, so he whispered the password and the panel opened. "Ladies first," he offered, and she moved pass him, casually grazing his mid-section with her hand. He activated the light and followed her up the spiral stairs, properly distanced to enjoy her bottom. When they reached the small room, she stepped to the window, opened the shutters and then stood awe struck by the view. He stopped a step behind her, looking out over her shoulder. The evening breeze swirled around them like a cool silk scarf, and Gale could feel himself tremble. If she touched him now... He struggled to get his feelings under control.

"Why haven't you let someone help you get past all this? We know how tough you are---you don't have anything left to prove. We just want to help you." Her voice was a comforting whisper, and when she turned to face him, they were nearly touching. He drank in her eyes, her inviting, full-lipped mouth, and the smooth skin of her throat. The chemical pull between them was overwhelming, and the urge he felt to touch her, to stroke her soft skin, was maddening. Gale swallowed, and he could barely speak.

"Why are you really here? I know you care about m..."

Her lips broke off his sentence, and the confusion he felt was honest. When she pressed herself into him, his arms circled her waist with a will all their own. She pulled her mouth away from his just enough to whisper breathlessly, "I want to be with you." What his heart wasn't sure about, his body confidently responded to. He pulled her back to him, letting the desire they felt carry them forward and beyond.

They kissed, Gale moving her back against the cool stone wall. His hands, mouth and eyes savored the excitement she was bringing to all his senses. She struggled passionately against him, and he felt like they were standing in a tornado. Their kisses were deep and hard, tongues playing and fighting like two starving snakes. Gale's hands were in her hair, on her back, gripping her muscular ass.

Then it all hit him square in the chest---guilt, fear, apprehension, confusion...His whole body jolted, and he pulled away from her. Helena opened her eyes, startled, gasping for both air and his lips. Chest heaving, he stumbled back a couple of steps, head shaking. His eyes were squeezed shut, as if fighting a battle from within. She stepped toward him, but he put up a hand and gave some more ground.

"I...I can't do this, Helena. God, I want you so much but I can't." He could hardly look at her, embarrassed, confused, and unable to find the words. He could feel her eyes on him, burning him like her lips had. He hadn't felt so on fire since his high school make-out dates.

"It's okay, Jefferson. It's okay." The words came staggering out as if they were all she could think off.

He stared at her chest, rising and falling, imagining the hot center of her wanting for him. He still had the taste of her in his mouth. But this couldn't happen. Not tonight. "I'm not ready for this. I'm not ready for you. If there is something between us, I want it to be real, not just a night or two. I need to get my head on straight before I take that step..." He looked into her eyes and was able to hold the contact. "I'm so sorry. I'm really sorry." He turned, embarrassed and frustrated, his thoughts racing in a hundred directions. Silence closed in around them, Gale not wanting to speak, Helena not sure what to say. Finally, she moved past him, a brief, feathery brush of her hand on his shoulder. She disappeared down the staircase, leaving Gale alone. He watched her in his mind moving down the second floor hall, then down the main stairway. He imagined that she might glance back just before leaving the house, and then she was gone, the machine of her body carrying her into the night. And still he stood there, in the spot where she left him. At that moment his body felt like his life--- unable to move forward.

And unless violence was involved, not able to move at all.

Two days later, Representative Whittington arrived at the Omni offices to meet with Gale, Jones and Maggie. Maggie greeted Whittington with a bright smile and the Representative did his best to return it.

"Jefferson and T.T. are expecting you, Mr. Whittington. You can go right in." He looked her over, sighing. The woman was absolutely radiant. Had he not read her Star Corp file, it would have been impossible to think of her as a battle hardened soldier.

"Has anyone told you how beautiful you look this morning?" Maggie's smile intensified, telling him all he wanted to know. She moved from her chair, her eyes reading his. She blinked several times, her cheeks showing a touch of color. It was his time for his smile to grow. "How is it to read the thoughts of others?" She had to think a moment about her answer. Her smile wavered just a tiny bit.

"It's not the thoughts. Its dealing with the absolute truth." Whittington saw a cloud of sadness passed behind her eyes, and he was sorry he had questioned her. "Thank you," she whispered. Maggie opened the doors for Whittington, and he immediately felt a different atmosphere than his previous visit. In fact, as he entered, Gale was laughing with the man seated at his desk. Whittington was relieved at the change of tone. Gale and Jones got to their feet, and the Representative turned on his best election smile. After handshakes and introductions, they all took their seats, Maggie standing a couple of steps behind Gale.

"So," Whittington started, eyes flickering to Maggie, "That's some executive assistant you have there. Is she as great as she looks?"

Gale smiled at the man. "Better, Mr. Whittington."

Whittington seemed to pause, then spoke, almost shyly. "Is this going to be a three person mission, Mr. Gale?" Gale nodded.

"Unfortunately, only three of us feel the urgency overrides the personal risk. So why don't you give us some mission details and we'll see if the three of us can handle it."

Whittington nodded. "I have no doubt of you and your associates' abilities, Mr. Gale. So, let me begin by telling you that preliminary authorization has been granted for this mission. At this time I am empowered to offer Omni Incorporated 22.5 million credits to perform a basic cargo transfer operation from Avaric to a research lab orbiting Earth's moon. The transfer would be of approximately 3,000 deceased plague victims, loaded into your cargo hold by robot ship. After loading is completed, the robot ship will self-destruct. You will have absolutely no direct contact with the bodies. Your hold will be modified from a double to a triple seal containment barrier. Once the transfer is complete, you and your crew will operate under Level Three regulations, which will require biohazard suits for the entire return leg. When you arrive back at the moon, you will be transferred off your ship by robot shuttle and put into quarantine for 30 days. We will transfer the bodies by removing the entire cargo bay. Your hold will be replaced, and your ship will be quarantined for 90 days of testing, then released back to your company. If your ship is found to be contaminated, or there is strong evidence of possible contamination, your ship will be destroyed. The government would then give you the option of replacement per your most recent set of blueprints, or the ship's cash value will be reimbursed to you within 30 days of the ship's termination. I also can offer that the government will cover any losses of income during the 90-120 day period, realizing that your company will be in great demand after the mission." Whittington smiled at the trio, obviously proud of the deal he had masterminded. "Not bad for a simple 11 day cargo transfer." The Representative made eye contact with each of them, took a deep breath and continued. "Now, there will be a few conditions placed on the mission. First, the contract pay off will not be accredited to your company's account until the mission is completed." That statement brought a grin to Gale's face, but he didn't interrupt Whittington. "And for the purposes of world safety, the government will install an auto self-destruct mechanism in your ship's reactors in case of an outbreak among the crew or any other problems that might arise to put Earth at risk from the mission." He smiled his politician's smile again. "That's about the size of it, Mr. Gale."

Jefferson rustled in his seat, his eyes locked to Whittington's. "It doesn't even sound like to you need us. This could all be handled with robotics."

Whittington's smile lost a little of its wattage. "It could be done that way, but human rights groups are forcing the 'dehumanization issue' of the colonists since the outbreak. Star Corp is refusing to use another manned ship at Avaric after the situation with the Merlin. And none of the commercial cargo carriers we have contracts with will accept the assignment with a manned crew."

"And why would that be, Mr. Whittington? For the kind of credits you're offering, it seems like someone would have jumped at the chance." Gale spoke, his tone amused.

Whittington's smile completely slipped from his face. "Details from the Merlin outbreak have everyone terrified." Gale reached into a drawer and withdrew a small disc. He tossed it on the desktop. Whittington looked at it, then back up at Gale, whose expression was no longer amused and barely under control. Gale leaned over the desk, his black eyes bottomless.

"A contact at Star Corp got me some footage downloaded from both Avaric & the Merlin." Gale shook his head slowly and Whittington suddenly felt nervous. "The Avaric footage was startling, but I kept in mind that it is a civilian outpost. The Merlin, on the other hand, was like a war zone populated by asylum inmates. There were things happening during the outbreak that made me sick to my stomach, and if my brother wasn't involved in this shit, I'd tell you to keep looking." Gale rose up from his chair, Whittington's attention jumping to the KILLER tattoo for just an instant. "But Chris is involved, and there is a chance, no matter how fucking small, he might still be alive, so I'll tell you what Omni Inc. will do for the government and for your presidential aspirations. I want a flat 50 million credit contract fee, of which half will be placed in the company account before departure. I want the latest biohazard suits and equipment shipped directly from the Center of Health and Disease Center in Atlanta. I want my engineer to be directly involved in the self-destruct installation. I want our quarantine time reduced to 10 days and the ship's quarantine down to 30." Gale's eyes skipped from the Representative to Jones and back. "I also want permission to board the Merlin once we get to Avaric to search for my brother." Whittington was pressed back into his chair, nodding with every demand. The light sheen of perspiration on the politician's forehead might as well have been a neon sign reading 'I really want to be President---whatever you want'. And that was the only signal needed, because Gale went straight for the jugular. "And one last thing, Mr. Whittington. If you become

World President, and we both know that if we pull this thing off it'll put you in a great position to get elected, I want your word of honor that you will grant me one favor, as long as it is not of an illegal nature." Whittington's eyes were wide and glassy from the last request. His lips moved as if to speak, but stopped. Whittington closed his eyes and rubbed his forehead like he had a headache, going over the alternatives. "We're your only shot, Whittington, but if we're going into the soup with that nasty bug, we have to get paid suicide pay. Huge suicide pay."

Whittington looked up, weary but not yet totally toothless. "But if you don't go, what about your brother? What if by some miracle he did survive Carnage?" Gale's eyebrows knitted and his head tilted slightly. Maggie and Jones also looked at the Representative quizzically. "Carnage---it's what we're calling the virus. Because of the violent, psychotic behavior it causes," he hurriedly explained.

"The media wanted a name, right?" Jones questioned. Whittington nodded, looking embarrassed. Gale stepped around his desk, but stopped, feeling a nudge inside his head. He turned, eyes locking dead on Maggie. She was focused on him, blinking rapidly.

"Stop it," Gale ordered, his tone sharp. Mentally she flipped a switch and she was just staring at him. The slight pressure he'd felt was gone. Unconsciously she took a step back.

"Sorry."

Gale turned back to Whittington, his anger barely in check. "Whatever you read in my file, I'm not that crazy, Representative. Christopher is dead and I know that. But if I have the opportunity to be sure, I want it. But I won't kill myself and my crew to find out." Gale took a couple of steps behind Whittington then stopped. He put his hands on his hips, took a deep breath, then slowly let it out. He turned to look at the back of the aspiring president's head. Whittington half turned in his chair. "When would we need to be ready?" Gale asked evenly.

The Representative blinked, the tension continuing to build. "I've been advised that we could have your ship modified in less than 24 hours." He paused, weighing the moment. "If I can get your demands met, do we have a deal?" Gale glanced at Jones and Maggie, got the answer he was looking for, then looked at Whittington.

"If you meet our demands, we'll accept the contract." Whittington exhaled in a burst, shaking a triumphant fist. Smiling like a happy child, he moved from his chair to shake all their hands with the eagerness of a campaign rally.

"Mr. Gale, I am extremely happy to have been able to come to terms on this agreement with you. I will have the documents drawn up and delivered to you by morning. With your permission, we will begin ship modifications immediately."

Gale nodded. "You can co-ordinate everything through Maggie. If I'm not available, she is authorized to make binding decisions." Maggie moved in front of the men, opening the doorway for their movement into the lobby.

"Surprise," Jones whispered. Gale glanced at the Omni doctor, then stopped dead in his tracks. The remaining Omni team members were milling in the lobby around Maggie's desk. Their expressions were friendly, curious, and anxious. Whittington looked at Gale, both men startled and slightly confused.

"Your team, Mr. Gale?" Gale nodded, dumbfounded. Helena stepped from the group, reaching her hand out. Without hesitation, Gale took it, smiling at her smile. Kurt stepped up behind her, patiently waiting for Gale's attention. When Gale looked at his friend, he was startled again. Kurt was clean-shaven and he'd gotten a haircut. His coloring was a still a shade on the pale side, but he didn't look like a barfly anymore. And when he spoke there was no hint of liquor or masking breath mint. They eyeballed each other for a long moment, then Kurt spoke.

"So, do we have a job, or what?"

Gale looked past him at the others, aware that Lauren was not among them. Everyone seemed to be waiting for him to answer the question. His attention fell back to Kurt, a tiny grin tugging at his mouth. "Yeah, we do."

There was an excited whoop from the group while Gale and Kurt stood facing each other. Kurt took a step toward Gale and started to speak. Gale stepped forward and let himself be hugged by his friend. He heard Kurt whisper, "I'm so sorry" and both men held on tight, happy in the moment to have re-found each other. The rest of the team gathered around them, joining in their happiness.

Jones made his way to Helena, squeezing her shoulder. She was smiling; her dimples making her look extra happy. Her eyes were also close to tears. 'I think Jefferson is on the way back." Helena hugged Jones hard, her eyes still holding on Gale.

Whittington quietly left the office, his thoughts racing. The real work was just beginning if he wanted to take full advantage of the publicity to come. There were press conferences to set up, various media interviews to do, and speculation to leak out to key sources. By the time the Omni crew returned, he would be the most recognizable public figure in the world. He would be

Representative Conrad Whittington, the savior of Avaric, champion of humanitarian causes. And less than a year from the next presidential, it just might be enough...

But would it be all for nothing if Gale didn't pull it off? Whittington shook the thought from his head. What could go wrong? It was a dangerous, but a very simple cargo transfer. Oh, and he had to remind himself that the cargo was victims, innocents whose lives were taken by a hellish, merciless virus called Carnage. That was good, really good. He could use that at his first press conference.

Smiling to himself as he stepped into the lift, he began to softly whistle, "Hail to the Chief."

PHASE II

A day later, amidst worldwide publicity, the Omni crew shuttled out to the ship, the various networks dispatching correspondents and telecam crews to document their departure. The media had dubbed the mission 'Operation Savior' and Omni Incorporated and Conrad Whittington were headline news. The Omni answering service was swamped with interview requests and job offers. One famous women's magazine wanted the male crewmembers to do a group interview. And pose nude.

Kurt and Torbeck were especially appreciative of the media flood. They used the attention to advertise their single status and hinted at using their generous share amounts to drive away the haunting images of death that would torment them after the completion of the mission.

As CEO, Gale fielded the bulk of the attention. His prior, highly decorated Star Corp career made him the darling of the evening news. When questions were posed regarding the additional danger of exposure by transporting a small group of survivors back for study, Gale merely shrugged them off, stating that there was really no additional danger to himself or the crew, and jokingly mentioned the sexiness of the biohazard suits.

Of course, Representative Whittington was the toast of political world. Rumors were already circulating about him winning the Nobel Peace Prize and possibly running for the government's presidential seat in the next election. Whittington ate up the media attention like a fat kid eats candy on Halloween night, but was careful to avoid addressing his future political aspirations, focusing instead on his gratefulness to the government body for allowing him to put his plan in motion.

Gale had guessed at the true intentions of Whittington prior to their first meeting. The Representative, despite his very public-minded demeanor, had stayed on a very steady, carefully chosen path up the political mountain. Whittington wasn't the only one with personnel contacts deep within the government.

Gale was very surprised at the ease in which he was able to convince Whittington to have the World Government authorize a transfer of a small group of surviving colonists for medical research. The scientific community had applauded the suggestion, and a biohazard lock-down dorm area was installed in a section of the hold for the survivors. Discussions had been held regarding the transporting of the colonists, and Gale had simply volunteered to transport them via shuttlecraft to the Omni ship. A special docking area that would feed directly to the colonist dorm was constructed, delaying the launch by nearly a day.

Just after 1:00am, dressed in comfortable pale gold with black trim jumper suits, everyone took their positions throughout the Omni. The ship itself was shaped like a wedge, with the engines positioned on the underside of the wider rear section. The Omni was connected to the huge cargo/hold section, much like old fashion diesel trucks were attached to trailers. The ship was covered in a black synthetic coating with the name OMNI written in white with silver trim over the front nose section. Take off would occur at their mark, and Gale hoped to be on their way within an hour. In general, this was the worst part of any mission. Once contracts were signed, everyone wanted to get on with it, get the assignment over, collect their credits, and take a vacation. But the Omni team went through the routine departure system checks, having learned that even the simplest mission could turn into a bloody nightmare. Pandora had proven that.

On the bridge, the only unoccupied station was engineering, where Pace normally perched. The tight schedule had Pace monitoring the engines and ship systems from the engine room. The high level of technology made the small operations deck a very simple design. Gale sat in the middle of the triangular chamber, staring into the infinite sea of stars. Impatiently he waited for the crew to give green lights for departure. He hated sitting around and waiting. Even on the most routine cargo mission, the last minutes before departure always steered his anxious thoughts to those of dark, unexpected surprises. Murphy's Law would gnaw into his mind and fester, turning the mundane into deadly perversion. This particular assignment, in all actuality, should be one of the most routine the company had taken on. But thoughts of plagues and psychotic violence and horrible, agonizing death nagged at Gale. As much as he tried to push away those thoughts, they continued to haunt him, refusing to be dismissed.

Along the rear wall behind Gale, Kurt and Julie Kimbro were stationed at the helm, going through the pre-flight checklist for the navigational and weapon/defense station. Maggie was seated at the communications console just in front of the command chair awaiting departure, her systems already checked and double-checked. Jones was in the sick bay, and Helena and Gii were down in the supply and armory vault checking over the emergency equipment and bio-suits. Gale had requested each team member have a primary and a back-up suit in case of life support failure or suit integrity being compromised. A malfunctioning suit was not an option on this mission. Gale didn't want to think about any of the team getting infected, and that's why he had Gii and Helena triple checking each suit.

Gale covered his face with his hands and tried to relax, and even as he slowed his breathing, he felt eyes on him. He was sure they belonged to Maggie, figuring if she needed him, she would say something. He knew she was probably stealing his thoughts right now, but that was something he had gotten used to long ago. Instead, his thoughts moved to his training regimen and the time he had recently missed. Physical combat techniques and conditioning took extreme discipline, and this mission had disrupted his routine. As he floated in the peaceful darkness of his own inner space, he realized that his routine, forged from depression and isolation, was not normal for a man of his position. He was no longer a wartime soldier, yet he spent at least 3 hours training every day, and that didn't include time spent at the weapon range. Since the Pandora assignment, he had felt an urgent sense to be ready for any future mission that might go to hell-in-a-hand-basket. He wanted to be able to sustain a much greater physical strain if and when the time warranted it. His hand-to-eye techniques had improved vastly. Even in the case of his quick dance with Albert, the bodyguard looked to be moving at half speed. The intense training had helped him get through the dark early days after the Pandora mission, but it had been far from a cure-all.

His heart hurt knowing he had been so poisoned from the loss that he would react like an assassin against Kurt. In that moment of rage, he might have hurt his friend. Kurt had been lucky he'd chosen a submission hold and not a strike. In his prime, Kurt had been a helluva soldier, but he was just a shadow of his prime self. He still had skills, but the booze and lack of training had dulled and slowed him. And Lauren certainly hadn't pushed him to stay fit. Her logic was 'why sweat in the gym when you can pull a trigger?' Kurt hadn't even remembered the escape move Gale had shown him for the chokehold he was in the other day. Thank God he had kept up his own training.

A smile played at his lips as he resettled in the chair. There were parts of him beginning to feel like his old self, despite his constant gruff front. One thing he couldn't fake was his excitement over a potentially dangerous mission. But weren't all the missions he contracted potentially deadly?

And just like that Maggie's voice broke into his chain of thoughts. "All systems have checked out and Pace has cleared us for departure. And Whittington and 'the world' wish us 'luck and God's speed.'"

Kurt glanced up from his station. "Oh, I bet he does," he mumbled. Maggie's mouth slipped half a grin.

"That's it," Gale sighed, relieved to be finally getting on with it. Orders poured from his mouth in a well-practiced cadence. "Maggie, alert the port of our immediate departure. Advise the rest of the crew. Julie, when helm is ready, please take us out of port and lay in co-ordinates for the Avaric colony, and once we're into clear space, please activate the auto-pilot."

"Aye aye," she responded, her focus welded to the navigational panel. Her fingers blurred over the control touch pads. After several moments she said, "Exiting dock now, Jefferson." Letting his mind glances over several details for a moment, Gale touched a soft pad on his chair arm. After a short pause, Pace's voice sounded.

"Engineering. Pace." Gale chuckled to himself. Who else could it have been? Pace Kimbro would have set up his and Julie's cabin down in engineering if he'd had his way. Of course, Julie had nipped that idea in the bud. They were trying to start a family and Pace spent enough time down there tinkering as it was.

"How's everything looking?"

"Everything checked out, but the self-destruct is very intricate and very sensitive. I'll be very happy when this thing gets out of our lives." Pace's tone had a thread of anxiety running through it, and with a quick head swivel, Gale and Julie acknowledged it. Apparently she had picked up on her husband's tone, and Gale knew where the apprehension was coming from. All Star Corp ships were equipped with a standard emergency self-destruct device, but it was a manual device that could only be activated by a series of codes fed in the shipboard computer that no single person on board knew. Self-destruct had to be a unanimous decision among the top five senior departmental officers. Only on top-secret assignments did the Omni ever utilize one, and it took Gale, Jones, and Kurt to activate it. But the unit installed by the government was the most sophisticated in existence. It was activated automatically by specific programmed variances outside normal perimeter conditions of the ship. These conditions included the ship's power, life support, internal cabin temperature and pressure, and unauthorized opening of the hold seals where the plague victims and survivors were to be contained. There was one emergency fail safe deactivation programmed into the device, so once that had been used, there would be no more turning back the clock. Once activated, the device would initiate a nuclear detonation in 15 minutes. It took almost 8 minutes for an experienced tech to deactivate the device, and Pace had made two practice runs around the 10-minute mark. There wasn't much margin for error. The idea that a simple computer malfunction could activate it, and the real possibility their one 'get out of jail free' card might not get used in time weighed in Pace's voice, and now on Gale's mind. Gale had agreed that the government couldn't take any chances with billions of lives at stake. The crew had accepted it, but Pace was going to have to live with it the closest for the entire mission.

"Good. Try to relax, Pace. Everything's going to go as smooth as silk. Out."

Kurt spoke, concerned. "He's really spooked, huh?"

Gale nodded, exhaling a deep breath. He tried to stretch the neck and shoulder muscles that had just tensed from Pace's tone. 'Can you blame him? He's the only one who can turn the thing off if there's a malfunction. We all had a walk through on it, but he's really it. And God knows we've had our share of computer and system breakdowns in the past." Gale stood up from the command chair. "But hey, the government had their techs completely check through our systems, so we should be fine." Gale glanced around the chamber, then said, "I'm going down to the rec-area if anyone needs me." Maggie nodded but didn't reply.

"Workout?" Kurt asked.

Gale shook his head as he stepped into the lift. "The tube." The doors closed and the lift took Gale away, leaving Kurt, Maggie and Julie to look at each other. Julie turned her attention back to her station, leaving Kurt looking perplexed at Maggie. And she knew why.

"Jefferson hates the tube," Kurt muttered. Maggie slowly swiveled in her chair, her mind echoing the same thought.

For some reason, Gale felt drawn to the sensory deprivation tank the crew had nicknamed the tube, and he didn't fight the feeling, though he had never imagined using it in the past. He had always held the opinion that if someone needed to relax and think, lying in a coffin half filled with fluid was not the way to do it. Gale preferred working through problems while training, but something drew him into using the tank to explore the battleground of feelings warring inside himself.

Gale thought about talking to Jones or Kurt, but it didn't feel right. And going to Helena was out of the question. That pretty much left babbling to himself and the tube.

He changed into a pair of skin shorts and carried a thick white towel to the rec room, which was a deck below the living quarters and conference room, and two decks below the bridge. Engineering, supplies, and the shuttle bay made up level three, while the cargo area of the Omni was level 4. Gale realized that he'd made a mistake by mentioning where he was headed, and he knew using the tube had to have struck a weird note with everyone, but he wasn't going to explain it now. Hell, they might have just chalked it up to more of his moody behavior.

57

He tried to relax as he activated the machine, his thoughts wandering to the moments of passion he'd shared with Helena. He felt his stomach tighten as it played in his mind, and he thought about all the flirting they had done in the past that he had laughed off and Grace had ignored. He knew he always had special feelings toward Helena as both a great person and a superlative soldier. They had struck up an easy kinship through their long hours in the gym, talking for hours and hours as they sculpted and forged their bodies, laughing, debating, theorizing. He suddenly realized just how well he knew her, and in turn, how much she actually knew about him. They had talked about everything over the course of the last two years---politics, sex, religion, their families and upbringing. They had talked about the military and their private war experiences. They had talked about their love lives---past, present and future. He had shared with her the vast majority of his thoughts, nightmares and dreams. He had never realized how comfortable he actually was around her until this moment. And he knew there was much more to their relationship than that.

He had watched her in the gym countless times. His eyes strayed to her from between sets, and during water and rest breaks. He had watched her push herself; powerful muscles working under smooth skin, hot sweat making her look sleek and sexy, despite her stocky, compact frame. The muscles just added to her curves, and she did have those in all the right places.

Gale remembered her initial interview with Omni Inc. Maggie had shown her into his office, and he had been stunned. He had seen her during a weight-lifting competition a couple of year's prior, and her service records had a photo, but he was surprised by the simple attractiveness of her, the dimples, her smile, her grace. When she had extended her hand to shake his, he could still remember several details. Her effortless grip was the equal of his, though her hand had been soft and warm. He remembered a tiny static shock had passed between them, which they both laughed and apologized for, and he remembered the gentlest waif of her perfume. The interview quickly turned into a catch-up chat between two budding friends, and they had eaten lunch together the next day. He had offered her a general crew position for which her jack-of-all-trades background would fit perfectly, and she had blended with the rest of the team by being honest, straightforward, and professional. She laughed at even the worst jokes, and had an easy to be around personality. And, as Gale stepped up into the narrow canister, he realized that Helena had chosen to be around him, with Grace and now without Grace.

The sensory deprivation chamber's fluid seemed strangely non-existent as it instantly matched his body temperature. He floated, waiting for the tank's lid to close. He felt a surge of panic course through him, fighting back an urge to cry out. He was suddenly reminded of an incident during his Star Corp active duty where he and a handful of survivors had been buried in a dark, tiny crawl space in the corner of a collapsed bunker. They weren't even able to stand upright, huge chunks of rubble entombing them until Star Corp soldiers had discovered and rescued them four days later. Eleven people had been trapped, but only six had survived until rescue. It had been that incident that had kept him from going in after Ted and Ursala on Pandora. Gale was now more than mildly claustrophobic, and when the lid slid shut with an inky blackness so absolute, no one heard him cry out...

Maybe that was why he had let the others know where he was going. He felt buried alive, and if something were to happen, at least they'd know where to find him.

As the tube sealed, he had a flash of the dream about Grace's burial. Gale felt his heart hammer, and he fought back panic and disorientation. After several moments he was able to slow his breathing, and he concentrated on the fact that he was really floating and all his external senses were void. He could feel his heart beating but little else. He was wrapped in an absence of light like a starless stretch of space, a preview of death minus the dirt and worms. Despite the clock in his head, time quickly dissolved. He closed his eyes without needing to and let himself drift into a strange existence where the boundaries between past and present, reality and illusion were blurred.

Gale revisited places he'd been, relived memories, boyhood dreams, and experienced the gray forgotten edges of his mind.

And suddenly he was back on the Pandora assignment...

Gale's black shark eyes blinked open, and he instantly knew where he was, realizing this trip down bad memory lane would be the same as all the others. He would only be able to flow with the situation, following the same pattern of events, fully aware the end would never change.

He glanced around, marveling at the detail of the surroundings. The soft burgundy sky gave the planet a surreal backdrop. The lush plant life was a spectrum of vivid greens, moist from the region's high humidity. The thick grass was an emerald carpet, and he watched a centipede-like insect crawl across his boot. Its stripes were blood red and black, nature's warning colors. It had a long pair of antennae, and a nasty looking set of shiny black pinchers. He looked up, not surprised to see team members hustling around him as a rescue attempt was in progress. Everyone was dressed like the centipede in bright red and black trim jumpers, and he found himself almost admiring the exquisitely camouflaged trap door that had surprised Ted McClanahan and Ursala

59

Edwards. The hole led down through a twisting, curvy tunnel and ended deep underground in some type of pit. Ursala and Ted had been in constant communication with the rest of the team, and according to Ursala, the higher ranked of the two, both she and Ted were stuck to the floor of a cave by some kind of ultra strong, quick binding adhesive. Grace and Jones had studied the trap, finally concluding that the two had stumbled into the lair of an alien or earth mutant insect. Ted and Ursala were probably potential prey for whatever was down there with them. With Pandora being a world heavily populated by biological and genetic experiments, it was going to be difficult determining the specific creature occupying the lair. Grace and Maggie were doing an insect crosscheck for possible predators, but the number one priority was getting them out. Immediately Gale hoped whatever had built the trap no longer existed, itself prey to some other diabolical predator.

On their second day of this assignment, Gale watched via remote camera as the scout team was confronted by a pack of large, dog-sized spiders. They looked like overgrown wolf spiders, and they seemed to co-ordinate their attack like African wild dogs. They used flanking techniques, they didn't display their total numbers, and they constantly shifted positions until they had decided to attack. Despite their quick movements and stalking strategies, the team handled the attack with relative ease. Gii had wanted to extract the oozing maw from the biggest of the pack as a trophy, but Helena, who led the team, hadn't thought that was a good idea. Gii had muttered his displeasure under his breath, careful not to let Helena hear him. For all his bravado and battle experience, Gii wasn't stupid. Gale knew everyone had heard stories of the Star Corp "Lady Atlas" long before she joined Omni. Gale remembered chuckling to himself at the amount of respect Gii had given her. Gii certainly never seemed to have a problem expressing his displeasure regarding decisions Gale or anyone else in charge made.

Ursala had described the incident as the two of them stepping through the ground, then sliding quickly through a narrow, curving tunnel. After several seconds, there was a sudden short drop to a cavern floor. Ted had landed flat on his back, and was now unable to move at all. His torso, arms, legs and the back of his head was attached solidly to the floor. He was able to lift his head just a tiny bit before his scalp screamed. Ursala had been more fortunate, landing on her side. She luckily still had an arm free—after the fall, she had put her free hand down to push herself up, but immediately jerked it away from the sticky floor, leaving some skin behind. Moments after the fall both felt a cool dampness soak through whatever clothing or bare skin was exposed to the floor, but had realized too late its significance. Ted had been stunned on impact, and had gradually regained his senses, but that was long after he was bonded in place. He had voiced his anxiety in his early statements, but now fear filled Ted's voice every time he spoke.

It had taken some time for the Omni crew to get to their position, and precious more time to formulate a plan. The only positive detail of the incident had been that only Ursala and Ted had been trapped. Had the salvage assignment not been in full swing, there might have been more of the crew literally stuck with them down in the dark.

Ursala had reported the den was pitch black. Using the hand light from her utility belt, she took a quick scan of their surroundings, but there was no obvious clue to what might live there. Both were very anxious to be rescued before they found out. She reported that Ted was laying just a few feet from her, and like her, had not been injured other than the jolt of the fall.

Crude, earthen walls that could have been dug by any number of creatures surrounded them. The floor, though, was another matter.

Ursala, forcing her voice to be calm, reported that the floor of the cave was covered in a clear, varnish looking substance that was obviously a fly trap-like adhesive. But she wasn't sure whether to be happy or sad over the fact that besides the two of them, the rest of the glossy floor was bare. There was no trace of bones or exoskeletons or left over carcasses. As she had studied their surroundings more, she noted that other than the opening in the ceiling from which they dropped, there was only one other way in or out of the chamber, but when she shone the light into it, there was nothing to see. There was an underlying, sickly-sweet fragrance in the stale, still air, not lending much of a clue to the identity of their possible host. And maybe the worst thing was the absolute silence---Ted called it "coffin quiet". If he was trying to make a joke, nobody laughed.

Ted and Ursala had been in the pit for nearly an hour when Ursala's voice burst from the crews' belt radios. "We can hear something. It sounds like soft, moist sounds coming from the chamber opening. Get us out of here guys!" Panic had edged into her voice, and Gale moved to stand over the hole, the trapdoor having been removed by Gii and Kyle. Gale closed his eyes for a second, suddenly deciding he didn't want to imagine what might be down there with them. He didn't take his eyes from the hole in the ground as he barked out orders.

"Kurt, Gii, get ready to go down. Kyle, hook them up to the towline. Maggie, send down the snake, and I want full audio/visual range on the camera, and attach a light globe to it. I want picture up before the guys go down." There was movement around him, and Maggie slid to a knee next to him, a heavy tech

vest dwarfing her torso. She started uncoiling 'the snake', which was a flexible, waterproof cable with a camera mounted on the end. She had already attached a powerful ring light, which would illuminate the chamber, and she was doing a quick double check before threading it down the tunnel. Gale pressed a button on his belt and spoke. "Ursala, Gii and Kurt are ready to rock right now, and Maggie is going to be sending down the snake in the next couple of minutes. Once it's down, save your hand light." Gale turned away from Maggie for a moment, lowering his tone. "Can you see anything yet?"

"Not yet, but that rotten fruit smell is getting stronger. Something is definitely going on." Gale could hear in her voice that she was fighting to stay in control.

"Do you have access to your weapon?" He closed his eyes to pray.

"Fuck yeah---it's in my hot little hand right now." Gale exhaled, feeling a little better. At least they weren't totally defenseless, and Ursala was an expert shot. Gale realized Ted hadn't spoken a word.

"Ted, you still down there man?" he asked, trying to lighten the moment. Ted didn't answer for several seconds, then spoke just as Gale felt a stab of real alarm.

"You gotta get us out of here, Jefferson. I got a really bad vibe going." Ted's voice was shaky, and anyone listening could tell he was nearing the breaking point. He was an adventure-seeking, biosciences expert Gale hired on from time to time when, like on this assignment, his expertise would be a valuable commodity. Ted had been a member of the government administrative team responsible for setting up Pandora several years ago. Right now, Gale knew Ted's mind was scanning through all the possibilities of what might be down there with them, and none were going to be a welcome sight.

Gale stepped away from the hole as first Gii, then Kurt, went belly down, head first in. Gale stepped around to look at the flat screen monitor on the back of Maggie's vest. The snake was still winding its way down, nothing to see yet except dark soil, rocks, and gnarled plant roots.

Suddenly Ursala spoke up, and everyone could hear the fear. "We have definite movement down here. I don't have line of sight yet, but I do have shadow movement low on the wall in the cave's ground entrance. It's moving slow but steady. And the stink is bad." Before Gale could respond, Gii's voice came over the frequency.

"We're in the hole and on the way, 'Sala. I don't how far down to you, but we're coming."

"Come on," Ted pleaded, the pitch of his voice noticeably higher.

Gale continued to watch the monitor, his anxiety and the humidity forcing him to wipe at his forehead. Perspiration was starting to fight its way through everyone's uniforms. The cumbersome tech vest Maggie wore was soaked with sweat.

Finally the snake made it to the cave, and Maggie activated the high-powered lamp. The crude chamber exploded into clear view, and both Ted and Ursala barked with the sudden invasion of intense light.

"Maggie, steer the snake down toward the pit's opening, and let's see what's coming for dinner." She nodded, the metallic fiber tentacle swaying its way from the ceiling toward the circular opening. It passed over Ursala and Ted, angling, focusing on the entranceway. Ursala cursed out loud as she saw with her own eyes what the snake camera projected onto the above ground monitor.

"What the fuck is that shit?" she muttered, wide eyed.

Ted, unable to see what was approaching, was franticly trying to find out what was happening. Gale was momentarily stunned, horrified by the sight.

"What's happening?" Kurt burst from the tunnel.

"Move your ass! We don't know what it is, but we're going to pretend it's a shit-storm!" Gale informed, entranced by the image on the monitor.

It was like a creamy white, gelatinous mass flowing slowly into the chamber, countless squiggling, squirming grub-like creatures swimming/sliding along in the soup. As Maggie zoomed the camera in for a closer look, Jones stepped up behind Gale. As Jones and Gale covered their headset microphones, Gale leaned back so Jones could whisper to him.

"I'm guessing that the goop around the grubs aids them in the digestive process. That mass' secretions will probably be extremely acidic." The quiet tone of his voice was just enough to get the attention of the closest team members. Gale's jaw flexed tightly, and his stomach clinched like a fist.

At its current rate, it wouldn't be two minutes before the massive spew of maggots made contact with the trapped Omni team members. Maggie spooled the snake into the passage from where the grubs were coming. Gale's mouth opened a tiny bit then closed. There was no end in sight to the mass, and there was more than enough to fill up the entire chamber, floor to ceiling. Gale's heart began to pound in his chest, and he had to remind himself to breathe. He'd had this feeling many times before in battle, but it never, ever got any easier. Ursala and Ted weren't going to make it, and there wasn't a fucking thing he could do about it.

The sound of Ursala's weapon firing snapped Gale back into the moment, and he knelt by the hole, pulling Maggie to a knee beside him. The rest of the

Omni crew hovered around, silently watching the events on the screen, listening with pained and anxious expressions to their headsets. Grace had closed her eyes, not wanting to watch, yet not wanting to turn her back on her crew mates. Kyle had pulled his mother's small gold cross from under his collar and closed his big fist around it, whispering the Lord's Prayer. Gale had seen him make that gesture in the past, but God always seemed too busy to intervene.

There seemed to be a surge in the flow of the grubs, not in speed but in volume, and now instead of just spilling across the chamber floor, part of the mass was flowing up the walls toward the ceiling.

"Pull the snake back to the ceiling drop point, Maggie," Gale instructed, absently swiping his hand over his sweat soaked face. Ursala continued to fire her gun into the mass, but the shots only managed to blast holes almost instantly re-formed after impact. Gale pushed his palm hard into his forehead for a moment, resolving himself for what was going to be the same horrific ending. He glanced over his shoulder at Kyle, switching off his mic for a moment. "Pull Gii back up asap." Kyle started to make a comment, but Gale's tight jaw and flared nostrils stopped it cold. Gale's attention flickered over to Helena. "Prepare some inferno grenades with remote detonation as quickly as you can." She scrambled to follow the order as Gale stared back at the monitor. He opened back up the frequency. "Kurt, I need you to be ready to use your weapon as soon as you get to the opening. You're not going to have a lot of time before the grubs have completely covered the ceiling." The mass was within several feet of Ted, but his head was turned and stuck facing away from the flow. He could see Ursala' face, and his whimpering was a direct reflection of Ursala's desperate expression. She kept firing her pistol until the twenty five shot load was gone, the rapid, empty clicking of the trigger the clearest sign of a soldier operating solely on fear. Unfortunately, her two extra loads were on the side of her belt stuck between her and the floor. As the reality of her defenselessness struck home, she began slamming the butt of the gun against the ground, tears streaking down her face.

"Fuck, fuck, fuck, fuck, fuck. Where are you guys, Jefferson? That shit is just about on Ted. We need some friggin' help down here guys. Right now, por favor." Her last few words had a strange resolve, as if she were just reading the words. That's when Gale realized that she knew the dark, inescapable truth of the situation. Gale stared at the screen, watching Kurt's upper torso burst from the ceiling, gun in hand. The grubs were almost on top of Ted, just a few feet from Ursala, and slowly swallowing up the chamber. The part of the mass that had climbed the wall and was spreading itself over the ceiling wasn't long from

being on top of Kurt. Through his helmet visor, Kurt surveyed the scene, hot sweat dripping onto the clear plastic of his face shield.

"Are you seeing this shit, Jefferson? We have to get these guys loose right now!" Gale took a deep breath, quickly formulating how he was going to word his next order. Then Ted's bloodcurdling scream sliced through his thoughts like a scalpel. The covered part of the ceiling began to undulate, and then hungry grubs began to drop onto Ted and Ursala like a hellish rain. Ursala was shrieking, flailing her empty weapon in a hopeless attempt to keep the grubs off her. Ted trembled and shook, so completely vulnerable to the attack, it sickened Gale and the others to watch. Ted and Ursala screamed and pleaded for help, for salvation. But a quick, painless death was not what they were going to receive from the blind, voracious abominations.

The grubs began to smother Ted, their secretions literally melting the flesh off his bones. He looked as if he were made of wax, the skin sliding off, mixing with the acidic mucus. Ted wailed like a man damned to his own private hell as he was gradually devoured alive. The grubs had begun to explore the exposed parts of him that had begun to be digested, and in moments his face, neck and hands were being penetrated. The maggots were driven by their instinct to seek the soft inner core of their prey, and they seemed to find access to this food source very easy.

"Oh God, oh God, oh God," Kurt was mumbling, watching the horror first hand, his eyes darting from the chaos below to the larva closing steadily on the ceiling.

"Shoot Kurt!" Gale ordered, emotion catching his voice in his throat. "Shoot Ted and Ursala. Now!"

"What? Shoot...?" Kurt sounded confused, like a small boy who didn't understand what the words meant. The agonizing screams from Ted and Ursala were deafening over the frequency.

"They're being eaten alive!" Gale cried out. "Take them out of their misery. RIGHT NOW, Goddamn it! Pull the fucking trigger!"

"Oh God oh God help me..." Kurt whispered to himself, slowly aiming at the top of Ted's skull, which was quickly devolving into something not recognizable as human. Defenseless, the wave of maggots poured over him, consuming him both inside and out. Blood burst from where his eyes had been, and no one in the world could have cried out in purer agony than Ted did at that moment. Satan himself must certainly be smiling at this unthinkable perversion. But Ted's cry quickly changed to a horrible, drowning gargle when the feasting grubs flowed into his mouth, Ted's tongue another soft entree. Kurt,

his face shield holding a small pool of sweat, pulled the trigger several times with a wail of his own, Ted's now silent face a dismantled, bloody, grub covered lump. Kurt quickly adjusted his aim, but had to hold his fire a moment as Ursala thrashed about. She was able to smash some with her free hand, but the contact with the larva started to liquefy the flesh from her fingers. She gazed up at Kurt, her expression a heartbreaking mix of pleading and pain and he darted out from the tunnel completely, dangling below the level of the ceiling. His free, out-stretched glove clasped her clutching hand, and her desperate strength tugged him toward her a little closer.

"Help me Kurt," she begged, wretched tears streaking her face. "I don't want to die like this. I don't want these things... feeding off me." Kurt jerked at her arm, but it was as if her body was welded to the floor. Countless things were flowing over the remains of Ted and washing up next to her legs, slowly creeping and sliding up along her torso. She held onto Kurt hand with an insane strength, crying and cursing and screaming in inhuman anguish. The mass slowly started to pour onto her, their digestive juices dissolving her uniform and eating at the exposed flesh. The grubs began to act more agitated as they fed, eating and burrowing into her softened skin and tissue. But somehow, through the violation and pain, she still struggled to survive, refusing to give up her life. Where her legs had been was now just a sea of grubs, stealing her life for their own. As the mass flowed up past her waist, she stared pleading into Kurt's eyes, bloody spittle spraying from her lips as she spoke in labored gasps. "Shoot me, Kurt. Don't let this shit happen. I can't take this shit..." She couldn't stop the shriek that leapt from her throat, the grubs continuing to feast, her body dissolving...

Kurt swung his pistol around, pressing the barrel against Ursala's forehead. His vision blurred as he blubbered goodbye, squeezing the trigger twice. He hung there, trying to force back the nightmare surrounding him, tears joining his sweat.

He heard a somber "Get out of there, Kurt," in his helmet, but he didn't respond. Gale prodded at his best friend, fully aware of the emotions Kurt was drowning in. "You have to go NOW, man."

Kurt opened his eyes to an unrecognizable heap covered in feeding, squirming things, and he still couldn't make himself release Ursala, watching the grubs slide up her arm toward his glove. Instinctively he holstered his weapon. Inches from the larva sliding from her dead hand to his, he tugged himself upward, Ursala's grub covered arm pulling free from her body, the flesh and connective tissue eaten away. The arm hung in his grasp for a long moment before Kurt's mind recognized the horror. He shook the arm free, it *falling with a wet smack into the bloody mire. Kurt scrambled back into the tunnel, the grubs flowing over the hole not a minute after he slithered back through.*

Most everyone had turned away from the monitor during the course of the incident, but no one had disconnected the audio feed. Gale could hear sobs around him, but he continued to stare at the screen, watching long beyond losing sight of his team members. As soon as Kurt emerged topside, Helena and Maggie used the snake to lower the grenades into the pit, landing with a thick, wet smack as if they were dropped into mud. With Gale's solemn nod, Helena detonated the extreme temperature explosives, turning the contents of the pit into nothing more than ash and charred soil.

Gale dropped to his hands and knees, head hanging. He felt Grace's soft touch on the back of his neck, but it couldn't ease the damage. The echoes of Ursala and Ted's voices during their last minutes swirled in his mind. Screams and pleas and curses blended into a hellish, haunting garble. Gale tried to get his mind around how it must have felt to be invaded and fed upon, helpless to defend yourself. He had lost two of his crew, two friends. There was no enemy to hunt down and drag to justice or just kill in cold blood. His friends had been nothing but food to another life form, no different than cattle or fish to men. And their deaths had no meaning---they had died for nothing.

Meaningless links in a severed food chain...

The vividness faded from the haunting nightmare, slowly returning Gale to the dark void he'd entered from. But could it really be a nightmare if the events really happened...?

Gale's eyes opened to the blackness of the tube, and he felt a tear roll from the corner of his eye. He reached into the darkness and activated the lid, the machine sliding open. Gale struggled, chest heaving, body trembling. He almost slipped as he stepped to the floor, Gii there to grab his arm for support. Gale roughly shrugged Gii off, grabbed his towel and headed to his quarters. He entered and went straight to the water room, dropping in front of the toilet and retching, his stomach twisting and rolling. When his stomach was empty, he laid his throbbing head on the cool lid, praying for even a moment of peace of mind.

Tammara stood at her hospital room window watching the workers dispose of body after body. The hospital rehab swimming pool had become mortuary, church, and liquid mass graveyard. She watched as pairs of workers grabbed each end of a body bag, lifted them from the motorized cart, and gently eased them down into the acid. The chemicals dissolved away bag, flesh and bones in a matter of minutes. There had been a mild backlash from the community's religious leaders regarding the unceremonious destruction of the victims, but civil and medical authorities were adamant about standard outbreak procedure. Tammara had no way of knowing how many had disappeared into the acid, or if any or all of her family had ended up there. It did seem like a reasonable assumption that her lover, who had been one of the first infected, had also been one of the first into the pool.

She wasn't sure how long she had been standing there, her face hot from the strong sunshine, when the door opened and her friend Lydia came in. Tammara gave her a weary smile, which wasn't even close to matching the one Lydia wore. Steam was rising from the lunch tray she carried in, and she hurriedly sat it down on the bed, the nurse's excitement growing out of control. Lydia practically ran around the bed and grabbed Tammara's hands as if to dance. Tammara wasn't sure what to make of the odd behavior. Maybe the stress had finally taken its toll...

"Guess who just found out about a rescue mission underway from Earth, and guess who saw a list of candidates to return to earth as test volunteers?" Tammara stared at her gushing friend, the words sinking in slowly through the hazy aftermath of daily sedation. Lydia started to bounce up and down like an excited child, her enthusiasm making her words come out in a giggle. "I think we're going to get a chance to go back to Earth! We're going to go home!" As the words sank in, a smile began to grow on Tammara's pale, slack face. She cocked her head, staring into Lydia's eyes. Her voice was a questioning whisper.

"We're going back to Earth?"

Lydia yelped happily, rapidly nodding her head up and down. "It looks like it, honey. I think Dr. Hollins is going to call a mandatory staff meeting tomorrow. Do you think you'll feel well enough to be a nurse for an hour or so?"

Tammara smiled, her body straightening, some energy seeping back into her voice. "No more drugs and I'll be fine." She glanced past her friend at the hot food. "Meatloaf. Who could ask for anything more?" Tammara chuckled, crushed in her friend's exuberant embrace.

Pace flexed and stretched the muscles in his back, stealing a quick glance at Julie, who was sitting at her dressing table in one of his old t-shirts. It was certainly too big for the petite blonde, but he could still see the golden curve of her calves as she sat using her fingers to comb through her wet hair. The shirt was tight against the globes of her ass, and as she looked into the mirror, she caught him admiring. She smiled as he flopped onto the bed, and scratched absently at his light colored beard.

"I don't want to talk about the mission, Pace," she started, splitting her attention between her husband and her hair. He lifted his head just off the mattress and peeked at his wife of six years. Her vanilla colored hair didn't reach her shoulders, with the bangs trimmed short in the front. Like most combat pilots, she found long hair a distraction, and it was an outlook she maintained when she returned to the private sector. The short hair didn't bother Pace at all. He loved to nibble playfully along the long, smooth skin of her throat, and there was no hair to get in the way.

"I hate t---"

"The self-destruct. I know." She half-turned, giving him a brief, though effective 'I'm serious' look. "No more mission talk for the rest of the night. I mean it." She turned back around, making final teases at her hair. When she was finished with her hair, she pulled the tee shirt up to her waist and started to work lotion into her legs.

Pace stared up at the ceiling trying hard to think of anything non-mission related. He rolled his eyes from the ceiling to watch her rub in the lotion, the light fragrance wafting to him. Wearing a dopey grin, he propped himself up on one elbow, content to watch the love of his life.

They had met in the service. She had been transferred onto his ship, ruffling more than a few officers' feathers when she took over the helm's number one position and was promoted to Lieutenant Commander in record time. Even though she had absolutely no designs on commanding her own ship, Julie made it clear that she was in total command of the helm. Pace had first spoken to her at an officer's function, interested to see if she were anything close to the circulating rumors. As it turned out, she was both nothing like and exactly like the rumors. In the weeks following that evening's introduction, through the lunches and dinners and off duty hanging out to follow, he had decided that she was the woman for him. It only took him three years to convince her that he was the right man for her. One of the things that had always bothered Julie was that he couldn't just walk away and leave the engines in the engine room when his duty shift was over. He always had his nose in a journal, was on the computer chatting with another engineer, or was working alone or in teams testing out alternate ship designs, engine systems, power sources, etc. Once they decided to get married, Star Corp regulations prohibited them being assigned to the same active battle cruiser. They put in for a joint transfer to an exploration vessel, where they worked together for almost a year before deciding to retire to civilian life and seek out the more lucrative employment opportunities of the private sector. Several private firms courted them, but when they received the message from Maggie DeLina, associate of Jefferson Gale, they knew their ship had come in. They had made more money in the past five years with Omni Incorporated than they had in their combined 20 plus years of military duty. Working with Jefferson had brought them just the right balance of professional continuation from their Star Corp positions, financial rewards beyond their wildest dreams, and just enough danger and adventure to keep their lives interesting and their skills at a high level. But now a new priority had taken the lead in Julie and Pace's lives.

They wanted to start a family.

This would be their last dangerous mission for a while. They had been trying to have a baby for well over a year, but the fates had kept them childless. If something didn't happen soon, they would seek medical intervention and have her artificially inseminated. They really didn't want to do that, still hoping nature would handle it, but the point was growing nearer and nearer to screw it, get out the turkey baster and get on with the baby making.

Pace watched her apply lotion to one leg, then the other, and then rub the extra into her arms. She glanced up at him, smiling more with her eyes than her lips. After a few moments, she looked up at him again, but her expression and her eyes were different. It was a look that Pace not only recognized but was extremely fond of. He smiled as she crossed the room, buttocks flexing under the thin material. When she reached the manual light switch, she paused, pulling the t-shirt off and dropping it to the carpet. Slowly, she turned around, teasing him with a full view before turning off the lights. As she moved through the darkness toward him, she whispered, "Let's make a baby." He felt her weight on the bed, and then she was sliding along side him, her mouth finding his. Her eager hands helped him out of his jumper and skin shorts, her desire forcing her body against his. Her fingernails trailed down his stomach, his abdominal muscles clinching as she found his manhood. Both groaned as snaking tongues played. Squeezing and stroking made him solid, then hard. His fingers found her moist crease, but soon she became wet and slick under his touch. Julie moaned as she broke off their kiss, her excited breathing like quiet gasps. He was using just the tips of his fingers, sliding them slowly up and down her slippery groove, and she opened her legs wider to allow him more access. Hungrily, she kissed her way down his neck, a sigh escaping his lips. Her mouth licked and teased his chest and stomach, his strong hands in her hair to keep her from moving away. Her hand squeezed him hard, and her teeth bit down on a nipple, causing him to cry out in pleasure. In response, he slid a pair of fingers deep inside her, his thumb teasing around her clit. She clamped her legs around his hand, a series of primitive grunts rolling from deep in her throat. She ground herself against his hand as fingers slid in and out hard, the sensations throbbing, building, carrying her away. The thought of making a baby was gone. Desire, wanting and burning need were everything. She flicked a nail at his neglected nipple, then attacked it with her lips and teeth. He was thick and throbbing, her hand pumping up and down its length. She nudged him over on his back, her mouth still locked to his chest. He protested with a whimper when she took her mouth away, but he groaned his approval when she slid her body over his and mounted him. Her tongue slid hungrily back into his mouth as she guided him into her hot, yearning wetness. She sat up and they both groaned, his hands on her thighs and hips as she slowly worked her body against his.

Pace's hands worked up to her small breasts, her flesh sensitive with excitement. She closed her eyes and leaned back, quickening the movement of her hips. Julie rode him, hands pinning his shoulders to the bed, nails digging into his skin, though not so hard as to draw blood. Their bodies coupled faster and faster as each became swept away in the tide of their pleasure. Both sought to push the other over the edge of release first, yet their bodies were racing on instinct to absorb as much carnal delight as possible. Like all extraordinary lovers, they fed off the others pleasure, their senses funneling the sensual stimuli through their brains then letting it flow throughout their bodies, making nipples even harder, groans louder and longer, breathing more labored, and the sweet release they sought closer and closer.

Pace forced himself up, his hands pulling her body toward him, his mouth closing over a breast, sucking hard. She grabbed his head, her fingers tangled in his hair, not wanting his lips to ever leave her, crying out as her body strained, the moist smacking of their bodies driving them both to the point of release. His fingers dug into the firm flesh of her bottom, and he pistoned in and out of her with all his remaining energy, feeling his orgasm gathering with the fury of a summer storm. And suddenly Julie came, her body slamming down onto his, her hips grounding herself against him drawing him into her as deeply as possible, her body bucking and trembling, her arms wrapped around her husband in a lover's clutch. Her molten center squeezed tight as the first wave of her orgasm pulsed through her, and that was enough to send Pace over the edge, the accumulation of pleasure more than his system could tolerate. He came, crying out as his hips bucked off the bed, lifting her again and again as his spewing seed mixed with her searing wetness. Her eyes popped open, and she almost laughed at the indescribable feel of his release inside her. "I love feeling you come inside me," she whispered, her voice husky. As his body relaxed he fell back to the bed, pulling her down against the sweaty sheen of his body. He moaned as her tongue pushed into his mouth to play. After a long, wet kiss, she pulled her mouth away just enough to speak. "God, I love the way you make me feel." Pace smiled, playfully licking at the salty sweat of her throat. He gently rolled her over and started kissing his way down her neck to her breasts. His tongue teased at her bellybutton, making her squirm at the tickle. He kissed her softly just below her navel.

"You don't mind if I kiss you goodnight, do you?" And he continued, not waiting for the vocal permission her opening thighs conveyed. His mouth slid down, down, mouth and tongue playing her, teasing in his gradual progress. When she cried out, ass lifting off the bed, biting her bottom lip at the sweetest of sensations, his talented tongue on her hot crease, he knew he was where she wanted him to be.

Pace smiled in his mind. Making love didn't always have to be about starting a family, and there was no reason you couldn't maximize the fun of trying to make a baby. But, at that moment, making a baby was the furthest thing from his mind…

The six-day voyage to Avaric went by quickly, despite Gale's absence from most of the meals and gatherings. It was not unusual for him to isolate himself prior to a mission, and he continued his normal exercise regimen. He was occasionally joined by Helena, and even once by Kurt, who, during the course of Gale's five mile run, folded to the track in exhaustion, arms and legs sprayed out like a dead frog. Gale could barely keep himself from laughing out loud as he had to jump over his friend several times prior to Kurt managing to get to his hands and knees and crawl off the track.

The crew was not even aware of their arrival until the bridge sensor alert went off throughout the ship. In short order everyone gathered on the control deck, the bridge crew quickly settling in. Gale spoke from the command chair, Jones and Helena on each side.

"Status report."

Julie quickly studied the helm readouts in front of her.

"In visual range of Avaric. Ready to disengage auto-pilot for manual orbital placement."

Gale nodded. "Do it."

Maggie spoke up. "We're also in communication range, Jefferson. Should we hail the colony?"

Gale thought a moment. "Let's wait until we've established orbit, then patch the council through to my quarter's private line." His response drew a couple of side-glances and knitted brows, but no one spoke. "How long until orbit?"

Julie scanned the panel. "Eighteen minutes."

Gale got up, heading toward the lift. "I'm going down to the hold. Contact the Star Corp ships to verify our approach, and let me know when we're in orbit. Kurt, you've got the bridge." Patrickson nodded, his questioning eyes shifting from Gale to Jones.

"Want some company?" Jones asked casually.

Gale shook his head, a weary smile on his face. "Not this time, thanks." Gale left the bridge. Everyone's attention went back to the view of the approaching world. Without really thinking about it, Pace swiveled to face his engineering panel to run a quick check of the engines.

Gale wandered around the huge hold area, letting the feelings of dread and anxiety flow over and through him. He wandered slowly across the empty expanse, large enough for more than one football field. The whitewashed walls, floor and ceiling made him feel like he was passing through some neutral world, a blank purgatory wedged somewhere between the mythic realms of heaven and hell. He stopped for a moment, looking around at the barren surroundings. If he had the choice between this for an eternity, or the general depiction of hell, he'd take the hot spot without a thought. At least there'd be people he'd know.

He continued walking toward the far corner of the massive, specially constructed container, eventually reaching the housing area built for the Avaric colony research volunteers. There were a dozen self-contained living quarters lined single file along the wall, almost looking like a small motel strip. Each unit had its own separate environmental controls, an entertainment screen with built in computer and water room. The World Government was setting up research teams and orbiting facilities in order to gain as much information as possible about the virus so an antidote could be formulated. But the mission had taken on additional hazardous responsibilities when the Star Corp computer link-ups designed to salvage and transmit data from any of its disabled military vessels failed to transfer any relevant outbreak research files. The puzzling absence of information was theorized to be nothing more than the simple fact that none of the data accumulated by the government's agricultural lab on the colony had been transferred to the Merlin's computer. The government declared the acquiring of that data vital, and it became the mission's top priority. Just hours before the Omni personnel boarded their ship, the contract was amended, an insane amount of credits were added, and now Gale and his team were being paid to board the Merlin and manually access the computer system the Avaric research lab had moved onto the Merlin. The added mission perimeters were of no consequence to Gale---it was an open secret among the crew that he had planned to board the Merlin to search for his brother's remains. Now, he and the crew were going to be paid millions more credits to do it.

Gale entered one of the simple but comfortable quarters, taking note of the thick, double-sealed doorway. Once the colonists were shown into their quarters, the doorways could only be accessed from the bridge or by a hand held remote control. He noticed the lack of windows, but there wasn't going to be any type of view to enjoy. The hold was going to be full of outbreak victims stored in double walled clear plastic body bags. Gale was sure the survivors had seen enough of what the plague could do, so the lack of windows was really a blessing. There was a small plexi-glass view plate in the door, if anyone really had to take a peek.

Gale walked out of the quarters, pausing to survey the empty expanse dwarfing him. The mission was finally set to really begin, and it wouldn't be long before he, like the colony survivors, would know firsthand the destruction the virus could inflict on the human body. And it wouldn't be long until he'd have to find a spot among the dead for his brother.

Tammara sat in the waiting area, her thoughts racing. The cargo ship would be arriving soon, and she and the others would be taken back to the Earth's orbit to serve as study subjects for continued plague research. Her feelings were mixed about the assignment; the knowledge that her family would be among those transported back extending her grief. But there was a growing part of her excited to have a chance to eventually return to Earth and begin a new chapter in her life. If she had chosen to remain at Avaric, she might never have the opportunity to distance herself and put these horrible, haunting events behind her. A new place, a fresh start...That is, as long as she didn't turn out to be a viral carrier, or didn't mysteriously start exhibiting symptoms. She was feeling better and more confident about having a clean bill of health since the last plague patient documented at the hospital had been nearly a week ago.

Terms were explained to her and the others. There was going to be an intense, grueling testing period of at least 6 months, but eventually, if there was absolutely no sign of infection, the subjects would be dismissed and be free to return to Avaric or go on to Earth. She felt good about her part in helping to find an antidote to the disease that had stolen her family. As a nurse she understood the swift and cruel thief death could be, and she would do anything in her power to help someone avoid the devastation that she had been subjected to. At the meeting the hospital chief of staff had mentioned the six-month examination period, but if at the end of that time the doctors and scientists felt like they were making good progress, she would offer to stay on for an additional half year. The loss of her family was worth at least that much of her life. Only with the discovery of a vaccination could she feel some sort of revenge against the microscopic murderer. Their 'volunteer' status withstanding, they would all be compensated with a generous research fee, which Tammara planned to use to set up a travel nurse business.

She had no intentions of returning to Avaric, which she had informed the hospital administration, and had begun to make a list of potential places to settle. She was passable in a few basic languages, so her scope was nearly worldwide. With nothing but time on her hands for the next several months, she was in no rush to make a decision.

One thought needling her was that she had been chosen at all. She had been the only person selected with a medical background, all the Avaric doctors and researchers continuing their studies here at the colony. Her friend Lydia had been crushed when her name wasn't announced, and Tammara had only seen her briefly a couple of times since. She felt sorry for her friend, and went as far as to question Dr. Hollins about how the volunteers were chosen. Tammara remembered he didn't answer her right away. In that uncomfortable pause she had taken in the total disarray of his office: the half-eaten food trays scattered around, the pile of unwashed clothing, research paperwork strewn around. And then for the first time she had really noticed the dark circles under Dr. Hollins' red rimmed eyes, the accusing emptiness of his stare. Normally clean-shaven, his face was covered in an itchy looking, uneven growth which had spilled down under his jaw. With a lean build, the past couple of weeks had taken a heavy toll. Even sitting at his desk, his lab coat seemed to hang on his gaunt frame. Had she not known him to be one of the top administrators at the hospital, he could have been a vagrant. It was obvious that he had been living in his office since the outbreak, and she had felt guilt and sadness looking at him. She was far from being the only one that deserved to escape from this hell.

He had looked at her as if he were imagining her standing there, as if he were trying to place her in his memories. Tammara could remember times she would pass him in the corridors, and more than once felt his eyes on her as she walked down the hall. She had been flattered by his respectful attention, surprised when he would notice a change of her hairstyle or some other minor detail. Now the look in his eyes was weary and hollow, haunted by the hellish chaos the virus had created. After a few moments, he finally forced a weak smile and told her to be thankful for the opportunity. He had walked her out of his office, a comforting hand on her shoulder, telling her not to worry about Lydia or any of the staff. Everything was going to be okay. The bug seemed to have run its course and that would allow the hospital to gradually return to normal operations, which would take a tremendous amount of the stress off the staff and administration. He had told her good luck and almost as an afterthought offered his hand. She noticed the slight tremble, born of extreme stress, sleep deprivation and low caloric intake, and she smiled and told him thank you, hugging him instead. She was not at all surprised that he hugged her back, both enjoying the comfort of another's arms for a moment that was all too brief. As she walked away, she could feel his eyes on her, wanting her not to leave, his need for her much different than it had been just days before.

Tammara looked around at the other members of the test group. The dozen were equally divided between men and women, half of them over the age of forty. The subjects comprised a racial rainbow of Caucasian, Black, Hispanic and Asian. And it was her understanding that, with only one or two exceptions, the plague had killed at least one member of their immediate families. It had been a very emotional scene at the colony government building as surviving friends and families said teary good-byes. Those like Tammara who had lost their entire families stood by silently, feeling the absence of loved ones all over again.

She still felt out of place among them, and was feeling anxious that at any moment someone was going to approach her and say, "There's been a mistake, Ms. Ward. You will not be leaving the colony." And then she'd see a smiling Lydia and a better rested Dr. Hollins with their travel bags set to take her place. When she resisted and refused to relinquish her seat, a pair of security men would have to drag her sobbing from the airstrip terminal. She tensed up every time someone walked near her, her anxiety building as the departure time grew closer. At one point she had gone into the ladies' water room and sat trembling in a stall; a pretty poor hiding place if they came to take her away, but it was all she could think of to maximize her chances. Realizing how silly she was acting she had rejoined the others.

When word had reached the waiting area that the cargo ship had established orbit, her nervousness reached its peak. As most of the others clapped and talked excitedly among themselves, Tammara began whispering childhood prayers, her stomach churning, a sheen of perspiration on her skin. It wasn't until her name was called with the others that she was going to be able to let go of her fear and really believe that she was going to take the first big step in escaping the nightmare her life had become.

Maggie hailed Gale when communication had been established with the colony council. Gale jogged to his quarters, excited to be closing in on his objective. Activating the com-box, he spoke. "This is Jefferson Gale, commander of the Omni. May I request audio-visual?"

A male voice, even toned but weary sounding, answered.

"Granted, Mr. Gale."

Jefferson activated his desk screen, settling into a chair. His attention flickered from the screen to the framed picture of himself, Grace, Christopher and one of his women in every port, fashion model/actress/showgirl, huddled together, wet and smiling on the beach at Rio de Janeiro. That had been about two years ago, when Christopher had some leave time and met he and Grace on vacation. Gale and his brother were as different as they appeared in the photo. Christopher was tall and lean, with youthful, model good looks. He had a swimmer's build: broad shouldered, lean washboard torso, and not much body hair. Gale shared the similar lack of overall body hair, but if his brother's body was a sleek jaguar transport, his was an antique diesel tanker. Gale really didn't care for his picture being taken, but he couldn't easily remember a happier moment in his life.

An image on the view screen appeared, as vivid as being in person. The transmission was originating from the colony council chambers, a large oval table in the center of a sparse conference room. Half a dozen robed individuals were seated around the table with a man standing behind a podium at the far end. Gale sensed a struggle beneath the man's strained or weary attempt at being cordial. Everyone at the table was facing the screen, similar expressions engraved on their faces.

"The Avaric council and all the colony citizens welcome you and your crew, sir. I am Thryall Roth, lead councilor of the colony's governing board." He paused, seeming to gather himself. "Your ship's presence is a symbol of the end of our ordeal, Mr. Gale, and I don't have the words to relate the gratitude we all feel for your assistance in this time of need." A warmth gathered in Gale's chest.

"We're honored to be of assistance. Are all the arrangements set?" The lead councilman nodded, Gale detecting a genuine effort from the man to raise his head from his chest. These people had been existing in a living hell, and it was grinding them to dust. They were all totally drained from the tragedy, some of them looking as if they were still in shock. Minds still trying to accept what had happened around them, to their friends and families. It was not easy to accept the horrible madness of the victim's behavior or the sheer volume of death surrounding them, changing their homes into grisly cages of fear and misery. Some were probably still in denial, unable to cope with the situation. Gale could understand their difficulties all too well, his own mind still easing into the acceptance of his own brother's death. Gale was happy to be in a position to ease their tremendous burden any way he could.

Councilman Roth spoke. "We have everything ready to begin the transfer. Shall we start the procedure?"

Gale didn't reply for a brief moment, his mind scanning the World Government plan once more. The plan called for Kurt to pilot a shuttle down to the colony to 'humanize' the transfer of the colony research subjects while the deceased were being transferred by two robot cargo carriers. Kurt would be in a survival suit, and would have no contact with the colonists, who would simply board the shuttle's specially contained passenger section and disembark via an airlock directly into their living quarters in the hold. Simple and safe, with Kurt's safety all but guaranteed. But for an instant there was something that didn't agree with Gale, and he rolled the plan over and around in his mind, searching for the flaw, the hidden danger he wasn't seeing but was suddenly sensing. But there wasn't anything.

"Proceed with the transfer. I'll notify my crew. And are we cleared to shuttle down for the research volunteers?"

Councilman Roth seemed to perk up a tiny bit, a weary smile curving his lips. "The volunteers are already gathered and waiting at the colony airstrip, ready to depart. You may proceed at your convenience. And you will be taking proper precautions for surface contact, correct?" Gale stared into the screen, tiny alarm bells going off in his mind. He looked into Roth's eyes and discovered the clue he had sought. Despite the body language and weary expressions, Roth's eyes were clear and shiny, not bloodshot or red rimmed or heavy lidded. And then Gale realized the same was true of everyone around the table. Their appearance gave the illusion of physical and emotional fatigue, but their eyes gave them all away.

Something wasn't right. And Gale was going to have to make a slight change in the plan. Gale smiled grimly, both relieved by his discovery and anxious over the looming intrigue. And if something was going to go bad, it was going to have to happen very soon. Gale nodded, his mind beginning to open up to all the dangerous improbable possibilities that might lie ahead.

"I'll arrive within the hour and set down at your airfield. You can begin the cargo transfer at your convenience. Gale out." Councilor Roth nodded then cut the transmission. Gale took a deep breath, letting it out slowly as he moved toward the doorway. Now for the hard part. Gale headed for the bridge to inform the others of his surprise trip.

"I don't like this shit," Kurt growled, pacing the control deck, glancing between Gale and the floor. "I don't like this last minute change of plan. I don't like you covering for me, and I especially don't like you getting a bad feeling about the colony." Helena stepped up to Gale, her body language telling everyone she was ready to go. Muscles taunt and flexing, she was impressive to look at, but it was her intelligence and attitude that allowed her to command attention. This was nothing personal now. It was all business.

"And even if we follow your hunch, why replace Kurt? And why does it automatically have to be you to take his place? We're all capable of manning the shuttle." Gale sighed, choosing his words very carefully.

"First of all, plan or no plan, it's always my call. Second, if there is trouble down there, Kurt is not in top condition." Gale glanced up at his friend with a slight nod. "No offense Kurt, but you're not really in top game shape." Kurt's face blushed in both embarrassment and anger, mad at himself, not Gale. He nodded back, his honest reply tight lipped.

"You're right. And no offense taken."

Helena was not to be discouraged. "So, what about me or Torbeck? We may not be a comic book hero like you, but that doesn't mean we couldn't handle a little action down there. That is, if something actually happens." Gale's attention slid over to Gii, who was leaning against the communication panel. Gii's expression was chiseled and hard, taking in the scene like a hawk. When he spoke, nothing moved except his lips.

"She's right you know. You're not sure there's gonna to be trouble. Me and wonder woman are ready, willing and able." Gale nodded, then looked into Helena's big brown eyes. Personal concern was seeping into her hard soldier look.

"You're both already set to board the Merlin with me. One direct exposure to the plague is enough."

"Except for you." She would not back down, and Gale wanted to kiss her for it, but he knew she wouldn't like it. He finally just shrugged and turned away from everyone for a moment.

"That's why I'm in charge. And I will be flying down there. If it weren't for the plague, I would be more than happy to leave the plan as it is. We didn't sign on for direct exposure until the wrinkle on the Merlin came up, which you and Gii volunteered. But I'm not taking volunteers on this one. And I'm hoping that I'm dead wrong about this feeling." Everyone just looked at Gale, not at all amused. "Well, maybe just wrong will do." He started for the lift, speaking as he brushed past Kurt. "You've got the bridge. And be ready for anything." Kurt nodded, moving to the command chair.

As Gale stepped into the elevator, Helena nudged beside him. The doors slid closed a moment after. "I'm going to double check your gear after you suit up."

Gale smiled. "I thought you and Torbeck had already double and triple checked everything?" Helena looked into his eyes as she leaned up and softly touched her lips to his. Only concern was in her eyes now.

"It's game time. Another once-over won't hurt." Clasping hands, they rode the rest of the way to the shuttle bay in a comfortable silence.

The shuttle, Arian, delivered Jefferson Gale down to Avaric in less than half an hour, and after a smooth slide through the planet's atmosphere, he touched down at the edge of the colony's air transport center. The shuttles looked like miniature duplicates of the Omni. The smaller crafts were wedge shaped, rear propulsion units capable of carrying up to twelve seated personnel if the supply area was empty. For this special trip, the World Government had supplied a shuttle from the Star Corp biohazard deployment team, which could comfortably carry two-dozen passengers in a totally self-contained cabin section. The shuttle was also equipped to separate the two-person operation section from the cabin section in case of emergency, which Gale and the team was particularly happy about. It wasn't possible to have too many safety devices and emergency back-ups on this assignment. Well, except for the Omni's self-destruct. The shuttles were silver and black, and not often used on missions. The Omni itself was designed to disengage from its massive cargo section and had the capability of entering atmosphere and landing. But today only Gale was taking the trip, and that meant the special shuttle.

During the brief voyage, he had hailed one of the Star Corp watch-dog attack cruisers. Gale had relayed an encrypted message to the cruiser's commander, receiving a brief 'message received in full detail' response. Gale had expected Kurt and Maggie to contact him, but they didn't. The crew was probably more focused on situations arising once he landed.

Two groups were waiting on the landing pavement as the shuttle set down. As the engines powered down, Gale carefully double checked his suit's communication and life support system, then patched his communication through the shuttle's exterior sound system. Despite himself, he had started to sweat, even though the triple layered suit was made for a high degree of comfort along with maximum safety features. Unlike the bloated, white space walking protective gear of the past, the bio- hazard outfit the mission had been supplied with was a black form fitting rubber polymer coated body sleeve. The boots were not much more than knee high extra thick socks with rubber soles, and the gloves, like the outfit, was computer fitted specifically for each crewmember. The black helmet was lightweight and comfortable, and featured a powerful light and fog-proof plexi-glass face shield. He deliberately didn't check the handgun strapped to his right thigh, at odds with himself more and more as each minute passed. The bad feeling was still worrying at him, but he also knew this was a good will rescue operation. He closed his eyes for a moment, breathing deep and slow. He thought about two of the many personal rules he had established for himself during and since his stint as a soldier. It's always better to err on the side of caution and he should never ignore his intuition. He opened his eyes, pausing before he spoke, surveying again what he had noted from the air.

At a distance of well over two hundred meters, armed security formed a ring surrounding this section of the airstrip. An armed assault hovercraft was circling the area. Wariness washed over him, his right hand slipping down to his gun, and he felt like he had just landed on enemy soil. After one final deep breath, he blew it out as the two groups started toward the shuttle, the groups distinctly different from each other. One set of people was the council members, led by speaker Mr. Roth. The other group was obviously the research subjects, and Gale could instantly see the difference in the eyes of the volunteers from the council members. The faces of the volunteers looked haggard and anxious and tentative, even the few who managed to smile. Their body language as a group screamed exhaustion, both mental and physical. On the other hand, the council members seemed alert and rested, their movements confident. Unlike the volunteers, there were no bloodshot eyes, slumped shoulders, or avoidance of eye contact, looking well rested, healthy and relatively unscathed by their colony's recent tragedy. The two groups walked around the shuttle to the front, stopping several paces from the craft but in full view of Gale through the large transparent titanium view port. Councilman Roth spoke, a strange smile growing on his face. It was almost comical in its falseness. Gale returned the gesture behind his face shield, his whole body tensing, preparing for action.

"Welcome, Mr. Gale. I'm sorry to see you made the trip alone, but we realize the tremendous risk you've taken on our behalf." Gale casually reached up to the bottom front of his helmet and activated the mini-cam, allowing the crew on the Omni to see what he was seeing.

"If the volunteers are ready, Councilor Roth, I'm all set. They can begin boarding through my side of the shuttle, and there are suits inside for the subjects to wear until they get to the isolation dorm set up on the ship." He glanced about the two groups, his eyes ending up on Roth's. He made himself chuckle. "I feel like the World President with all the security you've arranged."

Roth stared through the clear steel, his smile sliding away. "There are those who are desperate to leave Avaric and are willing to try anything, Mr. Gale." Gale frowned, and if he'd had hair on the back of his neck, it would have begun to stand on end. Something bad was in the works.

"But your world is quarantined by Star Corp battle cruisers with orders to vaporize any and all craft leaving the planet. They would be committing suicide." Roth forced a weary smile onto his face.

"Some would say your trip here is suicide, Mr. Gale." Gale nodded, accepting the thought. With no way to deny it, for the first time the real danger of the mission began to sink in. Gale stared out at the council, eyes narrowing, the truth materializing like a ghost before him. The plague was not the real danger here. The virus was never the potential merciless enemy they were going to face. And suddenly he knew the real reason the World Government hadn't forced Star Corp to just send in another bio-hazard/military operation. That fucking son of a bitch Whittington knew about this situation, but didn't bother to fill in the "oh, by the way," part of the mission.

The surviving Avaric colonists had become a rebellious, hostile force.

And the Omni had become the only way off this dead world.

Gale undid the Velcro strap that held his weapon in the holster. He'd have to play this shit out to the end. Maybe his end.

"Well, I am truly sorry about the tragedy that befell your people, and I wish you all the blessings you deserve for your resiliency and courage." Roth nodded solemnly, not speaking. And uncomfortable silence hung in the air, and Gale blinked back a bead of sweat. Finally he spoke up. "Okay, well, I guess we should get moving..."

"That won't be necessary, Mr. Gale," Roth spoke, his tone now all wrong, anger and pain barely under control. Gale was suddenly very glad the crew could see what was happening. "We will not require your services beyond this point." Gale noticed at the edge of his vision that the distant, surrounding ring of security had begun to close in. Councilor Roth slowly reached inside his robe and withdrew a laser pistol. He held it at arm's length, his aim swinging in the direction of Gale, but continuing past the Omni commander until the weapon was pointed into the group of research volunteers. There were cries and screams, people ducking down, grabbing each other and covering themselves. Roth threatened them to shut up and they all settled into quiet whimpering and sobbing prayers. The worst had just happened for Gale, his hand sliding helplessly away from his gun. If this was part of the plan they had made, no one had told the research subjects about it. They were all genuinely terrified, some shaking and crying and begging for their lives. Gale sat, momentarily powerless. "If you would please step out of the shuttle, Mr. Gale. And if you're armed, please leave your weapon. I know from your military record that you wouldn't want any of these innocent people hurt because you tried to play hero." Gale unfastened the thigh straps and the holster dropped to the floor as he stood up. He held his hands up so Roth could see them as he moved to exit the craft.

NOW things had gotten worse for Gale.

"Holy Shit!" Gii spat, eyes widening at the weapons panel. "Damn if he wasn't right." The bridge was quiet for a moment as events unfolded. Kurt suddenly came alive. Even as he spoke, his attention never wavered from the view screen.

"Maggie, signal Jefferson to let him know we're with him. Torbeck, I want you to lock in an area around the shuttle with a random pattern of particle charges. And be ready to fire at my mark." Gii's fingers swiftly manipulated the helm. Kurt stood up from the command chair, moving next to Maggie. "Pace, I want you to suit up and head to the shuttle bay. We may have to go down after 'em." Pace hesitated, glancing from Julie to Kurt.

"Kurt, beggin' your pardon but I'm the only one who can deactivate the self destruct unit. It might be better to send someone else down, just in case."

Kurt nodded his agreement. "Right. Helena, you're with Julie. Pace, you handle the shuttle bay operation, but wait for my go." There was movement behind Kurt, then Gii's voice.

"Uh, Helena's not here. I haven't seen her since she left the bridge with Jefferson." Kurt stood staring at the screen, brow furrowed, thinking. A tiny smile teased at the corner of his mouth.

"Pace, check internal sensors for Helena's location." Pace worked his panel for a few moments, then faced the others with a queer expression.

"She's not on board, Kurt." There was a stunned silence.

"That bitch went down with Jefferson? And you all think I'm the adrenaline junkie!" Gii laughed, clapping in delight.

"I doubt her going with Jefferson had anything to do with adrenaline," Maggie spoke, glancing around at the others.

Kurt quickly re-directed everyone's focus. "Never mind that shit right now. Gii, go with Julie on the double." The three moved toward the lift, pausing when Kurt called over his shoulder. "Take plenty of hardware and extra air. I want you ready asap." The three moved into the lift, Jones moving to join them at the last moment. Kurt nodded at them all as the lift doors slid shut. Kurt turned back to the view screen, moving to fill the ship's weapons post. Well, things were at least looking up a little with Helena's little riding shotgun stunt, having gone down to the colony with Jefferson. Kurt watched for the opening he hoped Jefferson or Helena would give him.

As Gale stepped out of the shuttle into the open air, he heard the three beeps in his helmet signaling him to the crew's presence. He knew Kurt would be watching his every move, looking for a sign. Gale walked, hands in the air, until he was just a few steps from Roth. Gale stared at the man, his shark eyes burning holes as the Councilor turned the laser on him. At this close range, even a blind man would have trouble missing.

"Think about what you're doing, Roth. You can't possibly think you can get away with this." Gale took a step toward the man. "Give me the laser, and let me get on with the mission." Gale extended his gloved hand, his eyes never leaving Roth's. The Councilor smiled as if he had a secret, then calmly raised his aim and fired. Gale was completely caught off guard. The concentrated light beam burst into his helmet, tossing him off his feet and onto his back with a staggering jolt.

On the Omni, the view screen suddenly went black as the bridge personnel flinched at the instant of laser light. Kurt cursed out loud, pounding his fist into the panel.

"Maggie, stop Gii & Julie, there's not enough time. Fuck! Fuck! Fuck!" Kurt shook his head as he stared into the dark screen. Maggie worked her panel, then reported.

"Jefferson's communicator isn't functioning, Kurt." Kurt growled in disgust and frustration, running his hand through his hair, trying to figure out the next move.

"Well, it's Jefferson and Helena's game now." He made a fist and blew air through its center. "Maggie, report to the watch dog ships that we are delaying the first colony transfer. Just make up something about fluctuations in our life support system and us not wanting to trigger the self-destruct. We'll advise when we're ready to resume operation." Maggie turned to carry out the orders, leaving Kurt to stare silently at the darkened screen. He tried to remain focused on the mission and the safety of the crew, but he couldn't help wondering if Jefferson was even still alive.

Gale let his body relax, even in the instant before it was flung to the tarmac. The laser had been aimed at his head, but not his face shield, so the blast was not meant to kill him. The Councilor had simply taken out the mini-cam and communications equipment. Very smart....which meant they still had a use for him. Gale didn't allow himself to smile, but for an instant felt like it. The longer he stayed alive, the better his chances of making something happen. Before he could sit up, there was the sound of footsteps, then a tangle of voices above him. Suddenly, a red haired woman appeared inches from his face shield, her face etched with concern. Gale felt blood trickle from his scalp, and he saw her green eyes grow big.

"His helmet's been damaged! His suit's integrity has been breached!" Gale sat up, barely containing the panic that shot through his system. Things had gone from edgy suspicion to near certain death in a matter of moments. He couldn't stop himself from gulping and gasping at the air, thoughts of plague infection bouncing and twisting and ricocheting around in his head. There was no going back now. He had been exposed to one of the deadliest viruses in the history of man, and there was no antidote.

As his mind wrapped itself around his situation, his soldier instincts and battlefield experience took over. Heart pounding against his ribs, his panic-fed thoughts stopped and his mind cleared. His first calm thoughts to himself: *I've got the edge now. The damage is done---I'm breathing bad air right now. They can't use the plague as a threat against me anymore, and I could already be infected so I don't have anything to lose. Not even my life.*

Despite the woman trying to hold him still, he got to his feet, his legs shaky for a moment. His head was beginning to pound, and he could feel blood on the side of his face. Gale stared at Roth with a naked malice he reserved for people he had decided to kill, and there was absolutely no reason to make an exception. Roth wore a poisonous smile like most women wore a new hat. He seemed to be relishing his role of civic leader turned dangerous man, and Gale wouldn't take him lightly when the time came.

"I apologize for wounding you, Mr. Gale. Hopefully, you will not become infected. But your crew had seen quite enough." Gale growled softly inside his helmet. He would enjoy taking this man's life. Out of the corner of his eye he gauged the distance to the shuttle's front hatch. It was several meters away, and there was no way he could cover that distance quick enough. He was going to need a diversion, and he prayed for Kurt to give him one. 'I'm sorry, Mr. Gale, but our situation is much more desperate than you realize. I'm sure you are unaware of the complete World Government plan implemented to deal with our circumstances." He paused, and the gun stayed pointed at the middle of Gale's chest. "The line of reasoning you're following is that in time a cure will be discovered and all will be well again. But the truth is that the government is on a specific timetable. If a legitimate antidote cannot be created in the next six months, the test subjects will be terminated; their bodies cremated." There was plenty of murmuring and groans of disbelief from the volunteers. The woman standing next to Gale seemed to sag a little at the knees, her eyes closing at the news of her possible six-month death sentence. Roth continued, the gun seemingly heavy in his hand. "Avaric will be 'cleansed' with nuclear radiation and declared an off-limit dead world. There will be no evacuation of those of us who survived. We have become an unacceptable risk to the rest of the human population." Roth chuckled without humor, his eyelids blinking nervously several times. "I don't really blame the government for their plan of action. But that doesn't mean we have to just lie down and accept it. You and your ship are our only chance at survival." Gale knew the desperate resolve this man and the other council members displayed by their expressions and body language. They were extremely dangerous, and like himself, had nothing to lose. But they weren't trained for this, they weren't soldiers, and they were operating on survival energy. Gale looked past the colony council at the distant armed security, steadily drawing near. This was going to get bloody.

The bridge was silent as Kurt sat thinking. Nearly two minutes had gone by since the loss of picture and he was still not sure what action to take. Working blind and by instinct usually did not result in Kurt's best work. But he also knew time was working against him. Until he received hard evidence otherwise, he would assume Jefferson was still alive. And he had to figure that Helena was waiting for the best time to help him too...everyone waiting for someone to make something happen... Kurt rubbed his hands over his face, squeezing his eyes closed for a moment. When he opened them, he had made a decision. He hoped to God it was the right one.

Wincing, Gale eased off the damaged helmet, Roth's laser still trained on him. When the helmet was off, he held it down at his side. From beside him, the woman edged closer to examine him. Calmly, she gave her diagnosis.

"You're still bleeding some, but it's already starting to clot. It looks worse than it probably is, but forehead and scalp wounds are like that. It's probably pretty superficial, maybe a stitch or two. But you might have a concussion." Gale glanced at the woman, his expression blank. Her professional demeanor told him she had a medical background and he gave her a slight nod as both acknowledgment and thank you. Mentally, he was focusing on putting the hot, stabbing pain of his head into a special place in his mind. He allowed himself to feel the mild stinging of the torn skin to keep him alert. His head was the least of his problems, though he knew the wound certainly increased his odds of catching the plague. Gale's black eyes rolled back to the councilor.

"So, how do you figure to make this escape work?" Gale questioned with mock curiosity. He was ready to move when Kurt made his.

"At this moment we're in the process of transferring the two loads of deceased, except instead of victims we are actually sending surviving colonists in one of the containers, armed and ready to capture your ship. Once done, we will use your craft to seek out a world outside of Star Corp territory and establish a new settlement. A very simple plan really. And just in case there is resistance from your crew, we have you as a hostage." Roth's smile wavered just a tiny bit, and Gale sensed real regret. "We have been forced into this, Mr. Gale. We really have no choice. And now that you've been exposed, you might want to consider joining us. Very soon your entire crew will be dealing with the same dilemma." The man's invitation sounded strangely sincere, but Gale just shook his head.

"I don't think so, Roth. None of this is going to happen. My crew won't allow you to use me as a bargaining chip, and I can guarantee you that your people will not set one foot aboard my ship." Gale took a strong step toward Roth, who actually slid back a little. Gale grinned at the man's giving of ground. "They didn't send the Red Cross or the Peace Corp to help you. The government didn't send a civilian biohazard team. They sent battlefield hardened ex-Star Corp mercenaries experienced in dangerous, alien environments, trained to adapt to hostile mission aberrations. We're soldiers, Roth. We weren't sent to negotiate with you in any situation. If you or your people are perceived as the threat you've made yourselves into right now, my crew will aggressively defend themselves, which means you and your people would have survived the plague to die at our hands." Absently, he wiped at the blood continuing to ooze from his head wound. Gale's shark eyes bore into Roth's and he took another defiant step forward. "And I'm no good to you either. They will assume that I am either dead or have been exposed, and I'm on my own and out of any equation. There will be no rescue or bartering or surrender, Roth. I sure hope you have a plan B." Gale was going to have to force the issue very soon, but unless he got extremely lucky, even with Helena's help, he was going to die here. At least if he went down the colonists wouldn't have him to bargain with. And hopefully Kurt would play hardball with them, but only use deadly force as a last result. This was still a humanitarian mission no matter how ugly things got. Gale looked over the now stony faces of the councilors. Desperate people did desperate things...

Gale felt a stab of sorrow. He didn't have time to decide if Roth was telling the truth about the government's plan of action, but he wasn't so naive to think that the government was beyond such activities. His eyes locked on his captor. The time was

"NOW!" Kurt shouted, actually talking to himself, his fingers responding at the weapons station.

Gale threw his helmet in a quick, underhand motion at the gun, instantly charging low behind it. The helmet did its job, catching Roth by surprise and causing him to jerk his arm upward. Just before Gale crashed into the man's mid-section he heard Helena's yell blended into a series of explosions around him, some sounding very close.

Roth grunted, the air exploding out of his body as Gale rammed into him, slamming him to the pavement. Chaos surrounded them, people running, screams of fear and pain everywhere. Gale disarmed Roth easily, the man older and slow with little fighting expertise. But Roth did put up a struggle, feeble as it was, which gave Gale the excuse to punch him with a combination of lightning quick blows to the head and mid-section. Controlling his anger, he pulled the punches, stunning Roth. Despite his attempt to limit the punishment he delivered, Gale both heard and felt the older man's ribs break. The blows caused him to cease his struggling, his body trying to curl up instinctively. Roth wheezed, unable to draw a breath without obvious pain, bleeding from his mouth and nose. As Gale started to move off the man, Roth clutched at Gale groggily, pawing at a chest pocket and producing a small disc. A hand grabbing at his shoulder from behind, Gale instinctively spun and applied a wristlock, driving the person to a knee as they were forced to follow the twisting torque of their wrist bone. In the following instant a gun barrel was pressed firmly against his forehead.

"Jefferson, it's me!" Helena burst from the other end of the gun. Gale released her like he was holding a red-hot iron.

"Sorry," he managed, "you'll have to excuse my manners. The hospitality," he said, with a side-glance down to Roth, "has not been five star." She nodded, her eyes scanning their surroundings. She spoke loud and fast, another series of explosions setting off around them.

"Kurt, Helena here. Are you getting this?" In that moment, Roth reached up to Gale, grabbing his arm with a desperate strength. Roth pulled Gale closer and looked him in the eye. Gale blinked back a drip of blood as Roth pressed the disk into his hand.

"Take this; the truth just might save you." Gale looked at the disk, hesitating before jamming it into an unzipped pocket. "I should have never become party to this madness. I was foolish to believe anything he and the government told me." Roth sputtered, coughing and gasping from the beating and the exertion. He now looked like the feeble old man he really was. 'My greed made me stupid. It made me forget my honor." Roth clutched with both hands at Gale, but the Omni commander batted his hands away. This whole situation was going all wrong. "The plague killed my wife and daughter. I brought death into my own house!" Roth's expression turned wild. "It was supposed to be a simple experiment, but they lied about everything! I'm responsible for the death of all those people. They trusted me, but I'm a murderer!" The councilman was beginning to babble, his mind crumpling. Gale quickly half-zipped the disk into the pocket, then he struck Roth one more time, rending him unconscious. Gale moved away from him in a crouch, grabbing the laser and quickly surveying the scene. There were a lot of people on the pavement, either hurt or scared. The security men surrounding the area had broken rank, some of them dodging their way through the particles blasts to make it to the shuttle. Burning debris was scattered at a distance, and Gale didn't see the assault hover craft, and assumed it had been struck down. The individuals close to he and Helena posed no immediate threat. All the other councilors appeared to be unarmed and seemed much more concerned with the explosions than dealing with the two of them. Helena tapped his shoulder, and nudged her helmet toward the shuttle. Gale followed after her until his attention caught one last detail.

He saw her laying on the ground, curled up in a frightened, fetal ball, her hands cupped over her ears. He scrambled quickly and knelt by her. His tone was soft, yet urgent. Armed men were coming, as desperate to reach the shuttle as he and Helena were. He blinked a couple of times to clear of vision.

"Come on, get up!" he shouted at the woman who had checked his head. "If we're going to make it, we have to go right now!" She looked up at him, her fear fading. Gale yanked her to her feet, half carrying her. Once they reached the craft, he turned and fired the laser in bursts, causing the onrushing security to dodge and scatter. Gale shoved Tammara into the shuttle, securing the hatch behind them. He quickly overrode the airlock controls, roughly pushing Tammara in front of him as he scrambled to join Helena at the control panel. She had already activated the propulsion and communication systems. Gale's head was pounding, the pain throbbing red hot behind his eyes. It felt like a needle-covered balloon was steadily expanding in his skull, his brain pierced by a hundred razor sharp points. As Gale spoke into the panel, a rough pounding echoed from the exterior hatch. "Kurt, we've got some uninvited guests trying to hitch a ride with us. We need cover fire close to the shuttle. We're in the air in less than 30 ticks." Another series of explosions was Gale's reply, two very close to each side of the shuttle. Yells of pain came from outside as the craft rocked.

Helena spat orders at the woman. "Strap in now---we're set to jump outta here." Tammara hesitated for just a moment, her mind trying to catch up to the chaos carrying her along, then moved quickly to one of the two open seats, securing herself as quickly as she could. As she worked the last strap, Helena called out. "We're off!"

The shuttle seemed to jump straight off the ground and in moments was climbing quickly into the bright mauve sky, their speed and angle alarming to Tammara. Small explosions danced around them, no one sure if they were being shot at or protected. She tried to fight back her fear and panic, focusing on the man that had grabbed her. She stared into the side of his blood-smeared face, watching the muscles in his jaw flex in determination. Though he was blinking a lot, his black eyes (were they really black or just dark brown?) were totally focused on the glowing instrument panels, and her hand floated out to his injured head before she realized it. Catching herself, she drew it back. He was clearly out of her reach.

It was several more moments before Gale and Helena relaxed, the shuttle finally out of reach of the colony airstrip weapons. Helena adjusted the ship's severe escape angle, her fingers barely finishing the course adjustment before Gale slumped against the panel. Tammara quickly undid her straps and moved to his side. Gale was sweating profusely, and his gaze was glassy. Helena was tight lipped behind her suit's face shield, expression tight with concern.

"Is it bad?"

Tammara eased him gently back in the chair, using her hands to steady his head. He was out cold. "His head wound is minor, but I think he has a concussion." Helena's attention oscillated between Gale's condition and adjusting the course to return to the Omni. His head didn't look good, but she was well aware that facial and scalp injuries always looked worse than they were. She fought to keep her feelings in check and concentrate on flying the shuttle. She spoke into her helmet communicator.

"Kurt, we've got a situation here. Jefferson's hurt---he's got a head wound and may have a concussion. And we have a single, spur of the moment passenger. I think we need a plan." There was silence from the panel for a long stretch. Long enough for Helena to glance again at Gale, then at the woman, not at all oblivious to the way the woman was looking at Jefferson. Helena reached down and opened a compartment, withdrawing a small medi-kit. She passed it to the woman. "See what you can do for him," Helena said, looking into the woman's crystal green eyes.

Tammara took it, returning the look. "My name's Tammara. I'm a nurse." She turned her attention to Gale, opening the kit and removing some of the contents.

"I'm Helena, and he's Jefferson." She watched the nurse begin to clean Gale up gently. "We should be docked at the ship in less than 20 minutes." Helena stared hard into the back of Tammara's head. "You were one of the research volunteers?"

The nurse nodded once. "Yes. I lost my family to the plague. I just wanted a chance to get away from the colony, even if it was as a guinea pig." She sniffled a little, half-glancing over her shoulder at the woman pilot. "I had no idea what the council had planned. I would never have been apart of something like that. And I'm so sorry one of you got exposed, much less injured." The two women didn't speak for a long time, Tammara continuing to administer first aid. Finally, Helena turned and asked the question Tammara knew was going to come sooner or later. Helena spoke in a hush, as if the nurse was tending to a sleeping baby instead of an unconscious man. And no matter what the answer was going to be, the whole crew was going to have to being fully informed.

"Do you think he caught it? The plague?" Tammara didn't look at her right away, carefully measuring the answer. Helena was just about to ask her again in a much more assertive fashion when the nurse met her eyes. Tammara's voice was equally quiet.

"If this was two weeks ago, the odds would have been nearly 100% positive. But new cases of infection mysteriously ceased days ago, and even with the all-out research effort, that was just another unanswered question." Both women's attention turned to Gale, who, at a glance, might have been napping. He appeared much better with his face and head cleaned and bandaged. "At the onset of the outbreak, rumors were flying about the colony lab facility somehow being involved, which is why the research teams were transferred up to the military transport. All kinds of conspiracy theories were being talked about, the religious right was busy finding bible passages for explanation, and the people with anti-World Government sentiments were convinced we were a test group for a new biological weapon. I even heard people at the hospital talk about the Devil; that it wasn't even a virus at all. Craziness about mass possession by damned souls freely acting out their unnatural, violent urges." Tammara sighed deeply, her eyes still on Gale, and Helena couldn't tell if the sigh was for the answer or the man. Or both. "He might not be infected, I don't really know. But I'm sure your crew will take all the proper precautions until you're sure." Helena's attention slid from the nurse to Jefferson before she focused herself on piloting the shuttle again.

Finally, there was a response from the control panel. "Dock at the quarantine section, and we'll meet you there. Kurt out."

On the bridge of the Omni, Kurt felt the tension seize his body, and he closed his eyes and covered his face with a hand trembling so slightly he hoped no one would notice. He was sure the others were too wrapped up dealing with the current situation and the news about Jefferson. Jefferson had followed his hunch, and ended up taking yet another bullet meant for Kurt. He should have been piloting the shuttle, and it should be him possibly infected. How many times over would he be dead if it wasn't for Jefferson? He shook his head, feeling his chest rising and falling, his breathing almost forgotten, guilt and fear and sorrow and anger forming a chaotic, explosive mix. Stomach churning, he could only stare into the infinite darkness inside his own closed eyes. This shit could turn out to be as nasty as bad shit got. If Jefferson was infected, he would end up like a rabid dog. The image of Gale struggling wild-eyed in a straitjacket, brain boiled, frothing and drooling... With no known antidote, it might become a matter of putting him down like a mad dog. And that decision would ultimately be Kurt's. Would he have the guts to have Jones give him an injection to take him quietly out of his misery, or would he gutlessly fold and just have Jefferson moved to a sound proof detention cube where he could scream and curse unheard until his brain completely turned to soup? Jefferson would never allow any of the crew to suffer one minute longer than necessary.

But Kurt was a long way from being Jefferson, laying off the booze or not. How many senseless deaths did their team need to suffer through? Kurt felt the weight of a hand laid gently on his shoulder, then Jones's voice.

"So, what's the plan?" Slowly, Kurt lowered his hand and opened his eyes, staring into the control deck view screen at the planet. It should have been him.

"Get suited up; the two of us are going down to see about our fearless leader. But first, Maggie, patch me through to the watchdog ships' commander. I need to fill them in on the current situation." Maggie started to speak, obviously in protest, but Kurt cut her off. "We can't hide this---we have to tell Star Corp something. They already know the shuttle didn't have enough passengers, and after our prior message about the delay in body bag transferal, they have to be sitting out there waiting for an explanation..." At that moment, an indicator flashed from the communication panel drawing everyone's attention.

"Speak of the devil," Gii mumbled, staring at the blinking light like it was a three-headed dog. Kurt took a deep breath, his mind sorting through the assortment of bullshit he could report, but in the next instant decided to simply tell the truth.

After getting suited up, Kurt and Jones, with the help of Gii, loaded up medical equipment on two floating anti-gravity gurneys and started for the hold. Gii accompanied them as far as the outer airlock door, remaining outside to operate the decontamination system for their return.

Kurt and Jones crossed the empty expanse of the hold to the volunteer quarters, maneuvering the gurneys into one of the cabins. Leaving the equipment, they steered a gurney to the boarding airlock and waited until Pace's voice sounded in their helmets.

"The shuttle is preparing to dock. Less than 2 minutes before contact."

"Copy that. We're set at the hatch." Kurt replied, nerves and the snug form-fitting body suit making his skin damp. He glanced at the doctor, who stood staring at the airlock like an uninteresting book. Kurt thought better of making meaningless small talk and just tried to slow his breathing. His mind teased at the memory of the Pandora mission, but he forced those thoughts away from him. This was no time to drudge up that nasty piece of business. Though his mind did pick up one point---this was the first time he had suited up since that mission, and he could not entirely avoid the stark, hellish images of the grub pit and the ordered mercy killings. He closed his eyes, forcing himself to shift his thinking and focus on taking command of the mission.

It seemed like an hour before Pace spoke into their helmets. "The shuttle is docked and secure." Kurt manually accessed the series of three circular airlock doors, and they met Helena in the small entry lobby between the shuttle and the subject quarters. The third airlock panel was still rolling back into the wall as Helena spoke. Her expression was concerned but under control.

"He's still unconscious, but stable. Tammara doesn't think it's serious." Kurt and Jones pushed by her as she spoke, Kurt guiding the gurney by hand held remote. Jones moved to Gale's side with little more than a glance at the female stranger attending to him.

After a quick once over, Jones spoke back over his shoulder. "Kurt, help me get him on the gurney so I can get a scan on his head, and then we'll move him into one of the cabins." Tammara stood and stepped aside as Kurt moved in, gently picking Gale up from under his arms as Jones took his feet. Carefully they carried him from the close quarters of the shuttle's control station to the gurney. Once Gale was placed on it, Kurt adjusted the gurney's hovering at normal table height and locked it in while Jones programmed the tests he wanted the gurney's diagnostic technology to run on Gale. Tammara stepped up on the other side of Gale, watching as Jones finished inputting.

"I don't believe he has a fracture, though possibly a small hairline in his left orbital socket from the laser. I've done a manual skull examination and felt no abnormalities..." Jones chuckled humorlessly, but didn't look up at the woman, his attention locked into the readings appearing on the gurney's small monitor.

"Well, Jefferson is a long way from 'normal', Ms.---" Jones eyes flickered to and away from the stranger.

"Wilder. Please call me Tammara. I'm a level one medical tech specializing in emergency medicine. I was due to return to the university in the fall to begin my first year of residency." Jones nodded, making a soft grumbling in his throat. He continued to monitor the data for a few more moments, then looked up at Kurt, his expression softening with relief.

"No fractures, though there is deep bruising under the laser wound, but we can deal with that easy enough. I would say he has a mid-level concussion, which we'll need to monitor for the next 48 hours or so. We'll need to limit his physical activity the next few days for sure. Of course, knowing Jefferson, we'll be lucky to keep him from training tomorrow." Jones paused, his shoulders sagging just a little. The relief Helena and Kurt felt also took a pause. "We're going to have to keep him in isolation because I have no information on this plague virus." The Omni doctor looked at the colony nurse. "Do you have any knowledge of the research being done? Anything at all could be a huge help." Tammara covered the lower part of her face with a hand, solemnly shaking her head.

"Since the outbreak, I've worked in emergency and the general ward. I don't have a background in research, so I was better suited for the direct handling of patients." Jones nodded, his eyes opening a little wider.

"You've been working directly with plague victims?"

She nodded. "I was on duty the day the first cases came into emergency. Of course, the medical staff had no idea what we were facing that day." Her eyes slowly closed as if she didn't want to see the images her mind was replaying, and just as slowly, her green eyes came back into view. "We worked under normal protocol for almost two days before we were issued bio-suits. I'm the only one from that shift who had direct contact with infected patients and survived." She glanced over at the unconscious Gale, then her eyes found Jones and held firm. "Just lucky, I guess." There was a silent pause, then Jones stepped away from the gurney, pulling the remote control from his belt.

"Let's get him comfortable," Jones spoke, slowly guiding the hovering gurney toward the nearest cabin. Kurt and Tammara followed, leaving Helena behind for a moment. After a thoughtful pause, she suddenly spoke up through her helmet communicator.

"Hey! Check the pockets on Jefferson's suit. Roth passed him a disk. It's important." As Jones and Tammara eased the corrupted suit from Gale, Kurt checked his pockets, discovering the small disk on the third try. He repeatedly flipped it in the air like a coin, then grabbed it in a backhanded swipe. His mouth curled into a cautious smile.

"Maybe we'll get lucky. Pace, have everyone gather in medical in about 30 minutes. We're tucking Jefferson in down here, then we'll go through decontamination and meet you all there."

"We read you. Jefferson going to be okay?"

Kurt glanced at his unconscious best friend. "With a head like his? You're joking, right?" Kurt listened to Pace's chuckle, wondering if a microscopic organism was going to be the death of one of the most dangerous men alive, hard head or no.

PHASE III

Gale seemed to awaken all at once, emerging from the black void he'd been set adrift in with a jolt. His eyes were suddenly open, his vision hazy for a moment. He bolted upright like a rising cobra, not sure where he was, his surroundings alien. Was he at the colony? Had the shuttle been shot down? Helena? Where was Helena?

Then the inside of his head flashed a blinding, electrifying flare of pain, causing his eyes to almost close and a moan to rumble from deep in his throat. Tentatively his fingers floated to the soft synthetic skin patch covering his temple and part of his forehead, lightly brushing the smooth organic substance that was formulated to bond with human tissue, match the patient's skin color, and provide enhanced healing agents directly into the wound and surrounding tissue. As the wound healed, the 'skin', as Gale called it, would be absorbed, leaving little to no scar behind. He thought a moment about the scars etched all over his body, the ones he wore like medals. The new one he would've had on his temple was not worth keeping. Soft hands were suddenly at his shoulders, gently pushing him back to the sleeper. The pain receded as he did so, a soft groan of relief escaping his lips. Tammara's face filled most of his sight, her beauty almost making all the pain cease.

She had freshened up, the loose curls of her scarlet hair pulled away from her face. Her smile rivaled Maggie's, and she smelled like fresh flowers. She wore a borrowed skin suit, her breasts straining the top. The smooth, creamy pale skin of her throat caused a slight stirring below his waist despite the ache in his skull. He smiled a little, trying to quickly organize his thoughts. She beat him to it.

"Don't worry---everything's fine. We're on your ship in the quarters set up for the research volunteers. You suffered a mid-level concussion, but Dr. Jones says you have a very hard head, so... you just need to rest and let the medicine do its work." Gale felt hypnotized by her sparkling eyes, as vivid and bright as emeralds. He wondered if the color was natural or artificial, and then fought back the urge to try to sit up again. He forced himself to speak, his head still throbbing.

"Have we gotten underway to Earth?" She shook her head, her warm hand lightly stroking the uninjured side of his face, an honest tenderness and caring to her touch. Gale couldn't help but close his eyes for a moment. A thought flickered through his mind---it had been an eternity since Grace had touched him like that. How could it feel so soothing and arousing at the same time? The memory of Helena's passion flashed, and his eyes blinked open. Despite his head injury, he could feel his body betraying him, on the verge of arousal. Teeth clenched, he sat up, swinging his feet to the floor, the wave of agony dousing the spark of pleasure. Tammara didn't step back, so now his face was nearly pressed into her chest. He drew her fragrance of fresh flowers into his lungs. For an instant he longed to pull her tight against him, to wallow in her obvious charms. His sense of smell was teasing him, and his other senses longed to have an opportunity to experience her as well.

"They called down just a little while ago, and they want to talk to you. They seem very concerned about what might happen to us when we return to Earth. I told them about what Roth said about the World Government's plan." Gale took deep breaths, trying to get control of the pain. Suddenly, his eyelids felt heavy and rough and he knew his body was telling him to lie back down, but instead he eased himself to his feet and walked slowly to the small communication panel in what would have been the colony volunteer's common room. Tammara walked with him, a supportive hand on his arm.

In front of the panel, Gale slid down into a black, high backed chair quickly patching into the conference room. Maggie picked him up and plugged him into the room's audio/visual. Gale could see the crew around the table, Kurt and Helena's hair still wet from the decontamination process. Handling the small disk like a coin or poker chip, it flipped and rolled around the fingers of his right hand, the motion as casual and unconscious for Kurt as blinking. Gale recognized it as the disk Roth had passed him on the planet. Gazing at the gathering, Gale realized Pace wasn't at the table.

"What's the word?" he mumbled, grimacing from the headache. The crew peered down at his image from the conference table's large, flat built-in screen, concern souring their expressions. If he hadn't already known, the looks on their faces spoke volumes about his appearance. The disk suddenly stopped moving, lying flat across Kurt's knuckles.

"You don't look too good," he spoke, a quick side glance toward someone off-screen.

"You probably shouldn't be moving around yet. You need to rest," Helena prompted, her whole appearance so much softer than when she had accompanied him to the colony. Funny how well a military biohazard suit and weapons can mask an attractive woman soldier. She was now dressed in a jungle fatigue tank top, and had a towel in her hand as she continued to dry her hair.

"You look like shit, but I still think you're faking it for sympathy," Gii sneered playfully. The other crewmembers shot him ugly looks. "What? What'd I say? Geez, lighten up people."

Kurt took a moment to organize his thoughts, then spoke, tossing the disk onto the table. "We took a look at the disk Roth passed you, and it was quite an eye opener. Roth basically kept a record of all his dealings with Whittington, and it's not hard to piece together the story. As usual, we've signed on for a shit load more than we bargained for." Kurt's attention flirted around the table, double-checking that he had everyone's undivided attention. Even Gii had on his game face and seemed focused on the matter at hand. Kurt wagged his head sadly. "Jefferson, I know you did some research on Whittington, but there would appear to be a few details your contacts left out about our benevolent Representative." Gale eased back into his chair, bracing his arms so his chin rested on his fists.

"So, kiss and tell already." Kurt resettled himself in his chair, his eyes locking with Gale's.

"We're all aware that this mission was just a trumped up public relations ploy, but the info on the disk spells out that we are actually the sacrificial lamb in a, can you believe it, government conspiracy. Whittington, who I will refer to from here on as 'that motherfucker', is still very much involved in all aspects of the agenda of the government's Military and Defense subcommittee, despite his very public resignation from that post. Unofficially, of course, that motherfucker's nose is in everything from budgets to personnel to weapons research." Kurt paused, looking like he wanted to spit. "Apparently during the Mandroid conflict a few years back, a bio-weapon was being developed specifically to use against the rebel cyborgs, but the situation took care of itself before the weapon could even be tested. When rumors leaked out that this bio-weapon had the potential to be devastating to unaltered humans, the project was officially scrapped and all chemical and germ warfare research product destroyed." Kurt paused and gave an exaggerated vaudeville wink. A flare of pain turned Gale's grin in progress into a smirk, and Kurt continued on with his report. "Unofficially, Whittington had the project resurrected at a lab on a distant Earth colony, going so far as to buy the silence and the cooperation of the colony council." Kurt watched Gale's eyelids droop. "Sounding familiar?"

Gale nodded, his neck feeling rubbery. He thought about how Whittington had sealed the bargain with the casual mentioning of Christopher. He wouldn't forget that when the time came. His voice was lazy and slightly slurred. "Finish this shit up---I'm sliding fast."

Kurt didn't hesitate, the underlying tone more urgent. "I'll skip to the big finish. The 'controlled' field test at Avaric went bad, the researchers panicked and never shared the supposed antidote with the colonists. They escaped to the Merlin for fear of retaliation from the colony population, infected the crew and forced Whittington to save his political aspirations. Fearing that his dirty little secret was set to explode over every major network, he worked both sides of the streets, lying to both the people of Earth and Avaric. He devised this 'desperate plan to salvage the lives and humanity' of the colony and hired the best paramilitary team in the world for the mission." Though Gale's sleepy gaze didn't reflect it, his mind had already skipped to the punch line.

"But we weren't supposed to make it back," Gale spoke up, almost exactly at the same instant that Kurt said, 'but he didn't want us to complete the mission.' The looks around the table were none too happy.

Kurt nodded, controlled anger creeping into his voice. "Pace is checking all the ship's systems for any programmed anomaly. We think we're set up for sabotage. Either the rebel colonists take over our ship, then the Star Corp guard dog ships destroy us, or our own self-destruct would take us out, or, who knows, Whittington might be forced to order us destroyed because of contamination. Either way, once we were out of the picture, the Government would be able to say that they made a valiant attempt, but that the situation was just too hostile. Then they could order a nuclear cleansing strike on the planet. They'd destroy the Merlin, and completely cover up the existence of their fucked up outbreak. It also makes Whittington look like the next coming of Christ." Kurt stuck his chin in the air, deepened his voice and spoke as though he was eulogizing an assassinated world leader. "He'll be portrayed as a man of action, yet compassionate and honorable." Gale's eyes dropped close, and he labored to force them open again. The lead weight of his eyelids was spreading quickly throughout his body.

Drowsily he said, "Call me if Pace finds something, and I'll put on my thinking cap as soon as I stop daydreaming about hanging Whittington with his own fuckin' intestines." Smiles cracked on a few faces around the table.

"I like the visual." Gii spoke, grinning ear to ear, genuinely amused by the thought. "And I might have the knife for the job too."

"The blade wouldn't be dull enough. I'd like to gut him with a spoon, cook his organs, then feed them right back to him, that slimy son-of-a-bitch," Helena spat, her expression dripping venom. Everyone's awed attention slid to her, Gii's mouth opening just a bit to speak, then closing, too stunned to come up with a witty response. The rest of the crew's faces were comical. Julie and Maggie were in total shock. Even Gale was surprised by the vivid picture painted by one of the sweetest, most even-tempered people he had ever known. There was a moment of startled silence, and then Julie spoke up sheepishly.

"I guess exposing him to the citizens of Earth as the cold, calculating, murderous bastard he really is wouldn't be enough?" After a long moment of pin drop silence, laughter broke out around the table.

"Yeah, we could do that too," Kurt blurted between breaths.

"It's not nearly as messy as the spoon thing," Maggie shrugged, playfully elbowing Julie in the ribs. Julie's expression wavered between being upset and tickled, but in seconds, amusement won out and she burst into laughter.

His head feeling like a bowling ball wobbling on the end of a straightened coat hanger, Gale tried unsuccessfully to get to his feet. Tammara was at his side to help him stand.

"I gotta lay down before I fall down guys, but my next thought is wondering why he chose us. He could have picked any government contracted salvage team. Kurt, you might want to check out any connections that might make Whittington want to bury us." Gale took a step, then glanced at the panel. "And see what you can find out about the 'supposed antidote'." He moved away from the panel without breaking the connection, the last trickles of laughter dying away as the crew watched in silence as he and Tammara wobbled out of viewing range.

Caught staring at the screen a little longer than everyone else, Helena glanced around the table, her mind and emotions whirling. She hitched her shoulders and tried to sound casual as she ran her fingers through her damp hair. She was suddenly aware that she was a long way from looking her best, much less looking attractive at all. Damn that nurse.

"She's got a medical background. Jefferson is in good hands."

Julie and Maggie exchanged a lightening quick glance, but Helena still caught it. Then Helena felt a gentle nudge to her head, causing her to blink rapidly for a moment as if something was in her eyes. Then the realization dawned on her---the nudge was at her mind, not her head. Her expression soured as she sent a glaring dart toward Maggie. "You really don't want to know what I'm thinking right now. Butt out." Helena's tone was more than enough warning, and Maggie withdrew herself, sheepishly dropping her eyes from the female power lifter.

"Sorry," she whispered.

Kurt raised an eyebrow. "Uh huh." He dared not say more. The woman from the colony was very easy on the eyes and she was obviously attracted to Jefferson. Kurt knew there was a strong vibe running between Jefferson and Helena, but shifting from friendship to romance was always much easier in theory than reality.

"Oh yeah, she looks like she's got great hands all right," Gii sneered, as he leaned back in his chair. "I wish I was lotion." Helena shot him a warning glare, and he was lucky to stifle the chuckle half way out of his throat. Kurt started to speak, but a beep cut him short. Maggie manipulated the small soft pad keyboard built into the table before her, and she looked at Kurt.

"It's Pace. On screen." The engineer's image filled the monitor. His forehead had a light sheen of perspiration, and that tiny hint of anxiety was like a fire alarm suddenly blaring in the middle of the night. His eyes caught his wife's for an instant before he spoke. He wasn't able to keep concern from bleeding into his voice.

"I found it." No one spoke. No one took a breath. There was no sound in the conference room. Pace swallowed. "It's bad. Whittington didn't buy us drinks or take us to dinner, but he sure as hell fucked us."

The crew sat in silence as Pace Kimbro relayed the bad news.

Gale was floating in a blackish, grayish void, faint swirling patterns moving throughout his surroundings. He wasn't dreaming, and he somehow knew he wasn't awake either. He was drifting in a twilight state, most of his body and mind shut down as the medication worked on restoring his jarred brain to normal function. Weightless in this mental purgatory, he allowed himself to simply just be. Other than his sight (or was it his imagination presenting his surroundings?), his other senses seemed to have stopped. Hell, he wasn't even sure he was breathing. Maybe he didn't have to breathe where he was.

As he drifted, idle thoughts past his mind like wisps of smoke, present but not really tangible. Time was no longer a working concept. He might have been in this state for a minute, an hour, a day. There was no way for him to tell how long he had been in the twilight. Nothing really seemed to matter; there was no emotional or realistic importance to anything. He merely existed.

Until he heard the voice.

Gale was so content watching the slow moving swirls around him that at first the sound hardly registered. When it did fully command his attention, he couldn't be sure from which direction it was coming, or if it was merely being manufactured inside his own mind. Slowly, and in an almost rhythmic cadence, the voice became louder and easier to distinguish. Gale became aware that the sound was indeed coming from inside his head, and he recognized his dead brother talking to him. With an underlying sadness, Christopher was almost singing the same sentence over and over again. It was the voice of a ghost in a place far away. Gale listened to his brother's message with a casual interest, but as the volume continued to climb, Gale had no choice but to pay attention. Steadily, Christopher's voice became so overwhelming that Gale had to jam the palms of his hands against his ears. Gritting his teeth as hot tears of pain rolled down his cheeks, he knew if he didn't do something immediately, the monstrous volume was going to destroy him.

Then Gale woke up.

He knew he was awake because the pain in his head, though not as bad as before, still drove a searing spike through one temple and out the other. He was fear-blinded for an instant, then, with a jolt, realized the colony woman was standing by his bed. She jumped a little at his sudden awakening.

Tammara had to step back as Gale slung his feet to the floor, the flare of pain already fading to a manageable throb. "I need to talk to Kurt," he mumbled to himself, standing and moving toward the communication panel. She watched him go, sighing.

"What a coincidence, they're on the line for you." Gale heard her, but didn't reply. He dropped into the chair and wasn't surprised to see Jones and

Kurt looking at him from medical. Gale flinched as he mentally shoved the pain to a special section of his mind.

"I had a dream, and it gave me an idea for a plan."

"Cool. I was hoping you'd pull something out of your ass," Kurt nodded, "You know that planning and organization are not my strong suits."

"Kurt, would you mind reminding us what exactly *are* your strong suits?" Gale inquired. Jones chuckled.

Kurt rolled his eyes. "Ha ha ha. You must be feeling better. Your comic timing has returned. So what's the plan?"

"We take the Merlin home," Gale announced. Kurt and Jones stared at him, his statement slowly sinking in. Gale waited a few moments for a response from either, but neither man spoke. "Okay, well, can someone tell me what's going on?"

Kurt and the doctor looked at each other, something good passing between the two, a tiny smile flirting with the corners of Kurt's mouth. A full smile bloomed on his face, and Gale could read relief was a big part of it. "Alright you two. Enough of the Laurel & Hardy shit. What's going on?"

"Funny you should mention the Merlin," Jones said, leaning back from his desk, his bulbous paunch hiding his waistline.

Kurt jumped in, his smile like that worn by a politician who had discovered fresh dirt to use against his opponent. "Helena, Gii and I did some random checking through the computer, and because of a relationship Julie has with the second in command of one of the watchdog battle cruisers, we were able to find some answers while you were getting your beauty sleep."

"How long was I out?"

"Oh, about six hours. You do look better," Jones slipped in. "A couple more days rest and you should be as good as new."

Kurt snorted. "I still wouldn't date you, but you do look like you're on the living side of half-dead." Kurt glanced down at something, then back at Gale. "Do you remember the name Joel Lott?" Gale's expression didn't change as he sped through his mental files as best his brain would let him. The name didn't exactly ring a bell, yet it obviously had some significance. The second in command threw Gale a hint. "He would have been a fresh faced grunt you met near the end of your Star Corp career." Gale continued to concentrate as he abbreviated his search to the last year or so of his military service. Nothing surfaced. Kurt read his blank expression and continued. "I don't really have anymore that would mean anything to you, so I guess I'll just spill the beans." Kurt took a breath, letting it out slowly. "Near the end of the Mandroid War, you had the misfortune of being at Mali Pri, a small colony on the edge of Star

Corp territory. Because you were just doing a preliminary tactical evaluation, you were accompanied by only half your War Dogs Special Forces unit, the balance of your manpower being made up from..." Gale broke in.

"From highly ranked academy grunts. The Corp wanted them to get some field experience on low-level operations," Gale finished, his eyebrows knitting.

Kurt nodded. "But then the colony was attacked, and you made the decision to stay and try to defend the colonists, despite Star Corp direct order to evacuate the situation and leave it for a reassigned battle squadron." Gale's jaw clenched, and his eyes narrowed, but he didn't respond, letting Kurt continue. "The records show that among the over ten thousand colonists, only fourteen survived, and out of the twelve man unit you commanded, only one soldier made it." Gale nodded, his expression angry and sad. The soldier had been a woman, and part of his Star Dogs unit, but he couldn't remember her name. "The rest, as they say, is history. You escaped Star Corp court martial, but were stripped of your rank and command and forced to retire at the ripe old age of thirty-three. Only the testimony of the surviving colonists saved your pension and allowed you to leave in good standing." Jones was having trouble keeping eye contact, Gale's intense stare burning like a welding flame. The doctor looked away, pretending something on his panel had caught his attention.

"You'd better be going some place with this," Gale warned, his voice bordering on a growl. Kurt glanced at Jones, clearing his throat for no reason then got to the point. "Joel Lott was one of the academy grunts assigned to you at Mali Pri that died under your command. He was also the grandson of Representative Conrad Whittington, then head of the Government's Military and Defense subcommittee. And the kicker is, that unofficially, Mali Pri had been deliberately misidentified as a strategic Star Corp star base to lure the cyborgs into an attack." Gale's lips parted and his face slackened as the truth hit him. He could hardly make himself say the words.

"Whittington was going to field test the virus. That fuckin' heartless sonofabitch-"

Kurt wasn't done yet. "Didn't you ever wonder why the massive overkill in the attack on the colony? The cyborgs were expecting a strong Star Corp presence. And behind the scenes of your court martial, Whittington was quietly pulling every string and cashing in every favor he had to not only get you court-martialed, but have you spend the rest of your life in prison. He wanted your ass bad." Gale sat shocked, completely blindsided by the statements. Whittington had done an incredible job of covering his tracks, to keep word, even rumor, from getting to Gale. Gale's mind began to click. Suddenly Whittington's choice of the mutated bodyguard Albert Tragin made sense. Albert hadn't been chosen to protect the Representative. Whittington had chosen him to attack Gale.

Gale's mind froze on a single thought, and Kurt saw the dawning of understanding on his friend's face. "You don't have to say it---Whittington probably had the Merlin assigned to Avaric because of Christopher." Though Gale was staring toward the screen, for a moment he saw nothing, an indescribable wave of black rage blinding him as he slammed his fists down on the panel, cutting off the connection. He howled in fury, getting to his feet and slamming his chair into the wall. Tammara watched him, shrinking back around the entrance to the room as he continued to take out his anger on the room.

"I'M GOING TO KILL YOU, WHITTINGTON! I'M GOING TO FUCKIN' KILL YOU!" Gale screamed, throwing another chair against the panel. He stood in the middle of the room, eyes wide and wild, chest heaving, head pain a million miles away, looking for something to smash, someone to hurt...

"Jefferson? Jefferson?" He hardly heard the soft voice, and when it did register, his head snapped from side to side searching for the source. He caught a glimpse of the colony nurse peeking around the doorway and started toward her, but the voice from the panel caught his attention halfway across the room. Gale looked at the cracked communication screen, and there was Helena. He moved to the panel, hesitantly putting his hand to her image. She pursed her lips, nodding at his warm gesture. While her features were calm, her tone had a steely resolve. "Don't worry, Jefferson, when we get home, he is as good as dead, I promise you that." His face contorting as the rage flared, he stared down into the face of a woman he could love. He might love her a little now.

"Get Kurt and Jones. We have a lot to do before we head home." She nodded and allowed herself an encouraging smile. She glanced off screen and moved so Kurt and Jones could sit in. She stood behind them as Kurt spoke.

"We've already put some things in motion that I think you'll approve of, but let me fill you in." Gale leaned on the station and listened. By the time Kurt was finished, Gale had settled down and almost wore a smile. But in the back of his mind, all the Omni commander could think about was the moment of satisfaction he'd receive when he watched the last drop of life ebb out of Whittington's body.

Within ten hours, the Omni cruiser had been abandoned by the crew, programmed by Pace to totally shut down in another twelve hours. After that the self-destruct would take care of the rest. Julie had calculated the explosion, re-positioning the ship in a wider orbit so any debris that passed into the planet's atmosphere would land harmlessly in the desert. Treating the Merlin as a biohazard hot zone, the Omni crew took everything from basic survival staples to weapons to extra bio-suits and air. They were going to headquarter themselves in the battle cruiser's research medical section the Merlin had set up for the Avaric mission. It had been described to Kurt and Jones as its own self-contained area, complete with independent life support, small armory, and second-generation bridge stations if an outbreak was declared. It should have survived any internal turmoil because it was designed to seal itself off from the rest of the ship in the case of any ship-wide emergency. It offered the colony researchers, Merlin medical staff and unaffected crewmembers a secure base of operations, and, in a worse case scenario, a place to hole up and wait for rescue. Whatever happened on the battle cruiser exceeded the worse case scenario tenfold. Before the Omni crew left their ship, they scanned the Merlin for life signs and when none were confirmed, Gale knew once and for all that his brother was dead. Supplied with ship layouts and operating codes, Gale and the others said goodbye to the Omni and headed for the Merlin.

Through assistance from the lead watchdog cruiser Neptune, the robot container ship carrying the Avaric dead was redirected and loaded into the Merlin's hold for transport back to Earth's orbit. There was going to be no disputing the fulfillment of their contracted duties.

Bio-suits on, Julie piloted one shuttle to the main shuttle bay while Helena operated the other, docking at the research/medical bay airlock. Helena's shuttle carried herself, Jones, Gale and Tammara. Once the craft was secured, Gale and Tammara moved directly from the shuttle to the isolation chambers in the temporary med-lab, while Helena and Jones checked out the condition and integrity of the section. The medical facility looked to be a genius blending of practical workspace, comfortable surroundings, and futuristic, cutting edge technology. The general medical area was very military in its use of space and organization, but the biohazard section was like stepping into another world. Filled with mysterious research equipment, the Omni doctor had no clue of most of the technology; its function, or operation. Even for a Star Corp ship designed for bio-chemical warfare Jones was impressed. Both he and Helena were somewhat relieved to find only a few bodies scattered in the section. On closer inspection it was discovered that the few bodies found outside of isolation had been killed with a laser, and one of the dead had what looked to be a self-inflicted head wound. Someone had apparently cracked, and as was usually the case, the suicidal impulse turned into a homicidal one. Once they confirmed the area was still secure and there had been no obvious breach, they moved to the central control panel and began a preliminary systems check.

Meanwhile, once the other shuttle docked, the other part of the crew embarked on a much more unpleasant task. They split up into two teams: Pace and Gii headed to engineering, while Kurt, Julie and Maggie set out for the bridge. The Omni crew had been briefed by the commander of the watchdog ships as to what they might expect to find on board. They had watched footage forwarded from Avaric to the World Government, which had then been passed on to Star Corp. Even for the battle hardened Omni team members, the images were very disturbing. The level of violence was nothing they hadn't witnessed or experienced before, but it was the idea that it was members of a peaceful, civilized population---men, women, children and the elderly---that had succumbed to committing vile, murderous impulses. The acts of savagery went far beyond the impersonal wartime and battlefield taking of life. The outbreak's mayhem was littered with sexual depravities, mutilation, cannibalism, and bestiality. At one point, Jones, a doctor and surgeon who had worked on the front lines of many conflicts, stood up, face ashen and drawn, and left the room. Gii tried his best to lighten the effects of the powerful newsreel nightmares, commenting dryly that the bloodiest, kinkiest images were not at all realistic. A tongue being pulled out of someone's mouth didn't sound like that; how all the screaming sounded like the same people over and over badly dubbed in. He even went as far as to say that the whole Avaric outbreak was probably just a government invention, a hoax. Gii continued to heckle the grim footage like an obnoxious movie patron until he saw the image of a girl no older than twelve tied eagle spread to the posts of a transparent bed that was a duplication of Cinderella's glass slipper. The crudely torn bed sheets binding her wrists and ankles were marked with bloodstains from her struggles, her pale thighs spread obscenely wide. Face bloodied, viciously raped and badly beaten, the girl's clothing and tender flesh were ripped and torn. Once shiny blue eyes stared lifeless at the ceiling, her expression under the bloody mask blank and empty, well beyond the pain that had broken her body and spirit. An enormous black dildo was still shoved into her bottom. Crusting, bloody stains splattered the sheets between her legs, on her thighs. The camera panned down to a bloated dead man slumped on the floor against the bed, a bloodied whip inches from his cooling hand. The buzz of flies droned in the background, and the camera caught a fat green bottle fly crawling out of the man's nose. It wasn't until the camera moved further into the room that life suddenly sprang into the girl's eyes, agonizing terror exploding from her throat as she started shrieking 'stop it daddy, stop it, it hurts' that Gii lunged and turned the video disk off. He slumped in his chair, hands covering his face. He stayed in his chair long after everyone had silently filed out.

As Maggie had watched the footage, she ignored the nudge in her head to read someone's thoughts, and forced herself to watch the monitor long after the film's point had been made. She was disgusted and angered by the pictures and sound bites, and was sure that her expression bared her soul to everyone in the room. As she left the conference room, Maggie's mind drifted to how Whittington had leered at her, tasting her with his eyes. Her skin crawled, wondering what nasty thoughts were writhing around in his head at the time. If she had spent more time with him, or had suspected for a moment Whittington had harbored such black secrets, she might have searched and found the dark, twisted sickness that made him capable of instigating such evil. It would have been too late to stop the hell he had helped create, but the Omni team wouldn't be in the kind of danger they were now.

She had been a foot soldier for the Corp, a grunt who had been handy with communications and electronics. She had been a team player, and was respected by the other unit members. She had also killed: in self-defense, following orders, in defense of civilians and her team members. Maggie had never taken a life in anger or for revenge or simply because at times she could. But for the first time in her life Maggie DeLina, after witnessing the atrocities of Avaric, hated Conrad Whittington, and if given the chance, she would kill him.

While full power was available in medical, the rest of the Merlin appeared to have been powered down and on standby, the red glow of the emergency lighting casting a hellish, shadowy pall throughout the rest of the ship. With the power placed off-line, the ship's elevators would be locked down and non-functional, which meant Kurt, Maggie and Julie would have to make their way to the bridge using hallways and emergency ladder accesses. All the Omni team members had served aboard vessels of this type during their Star Corp careers, so finding the most direct route to the bridge wouldn't be a difficult. The problem was going to be their surroundings along the way. They were prepared for the worse, and they got it. The Merlin had become a silent, blood shaded former battlefield with the war's horrible remains still on display. It had become an orbiting mausoleum for the victims of both a raging killer virus and demented, homicidal crewmembers. Like walking through a salvage yard made up of mangled, junked human remains, it was impossible to totally block out their surroundings.

The going was agonizingly slow at various points because some corridors were so congested with bodies Kurt, Julie and Maggie couldn't pass through without stepping on the dead. To ground troops, the action of walking on deceased fellow soldiers was both disrespectful and one of the more powerful superstitions for bad luck in battle. Of course, while at war, if a soldier is forced to trample over the dead, odds were the battle wasn't going well anyway.

Some of the bodies showed the obvious virus symptoms: grotesquely contorted, blood-filled eyes bulging, skin paled and stretched tight over the bones. But there were an equal number that had died hard, ugly deaths from the violence the virus drew from it victims. The footage they had seen of effects the virus could manifest in a civilized community was horrific. What the three of them were seeing was far beyond that.

Star Corp soldiers, even the most logical, intelligent and diplomatic, were conditioned from the first day of basic training for aggressive behavior beyond the realm of normal competitiveness, self preservation or other motivating factors. When wars were being fought against foes such as the non-emotional human/machine cyborgs or alien insect-like cultures, Star Corp worked hard on the psychology of its soldiers in order to match the single-minded focus of its enemies. To the cyborgs, humans were an inferior, yet dangerous rival for resources. The ant and spider societies discovered at the edge of Star Corporation explored territories simply viewed humans as an abundant food source. A simple purpose or a basic instinct fueled a more efficient fighting machine than a soldier dealing with fear while mentally processing orders, tactics and moral dilemmas. The Corp worked to give its soldiers an edge when dealing with non-human opponents through a variety of approaches: drugs, hypnotism, biofeedback, visualization techniques, psycho-manipulation. Fighting a spider the size of a large dog is much different than fighting another man. A different mindset is needed to fight "monsters".

Nearly 500 men and women with differing levels of "adjusted fighting awareness" had been exposed to a bio-weapon that made them violently psychotic. The infected citizens of the Avaric colony committed malignant acts of suicide, murder, rape, and arson. While these acts were horrible, they were somewhat contained by the depth of each individual's own anger or mental stability.

The same virus corroded a combat soldier's already shakier foundation for mental stability, inviting him or her to act out their deepest, darkest impulses. Impulses built around violence, monsters, and aggressiveness. A virus-infected soldier was capable of violence far, far beyond an average person. The three

Omni team members turned away at times, disgusted by the condition of some of the bodies. They had to continually remind themselves that the wholesale slaughter had occurred during a demented, homicidal frenzy amongst the crew and not by some attack by alien spiders or ants. It was almost impossible to believe that humans could do this to other humans, no matter what the driving force.

Had the elevators been working, it would have been a two-minute trip between the shuttle bay and the bridge. When the three finally arrived at the control deck, it had taken them nearly half an hour. All three were sweating profusely as they moved to their positions: Maggie to communications, Julie to navigation, and Kurt to the engineering panel.

Within moments, Maggie gave the first report. "The mainline system is functional, but there are a lot of units through the ship that are off-line. Engineering and medical appear to be operating. I'll have our suit communicators linked into the com-system in two minutes. Once I do that, I'll check out the ship's intel systems."

Kurt didn't respond to her, instead glancing to Julie. "How are things lookin'? Can she fly?" Julie focused on her panel, her fingers blurring over the soft touch pads. Nearly a minute later she was grinning behind her face shield.

"It's not all good news but she'll get us home, eventually. Engine power levels are very low, but the reserve system is online and functioning. It'll take us a while longer, but we'll make it."

Suddenly, in their helmets, Gale's voice sounded. "Kurt, what's the word? You on the bridge?"

"Yeah. It was a tough trip getting here. Once a disposal crew clears the bodies, they should destroy this ship. The place is full of blood and ghosts."

"I bet. It's pretty clean here in medical. What's the status?"

"Maggie will have com up in a couple of minutes. Navigation is operational but Julie said we have to use the reserves to get home."

"Yeah, I just spoke to Pace and engineering is a mess. He's working to see what he can do, but it's not looking good. We'll probably have to use secondary systems for the trip, but life support is stable."

Kurt glanced around the bridge, dark shadows hanging where the crimson emergency lighting didn't reach. "Well, I've been told that I look good in red," he said with a smirk, his attention locking on a body half hidden in the gloom. It was a woman, curled tightly into a ball, her fingers still clinched in a death grip around her knees. Unfortunately, he could see her face. It was demonic in the red lighting. Her eyes stared into eternity, her agony still painfully easy to see.

Kurt looked away, having seen enough death since boarding the Merlin to last him the rest of his life.

"And when you get a chance, don't forget that I'd like to pinpoint Christopher's cabin." Gale's statement was flat and sounded tired. Kurt shrugged, exhaling deeply. He had forgotten about Jefferson's brother.

"I'll check it myself and get back to you." Kurt tried unsuccessfully to imagine Gale's expression.

Finally Gale spoke again. "When we're green lit, Julie is clear to take us out of orbit and lay in a course for home. Have Maggie ready a linkup for me to talk to Whittington on a secured frequency. And Pace and Gii are using B channel while they work in engineering. We'll be on C here in medical, but once we get under way we'll all switch back to A."

"Gotcha. I'll get back to you with Christopher's address in a few minutes. Out." Patrickson glanced at Maggie and Julie. "You heard Jefferson. Let's get this show on the road and get the fuck back home."

It was nearly an hour later when first a soft beep, then Maggie's tentative voice sounded in Gale's helmet. He was lying down, eyes closed, on an exam/sleeper, preparing himself for the trip to his brother's quarters.

"Maggie here. I've got a secured channel through to Whittington's office if you're ready to speak with him."

Slowly, he opened his eyes, rolling a few thoughts around in his head. "Patch me through." There was a half-minute of dead silence on the line, then a bubbly sounding woman's voice spoke.

"Representative Conrad Whittington's office." She sounded like a happy, over-eager teenager. Gale pictured a ripe, freshly scrubbed, blonde haired, blue eyed air-headed cheerleader, complete with pom-poms and short skirt. Of course, for the benefit of the goodhearted Representative, she'd wear no panties.

"Jefferson Gale for the Representative please."

There was a quiet gasp on the other end of the line before she burst, "Jefferson Gale---the Avaric hero? Oh my God..." The woman's voice had slipped up an octave. There was dead silence again before a man's voice came on the line.

"Representative Whittington's office. Can I help you?" Gale repeated himself, his tone now bordering on a low growl. "Mr. Gale, please excuse our young intern's excitement. You and your team have captured the heart of the public. Can I ask you to please hold a moment? Mr. Whittington is on another line with the President."

Gale snorted, and his voice dropped even lower. "I've kinda got my hands full at the moment, so I can't hold. Can you give Mr. Whittington a message?"

"Surely, sir. What would you like me to pass on?"

"Tell Whittington that there have been a change in the mission table time due to some unforeseen developments. We will be returning in the Merlin, and will arrive approximately 3 days later than scheduled. I will check in with him about a day before our arrival. And please let the Representative know that after meeting with Councilman Roth, I have a complete understanding of the Avaric situation and I fully understand why it was so important I take this mission." Gale paused for a moment, listening to the man's soft breathing. "And one last thing---let Whittington know that I'll be seeing Christopher soon, and when I return, I'll do everything in my power to make sure he sees Joel soon too."

"Joel? Is there a last name?"

Gale cut the man off, fighting his temper. "The Representative will know exactly who I mean." Gale broke off the connection, jaws flexing, fists clenched tight. Now it was time to look for his brother.

Gale left out of medical, his flaring temper causing his head to ache. Absently, he put his hand to his head, forgetting he was wearing a helmet. Useless, he dropped his arm, and moved to the medical section's main entrance. When the double doors slid apart, and the bodies fell into the room, Gale's reflexes barely danced him out of the way. The tangled pile of the cold flesh settled inches from his boots, and he could only stare wide eyed at the grotesquely intertwined corpses, looking like a macabre version of the contents of the children's game Barrel of Monkeys. Arms and legs twisted and contorted, spines bent in unnatural positions, eyes and mouths stretched wide in a frozen silent scream. The virus had racked their bodies with indescribable pain, and they had come to medical, desperate for relief, perhaps willing to trade their hellish suffering for the quick, merciful death they might find beyond these doors. But their pain had clouded their ability to reason, and they had gathered one by one, screaming for help, pounding on the walls, crying out for help through the re-enforced alloy double doors that had been automatically sealed the instant the ship's computer emergency status program had been initiated. If a person had been standing in the threshold at that moment, they would have been cleaved into two bloody halves by the doors. So the dying had stayed outside the doors, some hoping to their last moments that someone might help them, others, brains too fried to think beyond the agony. Like a large litter of puppies they had nestled and crawled among themselves, some naked, some dressed, seeking whatever comfort they could find. Dying in a gruesome, tormented orgy only the insane could have imagined. Gale was still standing there, mesmerized and repulsed by the sight when Jones stepped beside him, shaking his head at the sight.

"Oh my God...what this ship must have been like during the outbreak," the Omni doctor whispered, as much to himself as to Gale. The two stood staring for another long moment, Gale starting forward, carefully searching for gaps to place his feet. Once he was in the corridor, he looked back into the well-lit medical section. In his helmet he heard Jones' voice. "You sure you don't want some company?" Gale shook his head, turning to head down the corpse-littered hallway, darkened by shadows and his own private thoughts. As he walked, he looked into the red emergency beacon casting the hellfire glow, thinking about all the wrongs he had committed compared to all of the rights. The shadowy hall beckoned, and he followed, blinking a drop of sweat from his eye. Halfway down the corridor he stepped around a woman's body spilled in the middle of the passage. She was laying face up, uniform in tatters, blood-caked hands clenched. A cord was knotted around her waist, tight enough to have broken the skin, and her crotch was splattered with dried blood. A knife was still plunged into her midsection. Slowing for a moment as he passed, Gale's mind drifted, wondering if the stabbing had been an act of murder or suicide. But unlike those who had been bunched up by the medical area entrance, her expression was peaceful, her eyes closed. She didn't display the outward symptoms of the advanced virus victims, and maybe that's what got her killed. He had taken a couple of steps past her when a thought struck him. He walked back to the woman's body, kneeling to take a closer look. She was wearing the basic gray with black trimmed Star Corp jumper, but she had an insignia on her shoulder. He touched it with a gloved finger, his head sagging. She had been part of the ship's medical staff, caught outside medical when the outbreak occurred. She had lost her life a very short distance from safety. But then Gale thought about the dead medical staffers they had found inside the med-lab. He stood and started down the hall. She probably would have died even if she had made it back inside.

As he continued down the passage, bathed in the pale blood light, he wondered if the price was right and the stakes high enough, would he take a contract to go to hell? The thought stopped him in his tracks. Gale stood alone in the long hall, feeling the unseen weight, almost marveling at the sheer number of the dead in his sight. He was surrounded by the cold, fleshy shells of those who were surely as damned as any souls cast down into the mythical fiery pit. The crimson glow of the emergency lights completed the hellish portrait of death and agony Satan would have been proud to hang above his hearth. Would he take a mission to hell? He shook his head inside the bio-suit helmet, starting back down the hall.

Perhaps he already had.

Gale, his eyes squeezed shut, slumped against the corridor wall, his body sliding down to floor, nearly finding himself on top of the only corpse in this passage. He sat for minutes, stunned, his mind whirling. At some point he opened his eyes, staring across the hallway into the cabin of his brother.

He had discovered the entrance to Christopher's quarters, and by reflex Gale's right hand had reached to his hip for a gun he realized he wasn't wearing. It was obvious an explosion had occurred. Once he had stepped into the cabin, it only took a moment to spot the body of his brother, but it would now take him the rest of his life to forget the sight of the remains.

He sat in the hall, staring into the darkness of the wrecked cabin, his brother's body hidden in the black. Gale was thankful the emergency lighting didn't reach into the room.

He was numb from the sight, too devastated to make tears or yell or act out his grief. Gale stared into the dark room, helmet light turned off, ignoring the voices nagging distantly in his headgear. He was certain it was his brother lying on the floor, but he couldn't wrap his mind around the fact that human beings--- Jesus, fellow crewmembers---had savaged Christopher as badly as any starving wild beast or alien insect. Christopher's body was faceless; a reddish-black mask of bloody muscle faced the ceiling. One eye and both ears were missing, his face skinned from forehead to torn open throat. He had died with his mouth open in a silent scream, teeth missing or broken. His bottom lip had been torn away, hanging by a strand of skin along his jaw and neck. Christopher's mid-section had been ripped open, intestines spilled out onto the floor. Crosses had been carved crudely into his exposed flesh, his uniform all but ripped from his frame. And Gale couldn't be certain one or more of the attackers hadn't taken or possibly eaten some of his brother's organs. Having seen the results of cannibalism in the past, it wasn't hard for Gale to recognize the signs. He identified the brutalized remains only by a close inspection that revealed a telltale, blood-crusted gift. Their mother had given them matching rings on their perspective graduation days from the Star Corp academy, and the ring identical to Gale's own stared up from the corpse's gnarled, three fingered hand. While Gale had stared down at what was left of his little brother, the evil of the virus and the horrible aftermath of what Whittington had helped to create began to stir inside Gale. His own flesh and blood lay at his feet torn open and apart.

Backing out of the dark room, he had stumbled when he struck the corridor wall, and now he sat. Eyes blurring, he couldn't take them from the darkness of his brother's tomb.

Then, suddenly, he wasn't looking into the dark. He was staring into the legs of two bio-suits. One pair of legs bent at the knees and there was Kurt looking at him from behind his own face shield, his voice filling Gale's helmet. The Omni commander winced at the volume.

"Jefferson, are you okay? We've been trying to reach you for almost an hour."

Gale waved him off. "I'm not fuckin' deaf." He turned his head just enough to see it was Gii in the other suit. Gii was holding something folded in his glove. "What the fuck are you doing here?"

Kurt met Gale's eyes, measuring his friend. "I thought we'd better check on you. Most of the ship's monitoring system is out. You didn't respond to calls." Kurt glanced up at Gii, who in turn peered into the dark cabin. "We started to get a little worried."

Gale's gaze slid from Kurt to the dark cabin. Kurt followed his friend's attention, understanding the message.

"Chris is there. It's...ugly." Kurt and Gii exchanged a knowing look, and then Gii started into the room. He stopped, seeing a touch of pleading in Gale's face. Gale realized that Gii was holding a black body bag. "Don't, Torbeck. Don't go in there. No one needs to see him the way he is. I'll take care of him." Gii's voice was hushed, solemn. "Let me do this for you, Jefferson. I never had a chance to meet your brother. Let me have this opportunity." Gale stared back in the dark cabin, his body seeming to sag just a little. He closed his eyes for a long moment, then gave the slightest nod.

"Thank you, Torbeck." Gii returned the nod, switching on his helmet lamp as he entered, the small, powerful light illuminating the room.

Gale and Kurt didn't speak while Gii was tending to Christopher's remains. When Gii reappeared from the room, he was hollow-eyed and pale. Sweat dampened hair was plastered to his forehead. His thick padded gloves had dark stains all the way up to his elbows. He had trouble looking up from the floor when he spoke.

"Christopher is all taken care of. I'll come back later with a gurney and we'll keep his body up in the medical lab isolation morgue, if that's okay with you."

"That's fine. I appreciate that."

Kurt patted Gale's knee. "We're going to head back. Are you done here?" Gale nodded, and Kurt pulled him to his feet. As they started their way back to medical, Gale's voice whispered into their ears, as cold a tone as either had ever heard pass his lips.

"I will have revenge for this; no matter what I have to do or how long it takes. And I want those responsible for Christopher to be looking into my eyes when they take their last breath." Kurt and Gii knew that if the team made it back to earth, Whittington, amongst others, was as good as dead. The threesome made their way back to medical, silence the fourth companion.

After leaving Avaric orbit, the first thirty-six hours of the return voyage were uneventful. The Omni team worked almost exclusively on the main bridge or in medical, Pace being the exception as he continued to tinker in engineering. The state of the art protective biohazard suits, though made for use by researchers and medical personnel, really bothered Pace as he went about his work. He complained constantly, despite the fact that he had done wonders with a ship that had been plundered and sabotaged by the very crew that ran it. The Omni engineer didn't like the bio-suits, and specifically didn't care for the suit's

119

gloves or helmets. Wearing the suit made him feel so...so...confined. And having to wear them any time he stepped out of medical... How was he supposed to get any work done? The engines were running, but well below normal operating parameters due to sabotage. Life support systems throughout the Merlin, with the exception of medical, had either been totally shut down or on emergency status. He and Gii had been able to re-establish regular status on the bridge and a few isolated pockets, though with the mandatory use of the suits, life support wasn't really as big an issue as it might have been. Pace had gotten the tube, the ship's multi-directional elevator working. He was highly motivated by the nightmare Julie had after her initial trek from the shuttle bay to the bridge. She had woken up screaming, covered in sweat, eyes wild in fear. She had whispered to him in the dark of their room about the images her mind played back to her. In her nightmare the dead Merlin crew were becoming the Omni crew, one by one. The sight of Pace dead had snapped her screaming into consciousness, but she'd brought the haunting spectacle with her, and even the strong, loving arms of her husband couldn't make what she'd imagined go away. He was still trying to work through some of the minor problems with the navigational and communication systems with Julie and Maggie, but at least they were to a point where they were going to get home at current system status. That was until he received a call from Julie on the bridge asking for a quick check of the ship's long-range sensors. After he'd cleared them at nearly 100% functional, she informed him there was something out on the edge of sensor range worth taking a look at if he could boost the juice. Of course, he did better than that, and in minutes the sensors were working short term at an additional twenty percent. After Julie quickly described the readout, Pace immediately headed to the bridge to see for himself.

Gale was hanging in twilight, totally relaxed. Mind drifting, he was not quite asleep. He had lowered the lights in the small isolation cubicle and stretched out on the sleeper, doing his best to separate his personal self from his soldier self. The mission had become a nightmare and despite his grief and anger, he had to keep his head straight until this assignment was dead done. There was no margin for error anymore. He drifted off thinking of when he and Christopher were kids, doing what boys do best: swimming, wrestling, tree climbing, building forts, having dirt clod fights, snow sledding.

When the communication panel buzzed, he sat up alert, though he had no idea how long he had been resting. He rolled off the sleeper, ignoring the painful flare in his head. He activated the panel. "Yeah, I'm here.."

Kurt's voice jumped out at him. The visual circuits from the bridge to medical were not functioning so the view screen remained dark. "When it rains, it pours, Jefferson. We have some type of energy pattern ahead of us. Julie has made alterations to our course, but this thing has compensated to remain directly in our current path. We've evaluated what the long range scan has revealed so far. It doesn't register as a living entity, and seems to be a collection of charged particles. Pace is a little concerned because the shields are not at 100%, so there is a pending threat, though we won't really know until we make contact. In about fifteen minutes it'll be close enough for visual, and I'll try to patch it through. You should be prepared to strap in for contact." Gale rubbed a hand over his face, thinking.

"Alright, keep me briefed, and have Helena and Gii and Maggie ready to assist Pace." Gale stared at the blank screen as if Kurt's image was there, leaning against the panel. He glanced over at his bio-suit and the airlock, his fingers brushing against his forehead. The pain was now manageable and lessening as time passed. "Do you need me up on the bridge?" There was a stretch of silence from Kurt's side until it ended with Kurt's throat clearing cough.

"I think we can handle this; there's really nothing up here you can do." Kurt paused again, and Gale knew what was coming. With everything else happening to him, he almost forgot about his own precarious situation. If he were infected, he'd start showing symptoms soon. "How are you feeling?" Kurt's tone softened noticeably, as if his question was half an apology. Now it was Gale's turn to take a moment. He closed his eyes and felt his heartbeat, the ache in his head. He didn't feel hot or achy. His body felt okay. So far.

"My head hurts, but that's it. I'm fine. Call me if you need me."

"Will do. Kurt out."

Gale lay back on the sleeper, hoping that when the time came, he'd still be able to lead his team. This mission was a long way from over and even after they returned safely to Earth, he still had to make plans to deal with Whittington. As he stared into the darkness of the ceiling, reality set in with the power of an explosion. In less than three days, he might very well be dead.

Minutes later and strapped into his chair, Gale patched through to the bridge. It was another full minute before Maggie was able to put the intercepting particle entity onto his screen.

A vast, cloud-like object made up of multi-colored flashing material filled the monitor. Kurt warned that contact was at three minutes and counting. Gale wished he were on the bridge where he belonged. He was still the commander, but no longer in command or control. He had become an unlikely passenger---no, a prisoner---on his own ship. And a bad feeling began to crawl up his spine as he looked at the screen.

"Any more info from the sensors?" Gale asked, wishing he really knew what he was looking at beyond the various flashing colors. It was Julie's even tone that responded.

"A collection of charged particles bonded into a free flowing formation. Some debris. The computer has designated it as a non-living entity, but the formation has matched every maneuver I have made to avoid contact. It seems to be attracted to us."

Gale almost spoke over her, anxious. The clock was ticking. "What about the particles?" There was a pause.

"What about them?" Kurt answered, sounding distracted.

Gale was growing frustrated. Something was not right...something he couldn't quite put his finger on, but alarm bells were going off in his head. He took a deep breath, trying to relax a little. If there were more info, they would have told him. He couldn't help gritting his teeth. "Give me a countdown before contact," he spoke.

"I'll give you a mark at one minute, thirty seconds, and the final ten," Julie responded. Her voice might as well have been automated.

Gale didn't take his eyes from the screen as Julie counted down from ten, nine...A terrible feeling of dread invaded him, a darkness bubbling up seeking to swallow him from the inside out. As he fought against it, Julie's voice faded into the background of his mind. When he heard her say three, he let the feeling have him and he braced for impact.

Then it hit. Hard.

The first jolt actually struck just an instant before Julie said one, and the ship was tossed sharply for well over three minutes. The visual on his monitor blinked out shortly after contact. During the turbulence, visible flashes of colored light passed through the ship, immediately causing Gale to worry about the Merlin's self-destruct.

Without thinking, Gale reached out to touch one of the floating lights. When his fingers made contact, it felt like a jolt of electricity shot through him. His body seized from the power of it. It was frightening---for a moment it felt as if his heart had stopped, and he did his best to avoid contact with the dancing lights, but there were so many he was shocked over and over, again and again.

When the particles seemed to have finally passed and the ship stabilized, he quickly undid the safety straps and attempted to contact the bridge. His panel didn't respond, so he moved quickly to suit up. The suit communicator seemed to be functioning, but after several tries he'd still received no response. Suited up, he moved through the small isolation area to Tammara's room. Strangely, the door to her cabin was partially open. As Gale stepped to it, her face peeked into the narrow opening. She looked tired and washed out, as if she had been awakened from a deep sleep. She sounded anxious to get out of her room.

"It started to open, then jammed." Gale nodded.

"Some of the systems are compromised. I'm sure Pace is on it. Are you okay? It got pretty rough." Gale heard her sigh, watching her head bob on her neck. She was having trouble keeping her head up. Her lashes fluttered as she tried to clear her head. Her green eyes were far from sparkling.

"I'm all right, I guess. It was those light things. It feels like I have no energy at all." Gale then realized that despite the painful shocks, he now actually felt pretty good. In fact, he felt great. And the throbbing from his head wound had stopped. "

Get on your suit and I'll be back." She nodded, stepping back from the gap. Gale continued down the short corridor, stopping at the airlock call box. There was no answer to his attempt to contact Jones in the main medical area, which meant he and Tammara, for the moment, were trapped. Disgusted, he headed back to Tammara's cabin.

Unable to force the door open with his own muscle, Gale sat down outside her door. The automatic night cycle was still in affect in medical, so the hallway lighting was dim. When Tammara was suited up, she slumped to the floor on the other side of the opening, her movements sluggish. It hadn't been that long since the Merlin had stabilized, but the silence made it seem much, much longer. Gale was pleasantly surprised to hear Tammara's weary voice in his helmet.

"Do you think everything is okay?" Her eyes looked a little pleading behind her face shield. "I'm starting to feel a little claustrophobic."

"I know," he agreed. "These suits have a way of adding to that 'walled in' feeling. Hopefully it won't be too much longer." Maggie's voice suddenly broke in.

"Jefferson? Jefferson, are you there?" Gale couldn't stop his smile. Her voice sounded good.

"Yeah Maggie, I'm here. What's the status?"

Her voice rushed back, relaying information in short bursts. "We're stable with no integrity breach. No injuries to report, but there are ship-wide system disruptions. Kurt had Julie put us at a full stop. Pace and Gii are dealing with the self-destruct which was activated during contact. Helena is working to get those systems back on line. The ship is still maintaining emergency status." Gale nodded as he took in the information. Everything was going to be okay. But then Maggie finished the report. "From everything the computers and sensors are telling us, the particle formation seems to have merged itself with the ship. Julie is in the process of identifying the ramifications, though there would seem to be no immediate health risk."

Gale glanced away from Tammara to the airlock down the corridor.

"Tammara has indicated that her contact with the particles has left her very fatigued."

"I'll alert T.T. to her condition. I'll keep you in the loop as situations present themselves. Full communication should be re-established in the next few minutes. Kurt just wanted to get word to you ASAP."

"Thanks, and keep me posted." Gale cut the transmission. Some of the feelings of dread slid away, and he felt like they had dodged another disaster. Now to just get out of isolation.

Gii wasn't much assistance, and he was sweating as if the engine room had become a sauna. The damn bio-suit wasn't helping in the perspiration department either. He watched Pace work through the intricate, yet routine steps, marveling at his crewmate's quiet confidence and surgeon-like focus. Gii was just glad that he didn't have to perform the re-set alone. The pressure would have him cursing and screaming and pulling his own pony tail, and thank God there would be no screaming today. Pace needed all his concentration, so Torbeck bit his lip and felt the sweat seep from his pores. There was only a 94 second margin for error due to the time it took for Pace to go from the bridge back down to engineering. Of course, that margin would be meaningless if Pace screwed up. There wouldn't be enough time for a second attempt. Pace didn't seem all that concerned, appearing to be locked in and as cool as a dead man. Hell, the goose that laid the golden eggs could drop one in Pace's hand and he wouldn't notice. And the notion of being as cool as a dead man almost made Gii laugh out loud. Like everyone on board, Gii was actually very confident in the reset process, and he knew that Pace had done this dozens of times. Of course, if this was the time he somehow messed up, Gii was going to spend his last 94 seconds kicking Pace's ass. And that thought did make him chuckle.

Pace felt in total control of the situation, but his bladder and bowels were a whole other matter. Talk about bad timing. As soon as he finished, he was going to have to go straight to the nearest water room and make a serious waste deposit. But first things first.

He went through the drill, trying to stay relaxed and focused. Despite all the wartime experience he'd had dealing with self-destructs, Pace usually didn't work around dead bodies. He and Gii had to move a couple of corpses for him to have comfortable access to the dummy panel that housed the self-destruct console. As he worked, a part of his mind drifted, thinking about how he and Julie hadn't had a chance to start the big family she wanted. This was going to be the mission that would allow them to start that family without the pressure of doing more than working only the most routine of assignments. Pace continued to work through these thoughts, and he suddenly wondered if he'd skipped something in the procedure. He sighed to himself, continuing to manipulate the panel's soft touch controls, wondering if Gii even noticed the instant of hesitation. Pace was certain he hadn't missed anything, but hell, if he had, it was too late. There was no turning back now.

Pace cracked the tiniest smile. If he had messed up, the worse part would be Gii kicking his ass for the last minute of his life…

The minutes seemed to stretch into hours, and Gale was contemplating his revenge on Whittington when Maggie's weary voice was in his helmet.

"The self-destruct has been deactivated."

Gale almost grinned. "Maggie, can you have Pace come to medical. Tammara and I are still stuck in isolation."

Kurt's voice joined in. "Uh, Jefferson, I think Pace is going to be busy with all the system damage from those particles. And I was thinking about pulling Helena from medical to help out. Things are a mess, Jefferson."

Gale closed his eyes and took a deep breath. "Kurt, go to channel B. Maggie, give us a moment, okay?" She didn't reply, and Gale trusted that she was no longer with them. There was a brief, uneasy silence. "Kurt; you wanna tell me something?" Gale heard his second-in-command sigh, then speak in a hushed tone.

"The ship is a mess, Jefferson. I have to make it the priority." Gale waited patiently through another pause. "You and Tammara should be fine in isolation until we get the systems back on line." Yet another pause. Then the truth. "You need to stay put Jefferson. If you start to, you know, develop symptoms, I can't afford to have you in a position to add to our situation." Kurt dropped the volume of his voice even more. "If it turns out that you are infected, we can handle you in isolation. If you were to get sick and have free access to the team and the ship..." Gale didn't have a response. "I'm just trying to keep a potentially bad situation from becoming much, much worse." Gale leaned his helmet back against the wall. He knew that Kurt was doing the right thing.

125

"I hear you and you're doing everything right. Keep me posted; you'll know where to find me."

"Kurt out."

Gale sat staring across the corridor at Tammara. She was sitting inside her cabin peering out the narrow gap of her partially open door. She looked as if she hadn't slept for days. With visible effort, she pushed herself to her feet.

"I'm going to lay down for a while," she murmured, moving out of his view. Gale wrapped his arms around his knees and let his head sag. Waiting for a sign of a symptom. Waiting for the beginning of death.

On the bridge everyone was busy at their stations working through system problems. Because of the extreme turbulence from the particle cloud, Kurt started a visual scan of the ship. The internal cam-system, like most of the others on the Merlin, had been sabotaged, and Pace had only been able to get about half of the system functioning. One of the areas where the system was intact was the hold/bay area, and when it was displayed, Kurt stared in disbelief. The Omni team wasn't aboard the Merlin when the bodies were unloaded, but apparently when the colonists had plotted their escape, the plan did not include a respectful handling of their dead. Containers had turned over, body tubes and bags spilled everywhere. Some tubes were leaning upright like brooms. The body bags were a glossy black, but the less plentiful plastic body tubes were clear, and the bodies stored inside them, at least the ones he could make out in the red gloom, had settled into twisted, unnatural positions. Kurt selected a different camera angle, noticing the large amount of bodies that had spilled right up against the airlock that connected the temporary medical lab to the hold. Kurt scanned the rest of the area, seeing more of the same, then turned off the cam-system.

As reports came in from the various sections, Kurt began to feel worse and worse. It felt like he had just recovered from the flu. His eyes had almost closed when someone reported in, startling him back to attention. How could his energy level have dropped so sharply in such a short period? He lifted a gloved hand in front of his face, looking and thinking about the particles that had shocked him repeatedly. That must be it, and probably what happened to Tammara. He glanced around at the others on the bridge, but everyone seemed to be holding up. Of course, with everyone's face hidden by helmets and face shields, it was hard to tell. He would have to work through it---as an active Star Corp soldier he had worked longer and harder in much more grueling battle situations. There was too much to do, and there wasn't going to be any rest until they could manage to get the ship's life support and engineering stable. Whatever was happening to him physically would probably pass quick enough.

The physical damage to the ship was minimal, but the particle bombardment had caused continuing across-the-board system disruptions. Kurt would have felt much better about the repairs if they had simply passed through the particle formation and put it behind them. The idea of the particles merging with the ship...it was proving very difficult to run an analysis because of the havoc the particles were causing. As he sat in the command chair, the emergency lights had dimmed to the verge of going out before flaring back to normal. Kurt jumped on the line with Pace.

"Please give me some good news," Kurt spoke, glancing at the ceiling lights as he waited for Pace's response.

"We've got problems, Kurt. The particles are circulating through systems, draining power from some and overloading others. It's a real mess. It's going to take a while to replace or re-route the fried stuff, and get the basics back on-line. Thank God we have the bio-suits." Before Kurt could ask the next obvious question, Pace continued. "We do still have enough power to get us home, and it shouldn't take too long to get us moving. I'm working on a program to isolate each of the major operating systems so that we can then eradicate the energy bits causing the damage systematically. There's pretty severe damage in the minor cores, so we might eventually lose all power for the lights, the Maze tube transport system & full life support. Talking with Helena, the medical area seems to be relatively unaffected, so as long as they have air, lights & energy there, I'm not going to worry about the rest of the ship. Julie is working to salvage the autopilot so we can all just camp down in medical for the return trip, but she says it's in bad shape and it'll take some time. I realize Star Corp will have a seizure, but I completely disengaged the self destruct because fluctuations in the power cores would keep setting it off."

Kurt wasn't sure he'd heard Pace's last comment. "You did what? Did you say you disconnected the self-destruct?"

"Relax, Kurt, relax. I was part of the original test team when the self-destructs were designated for fleet-wide use. And I know as an engineer that all mechanisms can be deactivated. I had a friend at the firm that designed it, and before I flew with one functioning aboard my own ship, I learned the secret to disconnection." Kurt was silent for several moments, a giddy smile spreading over his face. "You don't think Jefferson hired me because I was just a great engineer, do you? Jefferson hired me because he knew that I knew things about ships that weren't in manuals or in computers." Pace chuckled at himself. "There are a thousand engineers who are just as technically qualified as I am, but Jefferson recruited me because I know the secret shit."

Kurt had to laugh. "And I always thought that he was just partial to blondes." Kurt listened to Pace chuckle some more. "All right, we'll stay put. Keep me advised, please." Kurt cut off the line, then passed on the information to Gale. Suddenly the turbo lift opened and Kurt turned to see who it was. Nobody was there---another malfunction. The thought of ghosts haunting the ship struck him as he stared into the empty Maze cube. He didn't find any humor in the childish thought. Just as suddenly the door closed, and a slight chill ran up his back. His nerves were on edge. Boy did he need a drink.

Jones contacted Kurt on the bridge and informed him of his own case of severe exhaustion, the doctor learning of Kurt's and Tammara's. Jones asked permission to check on Tammara, though Helena still hadn't gotten the series of airlock doors connecting isolation to the main medical area to respond. Kurt complied, his attention riveted to the cam-system view of the hold. Something about the scene mesmerized him like a passerby to an accident, but he couldn't figure out what. There was still occasional movement as the piles of bodies continue to settle.

It was a few minutes later when Kurt's voice spoke into Gale's helmet. "We're having some trouble getting to you. Helena has not been able to get the internal airlocks to operate, and the hatch that faces into the hold area is blocked with body bags and tubes. Pace will be there soon to try to correct the problem, but I'm sending Gii to help Helena and Jones manually open the hatch. They should be to you in about ten minutes, all right?" Gale was still sitting on the floor in the hall. He hadn't heard or seen Tammara since she went to lie down. She was probably still resting.

"We're not going anywhere," he answered. "Out."

Just moments after Kurt spoke with Gale, Pace contacted him. As soon as he heard the run down slur in his voice, Kurt knew he was in for a double dose of bad news.

"I'm having problems implementing the system isolation program. Some of the particles that invaded the ship are not only re-circulating and damaging a system, but different particles seem to be jumping from system to system. It's not leaving us a lot of options." Kurt could hear Pace breathing heavily. "As for our continuing contribution to Ripley's Believe It Or Not, I've just completed a basic scan of the ship, and it indicates that while there are still particles in most of the systems, the majority of the energy has now re-settled into---are you ready for this?---the dead bodies scattered throughout the ship, with a high concentration of energy massing in the hold. How weird is that shit?"

Kurt didn't reply right away, and when he did it sounded like a vocal shrug. "Well, better the bodies than gumming up the works."

Pace paused for a moment to see if that was all Kurt was going to say, and then continued. "Julie and I attempted an analysis, but the system farted again." Pace blew out a deep breath, then went on. "To conserve power and minimize senseless repairs, I suggest we go ship-wide level one emergency status until the systems clear themselves or we get this thing figured out. What do you think?"

Kurt flipped through the cam-system until he could see the hold area again. "You're the expert. I'll have Maggie notify everyone."

"All right. Now, remember, that means no emergency lighting, no Maze, no life support, etc."

"I know the breakdown Pace," he replied sharply and a touch too loud. Julie turned a touch in his direction. There was a pause between the two men. "Sorry man. I'm just fuckin' tired." Kurt wished he could splash some cold water on his face and get a second wind. He needed a cold shower, a hot meal, and a good night's sleep. He needed to get out of this fucking suit... Kurt felt crushed and discarded like an old piece of dog shit scraped from the bottom of a fat woman's shoe. "We do need to keep all communications and the cam-system running if possible," Kurt finished.

Pace sounded equally gassed. "No problem, Kurt. I'll try to safeguard communications best I can. And I know that running on empty feeling. Out."

Though he would never admit it, Kurt was spooked minutes later when the red emergency lights went out, fading the bridge into a shadowy black, lit only by the faint, stand-by glow from the control panels and the variety of light beams from their helmets. Suddenly their surroundings reflected the truth---the Merlin was no longer a high-tech, Star Corp military vessel. The Merlin, the Omni crew's only way home, was a derelict ghost ship.

In the medical section biohazard ready room, Helena and Jones suited up to join Gii in the hold. Jones kept glancing at her, realizing she hadn't spoken in quite some time. Brow knitted and jaw tight, she appeared deep in thought. The lengthy quiet was making Jones edgy, so he tried to initiate a little conversation.

"It must be hard on you being so close to Jefferson but not being able to be with him."

Helena didn't answer him right away, continuing to check her suit. "It's not like there's a choice. I just can't stand this waiting around." She checked her helmet light, and the small life support mechanism attached to the side. 'I can just imagine what it's doing to Jefferson." Her tone was low, and Jones knew she was trying hard to stay under control and positive. Jones pulled on his helmet, feeling the fear begin to seep into his system like a cool I.V. drip. He knew the fear was appropriate and necessary for him to stay focused and do his job. The object was to get in and out of the hold as quickly as possible. Once they got the airlock accessible and the door working, he and Helena were heading right back into medical for yet another chemical foam shower and scrub. Once they were done with decontamination procedures, the Jefferson watch would continue. And if he continued to stay this fatigued, Jones would have to breakdown and give himself a stimulate.

Jones checked over his suit, waiting so Helena could give it a double check. As he stood there holding a small medical kit, it gave him a moment to think about what he was going through to earn his share. He might have to talk to a therapist when this was all done. They were all going to be wealthy when this was all over, but for Christ sake, was any amount of money worth this kind of risk and stress? At that moment, he had to positively say no.

After they had checked each other, Helena started toward the airlocks. Jones didn't move, suddenly feeling as if someone had snatched most of his energy like a thief snatches a purse. One second there, the next gone. Helen stopped and turned in time to see him take a wobbly step forward, his body sagging as he put a gloved hand down to a panel for support. She took a quick step toward him, but he waved her off, though he was still weak.

"Are you all right? What's wrong?" He looked up at her, and it was an effort to hold his head still. It felt like a small boulder was perched on his neck.

"The particles seemed to have affected some of us. I'm just tired. I'll be okay, but excuse me if I skip working out today."

Helena's mouth hinted at a smile, a hand going to a hip. "I've never seen you work out." Now it was time for the Omni doctor to grin. He couldn't resist patting his ample martini belly

"You know, you're right. Well, that really opens up the rest of the evening, doesn't it?" They both smiled, the mission fading away for a few moments.

Helmet lights on and Helena leading, they entered the first set of airlocks.

Kurt sat on the bridge, staring at the near pitch-black view of the hold, waiting for the first sight of Helena and Jones. He had almost gone to help them himself, but quickly reminded himself of what Jefferson would do, and he had sent Gii instead. So he sat, waiting for helmet light beams to signal their arrival. Gii was going to take a flood lamp with him now that the lights were temporarily off, with the exception of medical. Then he realized with a sudden clarity that their ship, the Omni, no longer existed. By now most of the pieces that had survived the self-destruct explosion had burned up as they had passed through the Avaric atmosphere. Whatever had survived was now scattered in the vast, uninhabited desert that encompassed most of that world. But the ship was no more. Kurt wondered if anyone else had thought about it; if it had crossed Jefferson's mind. There was a lot of history involving that ship and the places it had carried the team.

The thrumming of his nerves made Kurt feel like a piece of machinery plugged into the ship, and as he slipped closer and closer to exhaustion, the mission and all its missteps began to seep under his skin, burrowing into his subconscious and planting the seeds of future nightmares. Staring into the dark disaster area of the hold, something unpleasant inside him knew this mission was a long way from over.

It took a few minutes for Helena and Jones to exit the trio of airlocks, pass through the research section, and enter the main corridor outside of medical. Jones was particularly startled to discover that the emergency lighting was out and the hallway was now pitch black. Their helmet lights cut through the darkness and provided more than enough light for them to move about, but Jones was unsettled. He blinked back a tear of sweat, barking into his helmet communicator. "Kurt! What the fuck is going on with the lights? It's like the bottom of the ocean outside medical."

Kurt's voice sounded flat, as if he'd told the same story over and over too many times and had lost interest in the details. "Because of persistent system problems, we're conserving energy until we can work out a solution. Life support is off-line, which includes all lights. You've got your helmet lights." Jones' face blushed with anger as he followed Helena down the hall.

"You're damn right I'll use my helmet light." Jones continued to mumble a profanity laced tirade under his breath, the flare of emotion boosting his energy level. Kurt's reply was short and sweet.

"Just do the job and get the hell back to medical."

"And what the hell are you doing?" Jones snapped back, nearly tripping over the wood-stiff arm of a dead body. The Omni doctor was starting to slide from anxiety to real fear. There was nothing in his background to prepare him for this dark, spook house walk.

There was a lengthy pause before Jones got his answer. It was directed to Helena, and Kurt's words came fast and edgy. "Hold his hand if necessary, but get in and out of there. When you get to the hold I'll have you on the monitor."

Helena glanced back at the trailing Jones. "Copy that. We won't drag our feet."

By the time they reached the hold, Jones was hardly able to keep himself upright, and he cursed himself for not taking a speeder. There was only one dose in the small kit he carried, and that was for Tammara. But he was very tempted to take it. His strength was sapped, yet he also felt very restless in his fatigue. His mind raced without direction. Thoughts and memories were beginning to bounce around in his head from childhood, medical school, and the military in a rapid, random pattern that made him slightly dizzy. Jones was breathing from his mouth, drenched in sweat and muscles aching like he'd been jogging for miles. Blinking away a drop of sweat, he thought he saw movement on the fringe of his vision, where his helmet light faded into the surrounding black. He paused, searching; his mind telling him it was a shadow from Helena's movements. He turned toward the spot anyway, his head heavy on his rubbery neck. All he could make out was a transparent body tube, and Jones took an awkward step toward it. He didn't notice Helena continuing through the darkness toward Gii and the work light. His movements felt forced and sluggish as he was drawn to the tube, ignoring Helena's prodding.

Gii had worked up a serious sweat by the time he noticed the helmet lights coming from across the hold. He was just a couple of body bags from having cleared access to the airlock door, and he was feeling it in his shoulders and back. Dead bodies always weighed twice as much as they would have alive---that's where the phrase 'dead weight' came from. Gii had to snicker as he wished the colony had been populated with circus midgets. He could have just tossed those little suckers around like little couch pillows.

As he cleared the last body away from the door, he felt the hair on the back of his neck stand up. He instantly dropped the body and spun around, his headgear light scanning the area of bodies closest to him. He tried not to think about the gruesome, morgue-like atmosphere, but his instincts, along with his nerves, were jangling. He turned in a slow semi-circle, his back to the airlock, his eyes both searching for the cause of his alarm and yet not looking to see the details revealed in the transparent body tubes. His fingers formed loose fists, and he continued to look over the area as Helena stopped beside him. Even as he distantly heard Helena's voice in his ears, he realized something was wrong. He took a step past her then froze, not breathing, only eyes watching, watching, the bodies that surrounded him, towering over his head in sections, wall to wall. As he looked into the hellish graveyard around him, he could suddenly feel their eyes on him, hating him for being alive.

Helena wasn't sure what the hell was wrong with Torbeck, but it was creeping her out. She looked where he seemed to be watching, but didn't see anything besides body bags and tubes. There was nothing else there. Then she realized that Jones was still back across the hold, and she wasn't sure what he was doing, though something seemed to have caught his attention too. Both men had ignored her when she spoke to them, and she had no idea what the hell was going on. Helena heard something in the direction of Jones, and she stared across the area, barking into her helmet at the doctor.

Jones was just a few steps from the transparent tube when another one rocked, then slid from a nearby mound and rolled almost close enough to touch.

Jones took a heavy step forward, feeling as though he were moving in syrupy slow motion, and peered down through the plastic.

The body was of a girl, perhaps a young teenager, and she appeared to be intact. She was dressed in a hospital gown, but all the turbulence had worked it loose, exposing a smooth, fish-belly white hip and leg. Just a shadow of pubic hair peeked from the edge of the gown. Her pale face didn't show the unnaturally tightened skin of a virus victim, but there were purplish black bruises like a terrible necklace around her throat, offering obvious evidence of the cause of death. Though she didn't display the symptoms of from the bug, the chances were good that a psychotic victim of the virus had ended her life. Whether first or second hand, the virus was the equivalent of a microscopic killer storm. It made contact, and people started dying.

Unlike the images he'd seen earlier in the mission, she actually looked peaceful in her death, her eyes closed, her expression soft. Jones leaned toward her, drawn by the absence of brutality. It was so sad to see a young woman, barely out of childhood, stolen from her own future.

Then, as Jones watched, a dark stain began to spread across the mid-section of the gown. He knew instantly it was blood, and he was suddenly very confused, not understanding, wondering if she had been placed with the victims by mistake, ignoring the other subtle movements now happening all around him, his attention so locked onto her. Jones wearily bent his knees and leaned even closer, speechless when the young woman's eyes snapped open and stared into his. He was frozen, incapable of making a sound, watching in a state of morbid dread and fascination as she blinked a couple of times, trying to focus on his face. Then her pale blue eyes took on an inhuman malignancy that burrowed into his soul.

Kurt sat in the command chair, eyes straining through the dark, cave-like gloom of the hold. He watched either Jones or Helena fall behind the other as they entered, then one of them walked off to take a look at something. He switched camera views to have a better look at Gii and the airlock, but with the high positioning of the cameras, the massive size of the bay, and the absence of emergency lighting, Kurt could only make out what their helmet lights and the work light offered. Though the audio communication system was on-line, the bio-suits visual link-up system was not functioning. Growing more and more eye weary, Kurt closed his for a minute, leaning his head back against the crown of the high-backed chair. His energy slowly ebbing, he was glad not to be in the hold, moving those bodies.

For one moment there was a feeling of absolute stillness, and Helena suddenly felt the same wrongness that had touched Gii. Torbeck, his eyes continuing to probe the surrounding shadows, took a couple of steps and turned the powerful work lamp away from the airlock, facing it into the hold, illuminating a wide path. Jones' helmet light had disappeared from her sight, and now she too stared out over the darkness of the hold, not thinking, forgetting to breath. She and Gii simply waiting...

In the next moment there were subtle, eye-catching movement all around them. Tubes began to rock and move, body bags flexed, then stronger squirming and wiggling, tubes rolling. Gii's mouth dropped open, speechless.

Helena stumbled back a step, not comprehending this grotesque change in reality. What was happening was not possible, not even conceivable. She could see clearly into some of the body tubes, an unwilling witness to a perverse rebirth. Her mind would not accept the obvious answer to what she was seeing. She had seen a lot during her time in the military and since working with Jefferson, but nothing real or imagined came close to what was happening all around her. She felt herself move, legs stumbling until her back struck the airlock, and her frightened stammering joined Gii's voice in her helmet. Then Jones' scream, high and long, paralyzed her.

PHASE IV

Kurt opened his eyes and looked back down at the command chair view screen, the short break not doing much to relieve the tired roughness his eyes felt. It took him a long moment to adjust to the visual input his mind was being fed. He stared at the view of the hold, and for a moment he wasn't sure if he was asleep and just dreaming. His fingers adjusted the controls, switching the scene from the command chair small screen to the control deck's full wall monitor. He slowly rose from the chair, the ability to speak suddenly beyond his grasp. What he saw was inconceivable. It couldn't be happening.

Gii heard Jones cry out, jump-starting his brain. Jones was nowhere to be seen, but the entire hold seemed to have become a mass resurrection chamber. Gii had to glance around to see Helena had moved a few steps behind him, leaning stiff legged against the airlock door, her shocked expression like a mask. Her attention seemed to slide to Gii more than a conscious move, and they shouted at each other simultaneously, though Gii's voice was louder.

"What the fuck is happening?" Helena burst, stepping toward him, her eyes shifting from Gii to the situation around them.

"We gotta go---where's Jones?" Gii shouted, fear-fed adrenaline pumping through him like a drug.

"I don't know. He was behind me when we got here, and he stopped about half way here. I thought he was just tired." Then both of them heard Jones hoarse whispering in their helmets.

He was murmuring the same thing over and over. "Oh my God, oh my God, oh my God..."

Then Kurt yelled into their ears. "Get out of there! Get the fuck out of there right now!"

Gii and Helena watched as the Avaric dead began to tear their way free from the body bags, Helena's attention getting caught by a nearby body tube.

Inside was a small child, a boy, eyes open and tiny hands pressing against the inside of the container. Helena blinked several times, still having trouble processing the impossible. The eyes of the boy seemed to slowly become aware of her, and when their stares finally locked, what little strength Helena had melted away. The child pressed his face against the transparent plastic until his forehead, nose and chin were flattened, attempting to use his small teeth to gnaw through the plastic. As he did so, Helena felt her stomach sour and roll over, a touch of bile at the back of her throat. She yanked her eyes away from the child and grabbed at Gii's arm. "We got to go," she prompted, a slight tremble to her voice.

139

Gii was too busy shouting. "Kurt---can you see Jones? I don't have a visual and we have to go!" He felt Helena grab him and he nodded his acknowledgement.

Kurt spoke up. "I see his light about half way across the hold off the main aisle to your right. Go!" Gii and Helena looked at each other, Helena making a snap decision.

"You get Jones & I'll get the airlock open." Gii didn't bother to answer, running away from Helena down the disappearing main aisle, ducking and dodging and hopping over the colonists tearing themselves free of their plastic prisons. The bags and tubes were not designed to restrain anyone, and the revived deceased were shedding their containers with ease. Helena moved quickly to the airlock, coding the control mechanism to allow manual access. She would need every ounce of her strength to pull it open alone, but, after a quick glance behind her, she resolved to tear her arms from the socket in the attempt, chuckling morbidly as her mind added the phrase, 'or die trying'...

As Gii ran and Helena worked the airlock, both were conscious of a low, mournful wail beginning to fill the hold. It served to signal that the dead had truly risen, and from the sound of the moaning, their resuscitation couldn't possibly be a good thing.

Gii ran from the relative comfort of the work light, cursing under his breath. The once clear main aisle was quickly deteriorating into a moving, shifting maze of moving tubes, squirming bags and shambling zombies. As he moved deeper into the hold, he realized it was going to be impossible to get a bead on Jones without his help. The doctor had stopped his gibberish and now Gii yelled at his friend, leaping over a pair of tubes blocking the row. "Jones! I'm coming your way, but I don't see you. Where are you?" There was no response, and Gii had continued into the growing crowd, shoving a tall, very thin Black man out of his way. There were more and more of the things moving into the aisle and toward his light.

Shit! Gii thought, my fuckin' light is drawing them like moths. I'm gonna need some fucking dead repellent. He yelled angrily, "Jones? Are you there? Talk to me motherfucker!"

There was nothing for a long moment. Jones' trembling whisper finally replied. "Torbeck? What in God's name have we done?" Gii rushed through a loose pack of the dead, then slowed as he felt he was getting close.

"Jones, where are you? We gotta go now, man. I don't have time to play fucking games. Where are you?" There was nothing but heavy breathing from the other end.

140

Finally Jones replied, voice shaky. "I think I can see you." Gii stopped moving, searching through the shadowy chaos to his right. Angled to the right, about ten meters off, he thought he saw a flicker of light, then it was gone.

"Put your helmet light on high beam and turn toward the main aisle right now!" Gii directed loudly, easing forward. A fat, disemboweled woman pawed at him weakly, but he shoved her aside, the heavy thud of her body sounding from the shadows. Suddenly there was Jones' light, thankfully moving toward the aisle. The Omni doctor didn't seem to be in a big hurry, and when the light suddenly disappeared from sight, Gii burst into the darkness. Adrenaline was almost making him move too out of control. He stumbled into a small, relatively clear path and nearly fell over a crawling Jones. Gii dropped to a knee and grabbed up the doctor, then barked out an explosion of profanity when he realized Jones was no longer wearing his helmet. The doctor's face was pale and covered in sweat, his eyes rolling around in their sockets.

Grunting, Gii scooped Jones over his shoulder. Helena's voice barked into his helmet. "The airlock is ready, but I can't quite open it. And the things seem to be getting interested in me."

"Turn off the work light, and turn down your helmet light. I've got the doc and I'm heading back your way."

Suddenly Maggie's voice cut in. "You're closer to the hold exit than you are to Helena. Get Jones out of there. Help is on the way."

"She's right," Helena spoke. "Get out."

Gii tried to look back across the hold toward the airlock, only able to see the work lamp glow. "I'm not leaving Helena!" He took a couple of steps, but he immediately felt the dead weight of Jones, and the reality of the situation was clear. Carrying Jones, who was well over two hundred and fifty pounds, wouldn't allow him to make it back to the airlock, especially with the chaos and the darkness. "We need some help now!" Gii bellowed, pushing his way back to the main aisle. He didn't want to say what he knew he would have to do. "Helena, hold tight---I'm going to dump Jones at the entrance, then I'll come back to you." There was no answer, and Gii felt his heart being pulled from his chest. When he made it to the main aisle, he turned away from the faint light in the distance, and struggled his way toward safety.

Gale was pacing in the isolation area corridor, impatiently waiting for Kurt's arrival. Maggie had filled him in on the madness that had broken out and the irony was that despite his possibility of infection, he and Tammara were now the safest people on board. Tammara was still sleeping very deeply; she hadn't responded at all when Gale had called out to her from the space in her doorway. That was probably the best thing right now. She was one less life to be concerned about right now. Gale just wanted Kurt to get there and get him out so they could help the others. Jesus---those particles bringing the dead back to life---it was so laughably unbelievable that Gale instantly accepted the situation, and like a caged animal, could only wait until someone came and set him loose.

He tried not to think about the rise in body temperature he'd been feeling the last hour or so.

Helena strained against the airlock door with a strength forged of pure muscle, fear, and desperation. She could feel it slowly pulling free from its resting seal, but she couldn't gage if she had enough strength to pull it open enough to escape. She did know she was only going to get one chance at it, and she said a quick, silent prayer before getting a good handhold on the lever. Then the strongest woman in Star Corp history screamed as she pulled, attacking it with every ounce of her formidable strength, the stakes far, far beyond honor and her name engraved on a trophy.

The heavy metal door eased silently away from the wall, excruciatingly slow as the layers of different metals exposed themselves. Built like a bank vault door, the first foot of its thickness showed, and she sucked in a quick breath and strained some more, her face reddening with the effort. The door was starting to come a little easier, and she could feel the momentum easing her strain. The door pulled free and relief washed over her. Then she felt hands grabbing her. Dead hands.

Gii staggered to within spitting distance of the hold entrance, but there were a wall of zombies blocking the way. Gritting back the burning strain of his back and shoulders, Gii took a glance back, still able to see the distant fade of light. Not wanting to put the husky doctor down and have to pick him back up, and with no other ideas popping into his head, Torbeck Gii put his head down and charged the living dead between him and the door, not able to stop the maniacal laughter that poured from his lips.

Like a human bowling ball, Gii and Jones slammed into the milling colonists, scattering the dead like pins. Gii lost his balance and fell, Jones tossed from his shoulders into the dark like a big sack of grain. When he looked up he was at the hold exit, and he scrambled to his feet, searching for Jones. He quickly found him in the clutches of a small, naked elderly man who seemed to be stroking the Omni doctor with far too tender a touch. His eyes coated in phlegm, the old man grinned, not a tooth in his head, euphoric to have someone to have and to hold. The sight startled Gii, and the old man looked on the verge of tears when Gii grabbed Jones from him. With no time to think, Gii half-carried, half-dragged Jones out of the hold.

Despite her overwhelming instinct to do exactly the opposite, Helena didn't stop pulling on the massive door. In fact, closing her eyes as she felt more and more hands on her, she used her fear and disgust as fuel. The door continued to open. When a hand flattened itself against her face shield with a jarring thud, she prayed for just a little more time. But as she felt the crush of the living dead pressing against her, and the hands started to grab and tear and pull, the inhuman wail of the dead filled her helmet like water. For the first time, she begged for her life, but her plea fell on dead ears.

Kurt's voice burst into Gale's helmet. "I'm opening the second airlock door, and will be to you in a minute." Gale moved quickly down the hall, and when Kurt began to pull open the door, Gale helped push it open from the inside. Before Gale could speak, Kurt quickly turned and moved away. "There's no time---Helena is still in the hold!" The two men ran through the research section to the series of three airlocks that connected the hold area to bioresearch. Kurt over-rode the automated controls and the two men pulled the heavy vault door open with some effort. They moved quickly to the second door and pulled it open, stunned by the macabre scene.

It was a frightening, frantic Halloween mob, dead pale faces stumbling and staggering toward them, forced by the surging numbers behind those in the front. Many gray-lipped mouths were open and wailing, low and mournful. Gnarled hands reached out for Gale and Kurt, some hands missing fingers, some waving ragged, handless stumps. There was a victim in the crowd for every violent possible way to die. One poor woman in the front caused Gale to flinch. Her flesh was charred coal black, raw red flesh leaking through where burned sections had fallen or been torn off. Her face was missing lips, her yellow teeth bared in an unnatural clench. Where her eyes should have been were empty dark sockets. The woman's cheek and jaw was exposed, skin and muscle seared to the bone, but there were a few wisps of long blonde hair sprouting from a head scorched bloody black.

The living dead swarmed, hauntingly beyond life. They moved, yearning to leave the darkness of death and move toward the light of the living. It was so completely unnatural, so terrifying. In moments they would be totally overrun.

Faced with the surging wave of resurrected, it was more luck than skill that Gale was able to spot Helena struggling amongst the sea of reanimates. She fought to keep her feet, battling the zombies as the crowd pushed toward the next airlock. Looking into the crowd, Gale quickly sized up the situation. Gale rushed headlong into the oncoming mass, shoving and battering his way toward Helena. Kurt stayed at the airlock opening, fighting back those initial colonists attempting to continue past him. He looked beyond the mob into the hold, eyes widening. As far as the light in the hold carried his sight, there were frenzied zombies. And as far as he could tell, they were all surging toward the airlock.

"Helena!" Kurt shouted out, and she saw her two crewmates, doubling her effort as she saw Gale fighting his way to her. She became a whirlwind, fighting to move through the crowd and fend off grabs and clutches.

It didn't take long for Gale to reach her, and her exhausted, tremble-lipped smile made his heart feel warm and large in his chest. He pulled her against him and turned to wade back through the masses toward Kurt, who was having trouble holding his ground. There were just too many corpses flowing into the relatively small chamber, and the force of that many bodies was close to forcing Kurt back into the next chamber.

"Hurry---I can't keep them back," he urged, shoving a man no further than a foot back, the sheer number of dead overwhelming. Kurt was on the verge of being swallowed whole.

Gale felt pressure on his right biceps and he ripped his arm away, grimacing when he found it to be a young woman. Her grayish white form was exposed as her hospital gown hung open from only one shoulder. Her head was misshapen from a powerful blow to the skull, brain and shattered bone exposed. The young woman looked at Gale with glistening eyes, but he wasn't sure that she could even see him. He shoved away from her, not wanting to strike her, knowing she was dead but still sensitive to her once being a living, breathing young lady, and now certainly way beyond controlling whatever perverse impulse drove her. She was trying to bite---no, gnaw---through the material of his bio-suit. Sickened, he and Helena battled their way toward the front of the mob. Kurt was not going to be able to hold them off much longer, and even if he did, they were not going to be able to close the middle airlock door. Gale didn't enjoy the idea that only one door stood between the Avaric dead and free reign throughout the ship. Then his brain locked on the real bad news: if the infected colonists had been resurrected, then so had the hundreds of psychotic Merlin crewmembers. Including his dead brother.

Two life-saving things happened at almost the same time.

The first was the timely appearance of Pace at the middle airlock. Kurt was conceding ground and was only another step from being on the other side of the airlock door and losing any advantage to getting it closed when Pace was suddenly there. Gale and Helena had nearly worked their way to the front of the mob when they, Kurt and Pace heard Gii's voice. "Here you go dead people. Come on now, come back to papa." Gale glanced back toward the hold, not able to make out Gii, but it was clear he was using the work light and trying to draw the dead back into the hold.

Gii backed down what had minutes ago been the main aisle, holding the flood light, his mind recognizing a real sense of impending doom. He had gotten a glimpse of Kurt inside the airlock, but hadn't seen Helena, hoping that she had made it out. He also realized with the poor visibility she could be just beyond the reach of the light at the mercy of these things.

It was strange how some of the dead were very passive, simply milling around slowly, oblivious to his presence. It made Gii wonder if some might be blind or if their minds were dead too. But the majority of the newly undead acted more animated, twitchier in their movements. Some of the livelier ones had angry facial expressions, and they also seemed to be the ones doing the loudest moaning. Some were even attacking other each other. Some reached out very tentatively to touch, while others grabbed and clawed. For whatever reason, the bright light seemed to attract most of them.

Gii adjusted his helmet light to its lowest setting, realizing it would hinder his own ability to maneuver, but it would more than even out by making him much less a zombie magnet.

The work lamp drew some of the resurrected from the airlock that led into medical, though the lights inside that entrance were still attracting others. Well, Gii thought to himself, roughly shrugging clutching hands away as he sat the work lamp on the floor, he had done what he could. Now it was time to worry about his own ass. He backed slowly from the light, fading into the shadowy darkness before turning and running for his life.

Torbeck Gii was in good shape for a man of his size and weight. Far from fanatical about regular workouts, he still lifted weights and jogged, and he loved anti-gravity free form fighting. Still winded from his rescue of Jones, his leg muscles burning and his shoulders aching, he could feel his remaining strength draining away. The good thing was that he moved well when he had to, and this was certainly the time.

Still quite a distance from where he left Jones, Gii was moving on adrenaline, dodging and weaving and darting through the chaos. Gii was so focused on this deadly version of kill the man with the helmet he never felt his feet touch the ground. He could feel the violent intent from some of the things, and for the hundreds and hundreds of psychotically deranged colonists surrounding him, he was the only prize to be won. More zombies were on their feet than when he went after Jones, and where the center aisle used to be was nothing but a crowded dance of dead people.

Bumped and grabbed and jostled, he was suddenly knocked to the floor, surprised to find himself in a clutching tackle. He broke free of his attacker and jumped to his feet, stunned by the snarling figure that rose before him.

In the low light from his helmet, a Star Corp uniformed woman stood, her eyes burning in a hateful stare. Teeth clenched, she growled, but it came out in a thick, syrupy gurgle. Dark fluid spilled from bloated, blue-gray lips. Her hands were blood-crusted claws, and she was on him with surprising, savage speed. He toppled backward with her on top, her hands tearing at his helmet. She bit his face shield and he watched with disgust as one of her front teeth pulled out. He hammered her in the head, tossing her off into the gloom, and he burst back to his feet, staggering toward the exit.

Chest heaving as he sucked for air, he knew his body wasn't going to hold up much longer. Heart slamming in his chest, muscles on the verge of cramping, Gii looked into the gruesome gauntlet that lay between him and survival. He spewed a short tirade of mismatched profanity at the absurdity of even trying to pass through the sheer number of dead. But his will to live plunged him into the mob that surged toward him like a living thing, his dying battle cry muted by the deafening dead wail. A few steps into the crowd, he stumbled and fell, pulling a few zombies to the floor. Several others fell on him driven by their own reawakened dark hungers. A few just wanted to touch the screaming and struggling man, but most wanted to tear.

Without the strength or desire to stand, Jones slumped, legs sprayed out in front of him, sobbing. Eyes squeezed shut, tears streaking, body shaking as his mind continued to replay the image of the young girl coming back to life, fear and confusion in her pale blue eyes. It was an abomination, a cruel trick from the darkest of evil forces. The Omni doctor could still feel her gaze, pleading with him. He felt something deep inside himself shatter into a thousand pieces. Something that could never be replaced, healed or repaired.

So he sat, broken, the haunted wail from the hold not registering in his mind. Jones lifted his head to rest it against the wall, becoming aware that someone's boots were standing between his feet. He covered his face with a glove, shaking his head.

"Just leave me alone, Torbeck. Just leave me a-"

146

A strong hand grabbed his wrist and jerked the glove away. Hesitantly, Jones opened his eyes, blinking away the tears. Eyes straining in the dark gloom, he couldn't make out who was there. "Torbeck?" The figure leaned in, close enough for the foul stench of death and madness to overpower the doctor. Close enough for the man's tight-skinned face to become clear. Close enough for the necklace of severed ears to dangle inches from Jones' eyes, dissolving whatever remained of the Omni doctor's sanity. Many other faces pushed through the darkness to hover above him, and he could only cackle a broken man's laughter as they descended, bringing first horrific pain, then, eventually, a merciful release.

Gale and Helena pushed through to the front of the pack, nearly falling into their crewmates. Gale and Helena scrambled behind them and grabbed the edge of the massive airlock door, starting it to swing. Kurt and Pace gave a couple of well placed shoves, then jumped back through the closing gap. As all four pushed at the door, a few arms slipped into the narrow opening, and Gale turned his head as those arms were snapped off like twigs as the door closed. Kurt secured it, joining them as they closed the inner door that led into the biohazard research section. Helena immediately staggered to a wall and slid down it, crying out from exhaustion. Kurt bent down at the waist, hands on hips. Gale looked through his face shield at the heavily sweating, gasping for breath, second-in-command.

"Do we know where everyone else is?"

Kurt's head stayed down as he replied, still sucking wind. "I left Maggie and Julie on the bridge, but there aren't any bodies there. Hopefully Jones and Gii are together and okay..."

Gale immediately tried to reach Gii. "Torbeck, T.T., come in. What's your location?" There was no response. Gale eyed his crew. "We need to get everyone down here ASAP. We need to find Gii and Jones, then head to the bridge for Maggie and Julie." It was obvious that Kurt and Helena were totally exhausted, but Pace looked anxious, ready to go. Gale took a few moments, organizing his thoughts. Despite the exertion, his breathing had remained steady, though he still felt feverish. "Pace, you and Helena stay put in medical and see if you can keep working on the systems. We need to at least go back to emergency status for the lighting, and we need to stabilize communications." Before Pace could argue, Gale waved him off. "Even with Kurt gassed, he's still better with weapons, and we need you to work on the systems. We'll be back before you know it." Frowning, Pace nodded, and moved toward medical. Helena pushed herself from the floor and started after him, but Gale caught her arm. They looked at each other, Gale putting his glove hand tenderly against her face shield. "Check on Tammara, would you?" She nodded, her eyes locked hard onto his. Gale smiled a little. "If she needs it, give her a booster. We could use her help. And have Pace see if he can get the Maze tube operating for us. I'm not sure Kurt has the gas for a fight all the way to the bridge and back."

She nodded again. "Are you sure you don't want me to go along?"

Gale shook his head. "No, I need you here to keep this section safe. You and Pace need to get armed to the teeth, and wait for my call. If you get through to the bridge, tell them to stay put. Without some major firepower, it's too big a risk for them to try and make a run for it." Gale hardened his look. "You and Pace are not to leave medical without my knowledge. Am I understood?"

"I hear you loud and clear." She eased a weary smile and moved toward medical.

Gale couldn't resist one last barb as she walked away. "I'm surprised that opening the airlock door wore you out so much." Her reply was a simple over the shoulder middle finger salute. Even Kurt managed to smile. Gale watched her go, then patted his friend on the back. "I'll get the weapons. You need to go to medical and get a booster." Kurt's helmet wagged up and down. A moment later he walked slowly to medical and Gale headed to the section's armory.

Gale stood in medical double-checking his weapons as Kurt continued to strap weapons on. Gale had rightly selected only pistols, though he was sorry not to carry along a laser rifle. Heavy and long barreled, the laser just wouldn't be as effective in the kind of close range, tight quarters situations that loomed ahead. So he had holstered a force pistol to each hip, and shoulder holstered two more to his chest. He also strapped another to the side of his right leg, and placed one in the small of his back. He attached a packet of extra energizers for each gun, so he would have plenty of shots. He also loaded a large backpack with pistols and holsters for Maggie and Julie. He attached a pair of flash grenades to his belt, and tossed a few more into the backpack.

As Kurt continued to suit up, Gale checked in with Helena. "Any contact with anyone?"

"Negative. I've gotten no response from Torbeck or Doc, and I'm not sure why we can't get through to the bridge via the helmets. I'm working on it, but I don't have a good feeling about Torbeck and T.T."

Gale didn't even bother to pretend. There should have been word from one of them, or they should have made it to the bridge or medical by now. Gale didn't have a good feeling either, but was trying very hard not to think of them as...Gale blew out a deep breath. He'd believe it when he saw the bodies. "All right. Keep working on it. Kurt and I are about set. How are we doing on the tube? Will it be ready?"

Pace's voice responded. "I'm trying to isolate and micro-manage just the programs for the tube. It's touch and go. You'll probably have to start to the bridge on your own. I do have the emergency lighting up ship wide, but I can't guarantee how long it will stay on-line. When I get the tube running, I'll contact you." There was a pause, and then his voice continued. "Helena suggests that if we lose communication, we'll flash the emergency lights to signal you about the tube."

Gale watched Kurt checking himself over. "Pace, Helena relayed my orders to you?"

"Yeah. Just get Julie and Maggie down here, and we have no problem."

Gale caught the edge to the engineer's tone and didn't like it. Gale's voice went rock hard. "Don't leave medical, Pace. That's an order." Gale glanced at Kurt, who seemed ready to go but was listening intently to the exchange. "If you leave medical, you'll be putting us all at even greater risks. We need you here."

"I hear you." Kurt shrugged as if to say, 'what can you do?' and Gale couldn't keep his jaw from tensing. He headed for the connector between research and medical. "Let's do this."

Kurt quick drew the pistol from his right hip and followed the Omni commander. It was show time.

Her frustration boiling over, Maggie slammed her fist into the communication panel. She turned to see Julie still staring into the bloody gloom of the hold, her breathing not enough to alter her statue-like posture. Their helmet communicators were not operating, so Maggie had to shout for Julie to hear and understand her.

"Julie, I can't raise anyone. I'm not sure how safe we are here, but I think we need to get down to medical."

Julie didn't take her eyes from the monitor when she responded, her voice icy. "We need to stay put until someone contacts us."

Maggie moved from her seat next to the helm, the urge to use her power pulsing at her temples. Before she considered the weight of her statement, the words were in the air.

"What if there's no one to call us?" The silence hung in the air, a heavy drape dropped between the two women. Maggie didn't need her ability to read minds to know what Julie was thinking. The Omni pilot slowly swiveled her chair to face her crewmate. Julie's expression was unreadable. Maggie tensed, muscles twitching, ready for self-defense.

"Are you saying every---" The blood in Julie's face drained away. All the air seemed to have sucked from her body. Her bottom lip trembled as she forced the question out. "Is Pace dead?" Maggie blinked, the question catching her completely off guard. "Do you know? Can you tell with your power? Are we alone?" Emotion was playing with Julie's face. Fear, anxiety, indecision, shock, disbelief, anger. They were all there, and growing stronger by the second.

When Maggie didn't answer right away, Julie stood up, eyes narrowing, tone dropping. Julie was closer than Maggie wanted her to be. "If you know something about Pace, tell me." Maggie recognized the posture and the look. Anger had the upper hand.

Maggie slowly raised her hands, palms out. 'I don't know anything more than you do. You know I have to be close to someone to get a reading from their thoughts." Maggie didn't wilt under Julie's glare and the two stood in an awkward silence. Julie turned suddenly, bending to a knee by her helm station. She ran her glove underneath, finding and pressing a small panel.

A small compartment lowered, storage for two force pistols. Julie took them, handing one to Maggie. Maggie checked the gun's battery, acknowledging the full reading. Using her thumb, she made the adjustment to the highest setting, giving her 20 shots at lethal charge. She glanced up at the view screen, chilled by the thousands of dead milling around in the red glare of the emergency lighting. Twenty shots... Maggie really did not want to go anywhere near the hold unless she had ten times the shots available, but medical was the most secure place on board. She turned away from the large wall monitor for a moment to watch Julie manipulate the small monitor on the command chair. She didn't see any team members as she scanned through the ship, and the medical/research section was not monitored.

After a few moments Julie looked up, her jaw set. "We need to make a decision. I think you're right---we should try to get to medical."

Maggie nodded, but watching the monitor had dulled her interest. The more she thought about it, the less appealing the idea became. All she had was twenty shots. "Yeah, eventually we need to get to medical."

It was Julie's turn to nod. "Pace and Kurt went down to help. They might need us right now."

Maggie continued to watch the image of the hold on the view screen. "And like you said, someone might be on their way or trying to get in touch with us right now. But with communications out..." Maggie started to pat the gun against her thigh, thinking. She didn't like this either/or situation. There were too many of those things swarming the ship, and they didn't have any firepower. Not counting the fact that Julie, though a Star Corp vet, was a flyer, not a grunt.

Julie was comfortable with weapons, but far from an expert. Maggie had to stop herself from instinctively nudging Julie's mind to discover if she had ever killed with a gun. Taking a life up close and personal was a whole lot tougher than destroying enemy ships from a battle cruiser helm.

Nearly a minute passed before Julie nudged her. "Maggie, let's go. We could wait here, but what if communications stay down and it's too risky for them to try to get to us."

Maggie had to chuckle. "Too risky for Pace to get to you?" She snorted at the idea. "And I don't think there's a situation that too risky for Jefferson." Maggie paused, the flare of humor fading as fast as it came. "And if it is too risky for them, that doesn't say much for our chances."

Julie's face wrinkled with emotion. "You saw those things swarm into the airlock between the hold and medical. Medical might be overrun."

"But the emergency lighting came back on. That could be a sign."

Julie shrugged. "It could also just be the particles tricking the systems." Maggie closed her eyes for a moment, focusing on her breathing. She wished she had thought through getting to medical a little more before opening her mouth.

"All right, let's go," she decided, moving quickly to the emergency ladder hatch before she changed her mind. Julie's hard expression eased as she moved to follow.

It happened in a split second.

There was a complete darkness. Nothing else. The world had ended in a shadowy violence swarming all around him, all over him, his body the center of a maelstrom of pain, terror and fear. The sheer agony of the attack swept him up, his mind and senses overloaded. Just as his existence ended, his spirit or soul left his physical form, drifting away from the fleshy shell being ravaged by a horde of living dead. He didn't watch what happened to his body, concentrating instead on the warm white light.

Then came the blink into the darkness eternal. And then there was another moment... a moment both miraculous as childbirth and as unnatural as a man's body delivering an infant.

Torbeck Gii opened his eyes. Somehow he was still alive.

Gii couldn't really think. He lifted his head enough to see, his field of vision much less than usual. He was still in the hold, surrounded by walking

Avaric dead. He sat, unafraid, looking straight ahead, only seeing what was directly before him. He looked down at himself, vaguely aware that he was no longer looking through the face shield of his bio-suit helmet. He could see his own blood splattered remains in the red glow of the emergency lighting. His body was indeed sprayed out on the floor despite his lack of sensation. Gii couldn't feel anything. Nothing. In his being he knew that this was... was wrong, but he wasn't worried or startled or frightened by it. It just was. He just was.

The thought of getting up passed through his mind, and he rolled onto his side, then pushed himself shakily to his feet. He stood for a while, time no longer an important or graspable concept. As he stood teetering, a second thought took shape: they would still be his friends, and they would find a way to help him. Unsteady and awkward, he shuffled toward the hold exit, the same creatures that mutilated him minutes before now ignoring him, letting him walk amongst them unhindered. It seemed odd to him that the revived plague victims didn't seem so abhorrent and repulsive. As he moved slowly across the hold, his mind seemed to become more his own, though his thoughts were foggy and slow to form. He must really look fucked up if they thought he was dead like them. He stopped walking, closing his eye and trying to concentrate. The images in his head were a smashed collage, flashes of dead, ghoulish faces leering, snarling, snapping, drooling. Hands clutching, tearing at him. The only singular vivid image he had was as he stared at the floor through his cracked face shield. Gii could faintly remember his head being raised up and... Then nothing.

Black. Darkness. Infinity.

So here he was, body and mind numbed, but trying his best to focus on something simple. His friends.

Helena scanned through the limited camera views around the three accesses to the medical/research section. The outer airlock that connected to the hold was still attracting a lot of attention, while the mound of dead Star Corp personnel outside the main entrance to medical had risen and were trying to get inside by pounding and clawing at the doors. One soldier was butting his misshapen head against the metal over and over as if he was autistic. His efforts were producing zero effect.

That just left the section of hallway approximately thirty meters down the same main access corridor. Helena trained the camera down the hall, stopping when she got to the proper place.

She turned and looked at Gale and Kurt. "The area around the emergency exit is pretty clear. Because the access panel is camouflaged to look like regular corridor wall, most of the congestion is at the main medical entrance." Pace chimed in without looking up from his work. "If we're lucky, I'll have the Maze on-line in the next ten to fifteen minutes. Maybe you'll be able to use it for the trip back." Gale and Kurt nodded, then moved to the emergency access Helena had discovered in the medical section program.

"Be careful," Helena called after them causing Gale to grimace. "Sorry," she added with a tiny smile, having forgotten Omni commander's pet peeve.

As soon as they reached the panel area, Helena activated the doorway, the panel slid open, and the two men slipped out into the crimson shadows of Merlin's hell.

They broke immediately into an all-out sprint down the hall, though the hazard suit's boots were not designed for athletic performance. Conserving ammo, the walking dead they first encountered were merely dodged or shoved out of the way as they made their way to the first ladder. Because the emergency back-up system had been initiated, the ladders had automatically swung down from their positions high along the corridor walls and secured, ready for use. As they moved close, Kurt holstered his gun and leapt half way up the ladder, scrambling to reach the top and open the ladder hatch to the next level. Gale stopped a few feet from the ladder, his head on a swivel. There were several Merlin soldiers stumbling about, but most seemed to have no interest in Gale and Kurt. There were only a couple of zombies that seemed to have harmful intent, and after shoving both away a couple of times, he dealt with them each more forcefully. He snapped the thighbone of a tall, heavy woman with a sidekick, toppling her to the ground with the sound of a heavy sack of potatoes. Even disabled as she was, the dead woman still rolled over and began pulling herself to him. He quickly turned his attention to a flabby, crawling man in a tattered uniform, whose dog-like persistence irritated Gale enough to snatch his force pistol from his right hip holster and press it to the balding center of the man's skull. The force of the charge splattered the man's blood and brains in an explosive shower, some droplets getting on the lower legs of Gale's bio-suit.

With the hatch now open, Kurt drew a gun and glanced at his friend. "It's nice to see you give someone else a headache. Come on," he spoke, legs pumping up the last few rungs, quickly disappearing onto the next floor. Gale took two quick steps and jumped for the ladder, holstering his weapon while in the air. He landed midway up, his legs driving him upward. He shot out onto the next level, quickly re-drawing a gun. Kurt had shoved a soldier to the floor and was scanning the area around the T intersection they climbed into. There was

153

not much resistance in the hall to either side, but there were numerous resurrected in the narrower hallway where they needed to go. And to make it even more interesting, some of them seemed to have noticed their arrival and were limping/shuffling/dragging toward them. Their moaning seemed to increase as they closed the distance, their movements not much slower than if they were alive. Gale and Kurt glanced at each other, debating in silence until Gale quick-drew a second pistol, the quickness of his left hand just a fraction slower than the impossible speed he'd trained into his right. Gale grinned behind his face shield, daring his friend to try and match his dexterity, but Kurt only reached very, very slowly to his left hip holster and withdrew the gun in a smooth, syrupy motion.

"Showboat," Gale taunted, raising both guns to shoulder height, promptly dropping the two closest with exploding headshots. Gale mouthed disgusted profanity as he squeezed the triggers again, more headless corpses folding to the floor, bodies convulsing, limbs jerking. Gale kept watching for the spasms to stop, or at least lessen, but they didn't. Whatever the particles did to reanimate their cold flesh had returned the dead beyond living tissue, and it turned Gale's stomach as one of the headless dead flopped over into its belly and began to wallow in their direction.

In moments, a dozen or so zombies were on the floor in various states of disability, and the men danced through them, avoiding wanton hands that still clutched, some blindly, at the air.

Several levels above them, Maggie and Julie ran down a nearly deserted hall, dodging away from the half-hearted reach of a sitting zombie. They reached the end of the passage, stopping for a quick rest. Both were breathing hard. Julie bent at the waist, helmet sagging, her body slowly folding to a squat. Maggie kept an anxious eye out as Julie tried to catch her breath, glancing at the shot count display on the gun's grip. The small black digital number read 4, and Maggie blew air, her cheeks puffing out like a trumpet player. They still had several levels to descend, and Maggie would have bet that Julie's gun was empty. Maggie eased the weapon from Julie's hand and was surprised to see that she still had one shot left. Not that it would make a lot of difference. She handed the gun back to Julie and continued to watch as Julie rested. And then they finally got a break---regular lighting came on and stayed on, and Maggie grabbed Julie's arm.

"Let's go---if the power is back up, we might be able to use the Maze!" Maggie moved quickly down the brightly lit hall, Julie's shorter, less exercised legs struggling to keep up with Maggie's long, muscular ones.

"Don't waste any time, Jefferson. I don't know how long the system will stay up," Pace spoke tensely into Gale and Kurt's helmets. It took them a couple of minutes to get to a Maze station, and when Kurt punched the open pad, it lit up, and a few moments later the panel opened and an empty cube awaited.

"Yes!" Kurt exclaimed, jumping in, Gale right behind him. "Bridge," Gale spoke, and they felt the multi-directional elevator move toward their destination. Using the short break to their advantage, they checked guns for shot counts and exchanged power batteries, still in the process when they felt the tube slow, then the door slide open. Gale and Kurt stepped onto the bridge, instantly realizing they were too late. Maggie and Julie were gone, no doubt making a run for medical. Kurt kneeled quickly by the helm, seeing the empty compartment.

"Well, at least they're armed," he sighed. Gale stood looking down the open emergency ladder hatch for a moment, then turned away, glancing at Kurt.

"Pace, Julie and Maggie have left the bridge. We're going to attempt to get a reading on their location, otherwise, we'll try to find them on our way back." There was no response. Kurt moved to the helm to initiate a quick scan of the ship. By the time he had touched his first button, the lights on the bridge began to flicker.

"Shit!" Kurt cursed, trying to manipulate the panel faster.

"Damn it!" Gale burst as the regular working lights on the bridge blinked out. He and Kurt flipped on their helmet lights and stood quietly in the dark, hoping that the power would surge back on. A full minute passed and nothing happened. "Pace, Helena, come in." Gale's answer was dead air.

Disgusted, Kurt pushed himself away from the helm. "The system went down before I could complete the scan."

Gale moved over to the ladder hatch. He shouted into his helmet. "Helena! Pace! Come in." Gale looked toward Kurt, his eyes avoiding the powerful helmet light. "We wait one minute, then we head back, double time." Kurt nodded, moving to the ladder.

It was a very long minute, and Gale didn't speak as the seconds ticked away. It didn't take a genius to figure out that Pace wasn't going to take the news well. But if he had done anything to Helena...Gale's jaw muscles clenched and his nostrils flared as an angry, violent urge pulsed through him.

Kurt had dropped on all fours and poked his head down the ladder to take a quick peek. He looked at Gale and gave a thumb's up.

Gale patted him on the shoulder. "Let's go." Kurt swung his body around and dropped down the opening, hands and feet sliding down the outside legs of the ladder. Kurt hit the floor running, moving down the dark hallway with his pistol in hand. Gale slid down the ladder an instant later.

Helena stood, her large, muscular arms folded across her chest like a nightclub bouncer, between Pace and the emergency hidden exit panel. Pace had a gun in his hand and another in a holster tossed over his shoulder. He wasn't pointing the gun at her. Yet. But she knew that move was coming. Pace was red faced behind his face shield, and his body language was a portrait of conflict. Helena knew he had to go try to find his wife, but he didn't want to tangle with her in the process. Following Jefferson's orders, she moved in front of the emergency exit and waited for him as he had bolted to the medical/research section's armory. Here they stood, both not wanting any conflict.

His eyes flickering between her and the panel, he finally spoke. "Helena, we don't have time for this. I have to go." He took a hard, decisive step forward, but Helena held her ground, her large brown eyes staring. He suddenly spun all the way around, "Damn it Helena. Don't do this-"

"You don't do this," she spat. "Jefferson and Kurt will find them. We have work to do." Her arms unfolded and her hands dropped down to her hips. Instinctively, her right hand rested on her gun holster. The significance of that simple movement didn't escape Pace, and he quickly made his mind up. He raised his gun to point squarely at her chest. There was a slight tremble to his arm for a moment, but once he fixed his gaze on her, his gun arm went rock steady. His voice came out a whisper.

"Don't make me shoot you. Just get out of the way and let me go." Helena pursed her lips, her hand dropping away from her holster. She was going to have to do this exactly by the numbers or else he was going to shoot her.

"Are you going to shoot me or kill me? 'Cause if you have that gun set the way I think you do..." In the split second that the engineer's eyes dropped to the gun's setting switch, Helena quick stepped to him, grabbing the gun and forcing it toward the ceiling. Before he could react, she twisted his wrist counter clock-wise, which forced his whole body to follow the sharp torque. His yell had barely left his mouth by the time his back slammed to the floor and Helena's boot stepped into his gun arm's armpit. During his next blink he stared up at his empty gun hand floating above him, and the two pistols aimed down at him. In the next second she stepped smoothly away, well beyond his reach, the guns and her attention never wavering from him.

Defeated, he let his head drop to the floor, his arm flopping down to his chest. He closed his eyes as the pain, delayed by his surprise, now shot through his wrist and lower back. He spoke between gritted teeth.

"God, you're fucking good." His left hand rubbed at his right wrist. He pushed himself up to his elbows, his tone more his normal self. "Please Helena. I'm begging you."

Helena continued to ignore the sympathetic nudge in her chest, shaking her head. "I can't let you go out there, Pace. Let Jefferson do his thing."

Pace stared at her, a sneer forming. "Oh yeah. Right. Like when you let Jefferson 'do his thing' when he shuttled down to the colony?" Slowly, Helena lowered the gun, Pace's comment echoing in her head and her heart. She stood over him, shaking her head. In the space of a few moments, she weighed the risks, Jefferson's orders, the way she felt when Jefferson had announced he was going alone to the colony, how much she knew Pace loved Julie...

She tossed the other gun into his lap, then undid her own holster and dropped it next to him. He sat stunned, looking for a long moment at the guns, then finally raised his eyes to her. She pulled him to his feet, helping him quickly with the holsters. She smiled a little at her friend, and Pace nodded, waiting as she left to open the hidden access. She made a quick scan of the corridor, found the area around the panel clear, and opened the panel. On the monitor she watched Pace sprint up the hall, dodging through the first few walking dead he encountered. Once he reached the end of the corridor, he was out of camera sight. Helena stared at the monitor for a few seconds, then moved to re-arm herself. She wasn't in a rush to report her decision to Jefferson, but she touched a button on her helmet and spoke.

"Jefferson, Kurt, come in." There was no response, and by the time she returned to her panel, her monitor told her that the primary ship lights had failed again, and probably for good this time. Cursing, she tried again to reach Jefferson as she worked to bring the emergency system back on line. Of course, Pace would have been the best person for the job, but Helena was positive that repairing the systems was the last thing on Pace's mind.

One moment, Maggie and Julie were moving smoothly in the well-lit Maze cube, and the next they were standing still in what might as well have been a closed coffin. Cursing and switching on their helmet lights, they could feel the cube coasting to its next stop, where it would be locked down until power was restored. They stepped back from the entrance as they felt the slight jar of their arrival, dropping them somewhere mid-ship. The women glanced at each other, waiting for the door to slide open, anticipating the worst. A heartbeat later, the cube was lit up by the electric blue bursts of their weapons. Maggie & Julie emptied their guns into the surging crowd of dead, forced back against the rear wall of the Maze cube by the shambling rush of those still on their feet. As the masses closed around her, Maggie moved on pure instinct, flicking off her helmet light and dropping to her hands and knees, half-crawling, half-squirming her way through the hordes. That just left Julie, and her helmet light drew the wailing dead like angry, menacing moths.

Julie pushed and fought against the front line of the crushing wave of Merlin crew zombies, panic suffocating her. Her heart pounded against her ribcage like a sledgehammer. She tried to use her empty gun as a club, but there wasn't much room to move once the flood of resurrected filled the small chamber. In a glance Julie looked for Maggie, but she was gone, lost amongst the sea of reaching, clutching hands. The sheer numbers pinned her against the wall, then slowly forced her to the floor. She kicked and struggled for her life, but soon did so without hope. She was going to die at the mercy of these things, and her last thought, the last string of words that formed and passed through her mind was that she and Pace hadn't had a child, and now she was going to leave him all alone. She would die hating herself for doing that to him.

A large man, much bigger and stiffer of body that her beloved Pace fell on top of her, and she screamed, Fear was all she knew now. Feeling grabs and rough pawing all over her body, Julie realized that the large man was fumbling at the release for her helmet with his dead, uncooperative fingers. She screamed anew when she heard the suction release, and then her helmet was yanked away. The man's putrid, diseased smell was as much an assault as the hands tearing at her. She could feel her suit being pulled and torn, hair pulled from her scalp. Julie continued to howl as the things closed in around her, thrashing frantically. She stared into the milky eyes of the man on top of her, his face lowering closer and closer, his mouth opening... The idea of her lips pressed against the thing's mouth shut down her mind and sent a jolt through her system, stopping her heart. But Julie had misread the zombie's true intention, baring his teeth like a rabid dog and then lunging and biting into the soft, juicy flesh of her lower lip. He tore off that piece of her with a wet, ripping jerk, then used his gnarled fingers to force open her mouth and expose her pink, meaty tongue. The feast was on.

Maggie flinched at Julie's scream, which she heard from both inside and outside her helmet, but kept moving until she had gotten out of the cube and was clear enough to stand. She flipped on her light and spun back to the elevator, Julie no longer in sight, but her shrieking continued to pitch and wail as the masses swarmed over her. Maggie stood a moment, letting the sounds of Julie's death wash over and through her. Then she turned and ran, her light drawing too much unwanted attention.

Maggie ran through the dark halls, moving from ladder to ladder, descending through the Merlin as quickly as she could. It was a few minutes after leaving Julie that she rounded a corner only to see a light heading toward her from the far end of a long corridor. She ran toward it, relieved and grateful to see a crew mate. It was Pace, and her relief turned to grief. He shoved the last zombie between them to the floor, and then grabbed her by the shoulders. His eyes were like small saucers, wild with fear and adrenaline. He was so wired that he almost hit his helmet into hers when he spoke.

"Where's Julie? Where is she?" He was yelling through his face shield, the communication frequency between them not functioning.

Maggie dropped her eyes, knowing there were no words for what she had to say. So she said nothing. Pace shook her hard. "Where is she? What's the matter with you?" He froze, his hands still on her upper arms, his mouth snapping shut. Still looking at the floor, Maggie relayed the details.

"We were in a Maze cube when the power went out. When the door opened, there was a crowd of ...those things and all hell broke loose. We emptied our guns, but there were too many to stop. I managed to get out, but, but..." Maggie finally managed to meet his eyes, her own growing moist. "She didn't make it." Pace stood rock still. His hands tightened on her for a moment, then dropped away, useless. He didn't say a word as he stepped around her, clubbing a zombie in the head with a gun butt. He took several steps down the hall before he turned and shouted.

"Where is she?" Maggie started toward him but stopped in her tracks as he shook his head. She didn't bother to protest.

"It was the Maze station at the central hub, five levels...no, six levels up." She stared into the glare of Pace's light. "She may still be in the cube, Pace. I don't know." He stood there for a moment or two before turning away, heading the way she had come. Maggie started to say something, taking a quick step after him, but she stopped, watching him walk down the hall leaving zombies in his wake. She spun away from the sight, her heavy legged jog gradually accelerating into a full out sprint through the dark to medical. She tried not to think about seeing Julie and Pace for the last time.

Gii stumbled through the doorway leading from the hold, blind in the sudden darkness and limited by one eye. Without a thought, his hand went to his helmet and turned on his light, and he continued to shamble forward down the hall. He nearly tripped over something, and it was without reason that he even bothered to look down. The sight caused him to stop, something deep inside himself stirring. There was a man sprawled on the ground, head propped up against the wall, skin and muscle torn away, internal organs exposed. The face was slashed and gouged, ears and eyes missing. The man's throat had been gashed wide open like a hellish smile. The only sign that the man was alive, or had returned to the living world were his lips barely moving, bloody spit drooling from the corner of his mouth. There was a second man sitting beside him and Gii stared at the odd sight. The man was naked, covered in cross-shaped Ts or Xs that looked sliced into the skin. The Cross Man sat dipping a trembling finger in the butchered maw of the other man's mid-section, then smearing the blood into the shape of a cross onto the man's forehead. Gii stood over the two men, the fog over his mind clearing just enough for him to recognize... Acting before the thought manifested itself, he kicked out at the finger painter, his yell coming out in a moaning bark. The Cross Man bared his dark stained teeth, growling. Gii took a shaky step to kick again, but the Cross Man crawled quickly away, rabid malice twisting his expression. Gii's head slowly swiveled back to the other man, and Gii let himself half fold, half fall awkwardly next to Jones. He leaned to his friend and reassured him that everything was going to be okay. What actually came out of his mouth were wet retching sounds hardly classified as human. Several of the other resurrected was drawn to Gii helmet light, but once the zombies realized the wearer was as dead as they were, Jones and Gii were ignored.

After a while, again without an actual thought, Gii turned off the light, and he and the Omni doctor sat alone in the dark, neither dead nor alive, but not alone.

Pace was exhausted. The muscles of his arms, shoulders and legs were spent. His head pounded, the pressure tapping like a hammer behind his eyes. As he pulled himself up the rungs of the last ladder, he wondered if he would have the strength to carry Julie all the way back to medical. He hadn't been this tired since Star Corp basic training. He used to roll his eyes when he would listen to his crewmates talking about Jefferson's incredible work-out regimen, and how he actually worked out harder and longer now than he did when he was in the military. Pace knew Torbeck and Helena and Maggie worked out regularly, but he thought of himself more like Jones, who was a specialist, and not really a soldier. As he climbed out onto the floor where he hoped to find Julie, he fumbled his pistol out of the holster and wished he had gone with Julie on some of her early morning trips. Julie was the one who took regular long walks and watched her diet in preparation for motherhood. He could remember several mornings she nudged at him to get up and go with her, but he'd crack open an eye, see that their bedroom was still dark, then mumble and go back to sleep. His laziness and want of sleep all those mornings might very well cost him his life. And Julie's if she were still alive.

He got to his feet, following his helmet light the length of the hall to the cube station. The entrance to the cube was open, and there were dead people kneeling in the travel chamber. Pace felt his heart sink, and the truth slammed into him like a bullet. He knew that Maggie would never have abandoned Julie unless the situation was hopeless. He knew now that his wife was dead, and there was nothing he could do about it. As he moved down the hallway, he raised his gun to fire, not really aiming at any particular zombie. There were several milling around in the passage, so even an average marksman like himself could hit something. He squeezed off round after round, the blue flashes of energy knocking the dead off their feet, spinning some off balance with wounding shots. Some shots, without striking any of the dead, made it to the end of the hall. When that gun was empty, he tossed it to the floor, and drew another, continuing to fire and slowly close in on the cube. He began to think about what he would have Julie wear for her burial. Should he pick one of her favorites, or one of his? He liked her in anything that showed off her tanned and toned flesh. She was much more conservative about her appearance, always underestimating the extent of her All-American, Midwestern girl good looks.

When he tossed the second gun away, he took more careful aim with his third round of shots. The first zombie he approached was struggling to get back to its feet when Pace calmly pressed the gun barrel to the dead man's forehead and squeezed the trigger, skull and brain matter splattering like a dropped bowl of pudding. He stepped over the twitching body, all his attention locked on the interior of the cube. A hand grabbed him from behind, and Pace just swung the pistol behind him and fired once, twice, three times until he vaguely heard a body fall. Several steps from the cube he was able to see the sole of a biohazard boot and one small bare foot, the space between telling that her legs were spread wide. Three dead people were hunched over her, blocking his view of the rest of her body. Two steps closer, and he could see that Julie's legs were bare, and that her bio suit was bunched down around her boot. One of the three, a stringy haired woman, finally noticed the light, her eyes narrowing to slits as she stood. The woman was big boned and nude from the waist up, her heavy breasts sagging. There was blood smeared on her chest down to her waist, and with a gesture that chilled him to the bone, she smiled. It was the smile of a hooker that fucked for pleasure and not for money. In the space her movement created, Pace could now see Julie from the waist up, shocked to see her uniform totally ripped from her body, her tanned mid-section exposed, her torn, bloody bra waded up in the corner. Her small breasts were bare, and he had to blink several times before his mind absorbed what his eyes saw. Her breasts were bare and blood had run down to her waist in rivets from the raw wounds where her nipples had been. Feeling as though he was outside his own body watching, he leveled the gun and shot the woman in the throat and face, what was left of her head flopping to her chest, hanging by the skin and tendons of her neck. Her body fell off to the side as Pace turned the gun on the other two. He stepped right up to one and yanked his head up by the hair, shattering teeth as he jammed the gun into its mouth and pulled the trigger. He could hear a wet smack hitting the wall as he grabbed the back of the Star Corp uniform of the third person, a huge man naked from the waist down, who was in the process of sliding on top of his dead wife. Too big and heavy to drag off with just one hand, Pace holstered his gun and got two hands full of material and pulled the man away. The man roared as he flopped onto his back, and Pace flinched at the size of the man's engorged member. Pace's gun had barely cleared the holster before he yelled, long and loud, firing shot after shot into the man, his finger still squeezing the trigger long after the gun was empty. He stood over the remains of the man, chest heaving, breath rasping. As almost an after thought, he finally turned to Julie, and the sight stopped his heart. His mind couldn't register that the body, the thing sprawled on the floor, was the remains of his wife. The diamond stud glittering in the dead woman's left ear was the detail that locked the truth into his head and heart. Pace dropped the empty pistol and fumbled with the release to his helmet as his stomach twisted and the vomit gushed up his throat. He didn't quite get the helmet off completely in time, and he threw up down his front of his suit, the convulsions so strong he dropped to his knees, unable to avoid what his body so violently rejected. On his hands and knees, he hung his head, spitting and wiping his mouth on his sleeve. His helmet had bounced off a wall and rolled to a stop, the light pointed almost straight up, her body still very visible to him. He glanced at her, tears welling, and he looked away, shattered and alone. For God's sake, where were her lips...?

He didn't notice and didn't react as more and more resurrected lurched and teetered and crept their way toward him and the light. With his body and mind exhausted, he didn't put up much struggle as they descended on him, a dozen insane, with just as many perversions.

Some time later, when the last of them had crawled away, Pace was almost as unrecognizable as his wife.

Gale and Kurt continued to move through the ship, running and dodging more than fighting, conserving their firepower. At one point they moved into a more heavily populated pocket of living dead located by a cube station, and it was obvious that someone with a gun had been through this way. There were bodies covering the hall, some still twitching. Their quick glances didn't reveal any Omni team members among them, so they kept moving. Both men were startled to see a helmet, with the light still on, being tossed between two zombies like a toy. When they were close enough, Gale grabbed it from the air, turned off the light, then tossed it into the dark cube chamber, happy that there wasn't a head still in it. They kept working their way back through the darkened ship, steadily closing in on medical.

It wasn't until they were only a level away from the medical section that the first shot was fired at them.

Maggie had made it back to medical, literally falling through the opening waiting for her. Tammara was waiting with an adrenaline booster. Helena watched the monitor as a few of the dead moved to the section of the corridor where the emergency exit panel was, groping and clawing at the wall. She moved to join the other two women in the research area.

Helena was waiting for Maggie when she came out of decontamination. It was almost strange to see someone out of a bio-suit. Maggie mustered a trembling smile but it quickly faded as Helena spoke.

"Julie?" Maggie closed her eyes and shook her head. "What about Pace? Did you see him?"

Maggie opened her eyes and looked into Helena's. "Yeah. I met him in a hallway a few levels up. He went on after Julie." Maggie turned away, moving to the water room. She emerged a few minutes later, and Tammara had her lie down as she administered hydration therapy.

The Avaric nurse looked at Helena. "This certainly wouldn't do you any harm. She'll be done in less than half an hour." Tammara glanced between the two women "If you'll excuse me, I'm going to isolation to clean up and change out of my suit. I'll be back." She didn't wait for an okay, leaving the room quickly.

Helena moved to bed, sitting on the edge. She looked down at the floor. "I shouldn't have let Pace go. I should have just stunned him and secured him in isolation until I got word from Jefferson. Unless he and Kurt find Pace..."

Maggie spoke softly. "Any word from T.T. or Torbeck?" She watched Helena's shoulder shrug.

"Nothing. And T.T. wasn't feeling great when we first went to the hold. And neither of them were armed." She glanced at her friend. "Communications have been out since the power off-lined again. I hoping they're just holed up somewhere, but..." Helena's hand went to one of her right hip holsters for comfort. "Jefferson and Kurt should be on their way back, but I haven't heard from them since they were on the bridge." Maggie started to speak but stopped. Helena finally looked at Maggie, her expression soft. "Don't even think about it."

Maggie turned away from her friend, a sob catching in her throat. Helena could see her body trembling, and she could feel her own emotion welling up. Gently, she reached out and touched Maggie's cheek, feeling moisture coming to her own eyes. She pushed away from the bed and headed for the door, talking over her shoulder. "When you're able, I could use your help getting communications back up." Maggie didn't reply, and Helena didn't expect her to.

Helena was watching the monitor when she first saw Jefferson's and Kurt's lights, moving at a full out sprint, on her screen view of the long passage outside medical. As they grew near the emergency panel, she opened the doorway, watching on the screen as the familiar blue flashes from more than one force pistol fired from the way they had come. Jefferson slid as he reached the entrance, catching the opening's edge and flipping himself onto his belly. He rolled back into the middle of the hallway, drawing and firing a pistol from each hand as Kurt dove headlong to safety. Once Kurt was clear, Gale bear crawled quickly through the opening, the panel sliding shut an instant behind him. As he followed in Kurt's hurried footsteps to the armory, he shouted out instructions.

"Helena, Tammara! Get strapped right now! We've got company coming, and I don't mean for dinner!" Gale arrived at the armory as Kurt opened the access, and was happy to see Maggie jog into the room. She had a bio-suit on, but was not wearing a helmet. Kurt tossed out a long barreled laser rifle Gale caught, then passed to her. Helena then joined them, asking for shoulder and boot holsters. For the next couple of minutes, the four of them fastened and adjusted holster after holster, Helena helping Maggie adjust the back sling for the laser rifle. In a quick, orderly fashion they moved through the armaments, selecting force pistols, grenades, and extra gun batteries. They were all close to being completely strapped, when Tammara ran in, smiling from ear to ear. She just stood there, hands behind her back until, one by one, she got the attention of all four soldiers.

"What? What is it? And you need to grab a gun or two." Gale glanced at Maggie. "Get a couple of holsters on her while she shares the joke."

Words burst from her mouth. "I was in the research supply cooler, looking for a stronger booster to give myself, and I stumbled upon this." She whipped her right hand out and in it was a small vial, made for loading onto a standard injector. Even Maggie stopped in the middle of adjusting a strap as they all stared.

"What is it?" Gale spoke softly, his attention shifting between the vial and the nurse.

"I think it's a vaccine for the virus. It was coded under the emergency provisions brought on board by the Avaric research group. There were two small canisters---one was empty and the other had been opened. There are enough doses for everyone."

"If that's what the shit really is. Maggie," Gale directed, "man the panel and see if there are any systems you can try to get online, especially communications. I don't think we're going to have a lot of time. They might be dead, but some of them have re-discovered the joy of firearms." She moved, Helena taking a step to follow, but Gale shook his head. "Kurt, why don't you see if you can lend Maggie a hand? Concentrate on communications, then whatever else we have time for. We're on the clock." Kurt was already out of the room as Gale spoke the last sentence. Then he looked back to Tammara. "Finish getting on your stuff, then go back and get the vaccine. After that, go to main medical with Kurt and Maggie and wait for us."

The colony nurse frowned. "Where are you going?" Gale looked at Helena, softly taking her hand. He spoke as he turned and led Helena from the room.

"The morgue."

Sharing a wall with the isolation quarters, Gale and Helena passed quickly through the coroner/examine room, all white tile and gleaming metal. Strangely, there was no smell. There were a half dozen examination slabs built into the floors, high tech autopsy equip at the end of each. Gale had to access the large shiny metal door before they could enter their final stop. Opening the door, the muffled pounding and wailing from the now revived dead inside the coffin-like confines of the morgue drawers gave the open, ultra-clean room a chilling, haunted feeling.

The metal doors to the body storage and preservation units took up nearly all the space on the gray walled chamber. Only a submarine-type hatch built into the floor in the far corner of the room disturbed the simple, efficient redundancy of the room.

Once in the room, Gale paused for a moment, deciding between leaving the room immediately or opening the drawers one by one and silencing the occupants. He ignored both options and, leaving Helena by the door, walked slowly across the room to the drawer Torbeck had marked clearly for the Omni commander. A bloody strip from Christopher's uniform hung from the handle of the bottom end of the wall to Gale's left, and he stopped beside it, confused by the lack of sound. He grasped the handle and twisted it to the right, hearing a faint click. He glanced back at Helena, and then slowly pulled the drawer open, revealing the body bag containing his brother. A body bag that now housed a moving corpse. Gale pulled the tray all the way out, then reached and unzipped the bag slowly, stepping back and steeling himself. Like a caterpillar squirming out of a cocoon, his little brother emerged, and all the love inside him was not enough to keep Gale from taking another step away. Once a young man with a model's good looks, Christopher was now an abomination, and Gale drew a gun and let it hang at his side. Christopher sat up, his face a raw, bloody mask, but his one good eye wandered in its socket until it fell on Gale. That clear brown eye locked onto him, and after a few moments recognition dawned, and Gale stepped up to the drawer, raising his gun as if it weighed pounds more than it did. Christopher's smash lipped and almost toothless mouth moved as if he was trying to speak, but nothing came out but a whispering moan. Gale inched closer, his chest tightening and his features pinching as all the welled up emotion began to bubble to the surface. He was just a step from his brother, the barrel inches from the middle of Christopher's brow. His brother's head appeared unnatural without his ears, bloody gaps where they used to be. Lifting a shaky hand, Christopher slowly reached out for the gun, grasping the barrel and gently pulling it against his blood caked forehead. Gale's gun arm trembled, a tear rolling down his face as they looked at each other for a few seconds more, then Christopher closed his eye. Gale sniffled, chest rising faster and harder, blinking back the moisture filling up both eyes. He closed his eyes, forcing more tears down his cheeks, and he felt his finger balanced just so on the trigger, awaiting the mental command...

Gale jerked the gun upward, spinning away, shaking his head, totally at a loss at what to do. He looked to Helena, but couldn't read her expression through the face shield. He turned back to Christopher, his brother's eye still closed. Slowly, he holstered his gun. Kneeling down, he carefully gathered the body bag up, his brother's eye slowly opening.

"I'm taking him to isolation," Gale spoke as he walked out of the room. Helena closed the morgue door, close to tears herself.

On the way back through the section, Christopher managed to point Gale away from isolation and into the main medical area. Gale stopped as he entered, Kurt & Helena & Maggie stunned to silence by the sight. Christopher managed to wave his finger toward the central panel. As Gale carried him forward, Maggie quickly moved, giving up her seat. Kurt jumped up and helped Gale lower his brother into the seat. Maggie leaned in and adjusted the screen, then they all stepped back as Christopher stared down at the keyboard, his chin resting on his chest. Awkwardly he began to manipulate the keyboard with his good hand, and they watched as he typed out a message.

Jef Jefersson plese plesse help mme

There was pin drop silence and Gale turned away, the message clear. He could feel the others looking at him, to him, and he turned to face his friends, his expression tortured.

"I went to the morgue to...to..." Gale's voice caught in his throat. "But I just couldn't... help..." Kurt stepped up to him, their helmets almost touching, speaking in a whisper.

"Maggie ran an analysis, and the particles seem to be dissipating. If we can hole up here..."

"Guys, we just lost the camera outside our entrance," Helena burst. Christopher's head rolled on his neck toward the entrance, his eye staring hard. Gale stepped around Kurt toward the panel but noticed his brother's focus on the door. Before he could say a word, take another step, think another thought, there was an explosion. Gale was lifted off his feet and the war began.

The world went from moving in super slow motion to everything moving at double time. Gale felt like he was floating forever with the force of the bomb, seeing the main entrance disappear in a flash of lightening and black smoke. Kurt was tossed off to the left, out of his sight, while Maggie, Helena and Christopher were thrown to the floor by the blast. When his body struck high on the wall behind him, Gale felt the sudden impact, the air exploding out of his lungs, his head snapping forward. He felt his body twist and hang in the air for a long moment, then the floor rushed up to meet him face first. Gale's helmet absorbed most of the jarring collision, but enough got through to his head to make him see stars. His belly to the floor, he shook them away and quickly took stock of the situation.

There was swirling smoke and motion everywhere. There was gunfire and zombies pouring into medical, and like a magician, Gale was on his feet, guns appearing in his hands. Helena was on one knee, firing into the mob. Maggie seemed to have just regained her senses and had put her back to a wall before her finger found the trigger. Kurt was still on the floor, spider web-like cracks across his face shield but he had a gun out and was defending himself. As the smoke cleared and visibility increased, Gale could see just a handful of undead

Merlin crewmembers actually using force pistols, and though their aim did not seem particularly good, it was enough to put the Omni team momentarily on the defensive.

Gale targeted the shooters, and fired a first quick round, his attention skipping to Christopher for a split second. His brother was still lying on the floor, half under the panel, and seemed to be staring into the mob. Gale's first shots hit where he aimed, and two of the zombie shooters were put on their backs. He targeted another, but couldn't squeeze off the shot before a soldier rushed at him brandishing a piece of metal pipe. Gale stepped into the man's methodical overhead swing, catching his pipe hand and rolling the man's wrist sharply. But instead of the man's body following the motion of the wrist bone, there was a loud snap like a tree branch breaking, and the man's hand flopped at the end of his arm, useless but still clutching the pipe. Both he and the zombie paused for a moment looking at the man's hand, then Gale snapped his right leg nearly straight up and back down against the side of the man's head in a slashing scissors kick. Even before his foot had landed the blow, Gale's attention had moved on to the next opponent, and before the man's body had hit the floor, Gale had quick-drawn with his left hand and fired a single shot into the man's head. His movements a blur, he returned the pistol to his left hip holster, his attention sneaking back to Christopher. His brother was trying hard to push himself to his feet, and he was still staring at the attacking group. Gale took the extra moments and followed his brother's line of sight. He searched the surging crowd, eyes finally landing on who seemed to be the leader of this loosely organized attack. As Gale watched the man move closer, all his emotions melted into raw, undiluted fury. Fixating on the man with the necklace of severed ears, Gale drew down on the Ear Man. Kurt suddenly called out from across the room.

"Shit! Son-of-a-bitch, they're all over me!" Gale twisted to his left and could barely make out Kurt through the crowded, shifting room. He was on the floor, surrounded, and the numbers were getting worse by the second. Gale started shooting with his right hand, his left hand joining a split second later. He was shooting only for their heads now, trying hard to drop a zombie per shot. Gale took a quick peek to his right. Helena and Maggie were more than holding their own, and the Ear Man had stopped just inside the entrance, his head slowly turning from side to side, surveying the action. Gale concentrated on clearing some room for Kurt.

"Helena, Maggie, get to Kurt and retreat back through the research section. Get Tammara and make a run to a shuttle. I'll meet you guys at the shuttle bay." Helena and Maggie started across the room in tandem, clearing enough room for

Helena to help Kurt to his feet and start their way back to research. Helena let Maggie take Kurt, who seemed able to walk but whose right arm hung limp at his side.

"I think it's dislocated," he grimaced, continuing to fire his weapon. Helena made her way near Gale, shouting as she holstered one empty gun and drew another.

"What's the plan?" She received no answer, watching as Gale started forward, the dead beginning to thin under the continuous barrage. "Jefferson? Jefferson!"

"Get to the shuttle," was all he said, his tone a low growl, meeting the charge of a frenzied woman with a powerful right jab, the gun meeting her face with such force that the barrel jammed into an eye socket with a moist sucking sound. She stood there, convulsing as if an electrical current was flowing through her body until Gale's trigger finger flinched and her head shattered like a dropped pumpkin. There was a bloody chunk of brain matter stuck to the pistol, but he slung it off and continued to fire. The Ear Man had moved from his spot toward the main panel. He had a pistol in his hand, and seemed to be focused on the main consul. Or Christopher.

Tammara was on her way out of the research supply room when she heard the explosion. She dropped her small hand held computer and moved toward main medical. As she approached the last set of doors separating the areas, Maggie and a limp-armed Kurt burst through, firing their guns back into what was now a smoke hazed main medical. Zombies swarmed within the haze, their telltale death wail their battle cry.

Maggie put herself against the wall just inside the doorway, as Kurt, looking behind himself as he fired, nearly ran over Tammara.

"They're going to overrun medical. We need to get to a shuttle," Maggie called out. Tammara was stunned for a moment, all of her attention locked into the swirling gray air of medical, and the chaos that lay within. Maggie began to give ground as the flow of living dead pushed its way closer and closer to them. Snapping out of her trance, Tammara started to turn away when a balding, gray haired man caught the corner of her attention. He seemed to notice her, and he directed his awkward stumbling toward her. She peered into the smoky room, losing sight of the man amongst the dense party of zombies for a few seconds, and then he was there, less than twenty feet away, staring at her with those red vampire eyes. Her breath caught in her throat and, despite her fear she felt herself take a trembling half step toward her father. The piece of her mother's flesh still stuck to his jaw, he shuffled forward, raising and extending his arms as if he were inviting a hug.

Maggie glanced at Tammara as she continued to give ground. "What's going on? They're almost on top of us. We gotta go."

Tammara's attention was locked on her dad. She tried to speak, but it came out in a whisper. "That's my father." Maggie continued to fire back into medical, ignoring her very strong urge to drop the advancing man. Another few seconds and he would be on this side of the doorway and just a step or two from being very dangerous. With another glance, Maggie could see the tears welling up in the Avaric nurse's eyes. She tried hard to keep her tone calm and soothing as she spoke.

"He's not your father anymore, Tammara. Your father died back at the colony. Those particles are just playing a nasty trick with his body." Tammara's father was at the threshold. "Don't let him touch you."

Kurt stepped up next to her, his gun down by his side. "Turn away. I'll take care of it." Tammara stepped away from Kurt, closing the gap between her and the man who used to call her Angel and tickled her until she cried. She searched her father's pale face, longing for just one sign, one minute detail to let her know that there was something still left in the forsaken shell of his body. Then Julius Wilder, agricultural systems analyst and ex-father of three opened his mouth and moaned. Soft and low, it was the sound of a cold midnight cemetery breeze, and its total absence of humanity chilled Tammara to the bone. A tear ran down her face and she turned away, putting her face into Kurt's injured shoulder. He bit his lip from the sharp pain, raising his pistol as Mr. Wilder closed to within just a few feet. Kurt seemed to hesitate for a moment, then pulled the trigger, turning away as he did, not interested in the sight. He pulled Tammara tight against him, and they moved back into research. Maggie emptied her gun, stole a last peek to assure herself that Jefferson and Helena were still holding their own, then followed Kurt and Tammara's quick exit.

Gale moved to intercept the Ear Man, but unlike the Merlin soldier, Gale had to fight his way. Halfway to his brother, someone grabbed him from behind in a bear hug, and he could feel the tremendous strength of the man. His body instinctively relaxed, and he let himself drop, slipping through his attacker's grip to the floor. He spun on his back and fired a quick, decapitating shot through the man's chin, only to have to quickly roll out of the way of the massive man's falling body. Gale popped up to his feet, and realized that the Ear Man was going to reach his brother long before he could, and he yelled across the room.

"Christopher! Christopher, look out!" But Gale's brother had been watching the Ear Man approach, and when he was close, Christopher's good eye found Gale. "Christopher!" Gale cried out as the Ear Man raised the gun and fired point blank into Christopher's face.

Gale flinched at the sight of his brother's second and final death, the sound of Christopher's body striking the floor hung in the air, echoing in Gale's ears. He stood staring at the Ear Man for the eternity of several seconds, then watched as the zombie began to manipulate the panel. Gale holstered his guns and charged forward, bulling his way toward his brother's killer. Twenty feet, ten feet, five feet...

Gale jerked the Ear Man around, and slammed a punch into his face, knocking the man with the grotesque necklace onto the panel. Not as fast as a living man, but still quick, the Ear Man reached to the small of his back and pulled out a large, blood-crusted knife, his fingers sliding into the ringlets carved into the handle. He stood slowly, an ugly smile spreading. He glanced at Christopher's body and the smile grew even more. When the Ear Man spoke, his voice was half gurgling, half hiss.

"You look... like him. In the face...before...we had...fun." Gale stood, weight on the balls of his feet, arms loose at his sides. The knife in Ear Man's hand began to cut a slow, lazy figure eight in the air. The smile grew to cartoon proportions. "Now...I can have....fun...with you." Suddenly a cord slipped tight around Gale's neck an instant before the Ear Man lunged. Gale ignored his choker and side stepped into the knife thrust, the large blade sinking up to the hilt into the soft belly of his surprise assailant. Gale reached back and closed his left hand over the Ear Man's knife hand, then slammed the crown of his helmet into the Ear Man's face. There was a nasty crunch, and Gale guessed it came from his brother's murderer' nose, though maybe cheekbone or eye orbit too. He followed it with another butt to the face, driving the Ear Man to let go of the knife and drop to his knees. When he swung his arm up to fire the gun, Gale used his right arm and swept the man's gun arm to the side, the gun firing several feet to the right. Gale suddenly dropped forward to his right knee, flipping his choker over his shoulder and head over heels into the air. The man slammed into the panel face first. Free to move again, Gale sprang to his feet, the Ear Man pulling the gun back around to shoot. Gale used his right leg and snap kicked the gun from the man's hand, and repeated the same fast, powerful kick into the Ear Man's face. The Ear Man sprawled, sliding onto his back, the man with the choking cord sliding off the counter and half falling on top of him. Gale drew a force pistol and blew the head off the choker, then turned and dropped three or four revived soldiers that seemed unsure whether to attack or retreat. A split second later, Gale had made a third, more permanent choice for them. As Gale spun back to face the Ear Man, he saw that Helena was still fighting and more than holding her own at the open doorway, the number of attackers falling steadily to a manageable number. He'd yell at her later for disobeying his direct order.

He took a couple of steps and stood over the Ear Man, for the first time seeing the bloody but readable name patch on his uniform. It read Hopkins, and he knew the name had significance, but the answer would have to wait.

"Get up," he challenged, slipping his gun back into the holster. "I'm not even close to being done with you." Hopkins gathered himself, his narrowed eyes searching for a weapon. He quickly made a half turn and snatched his knife from the chest of his follower. He spat crazy gibberish at the Omni commander.

"Do you know...what kind of gift this...could be...this Devil's doing?" He slashed the knife at Gale, who easily stepped away. Hopkin's face split into that insane smile, his eyes boring into Gale's. "Did you know...brother... pissed himself when...I took...his ears?" His free hand reached to his trophy necklace. "Acted...a little girl...my men...wanted to...fuck him." Hopkins eased forward, his eyes flickering to Gale's right. Gale noted that, expecting an attack from behind to that side, but in the next moment Hopkins made his move, rushing forward, the knife high. Gale sidestepped and met him at the wrist and elbow, snapping both. Using the man's own momentum, Gale executed a simple hip toss. Hopkins tumbled to the floor in a heap, but Gale realized too late that he had played into the deranged man's hands. As he watched Hopkins grab up the gun he had kicked out of his hand earlier, Gale pitched himself to the side, cursing the lack of body armor. The first two shots missed wide, but the third caught him in the helmet, and he marveled at the brilliant blue flash. When his head banged off the floor, the room doubled and began to swim in and out of focus. He didn't feel his body hit the floor and slide, and he couldn't seem to make his arms do more than flop, his hands unable to draw a gun. He was able to see a double image of Hopkins walk slowly toward him, leering like a mental patient on Christmas Day. The Ear Man dropped the gun and used his good arm to pick up his knife. He stood over Gale, his head tilting from one side to the other as if keeping time to music only he could hear. The Ear Man knelt, slowly leaning forward, his putrid breath reaching Gale through the shattered face shield. Hopkins stared, his joker's smile transforming into a taunting pout, then back to a smug leer.

"Can you... see...hell with those...black eyes?" He waited for Gale to answer, but when he got no reply, he continued. "Once...your helmet off...can make you...brother's...twin. Like that?" He leaned even closer, the knife sliding out of Gale's warped sight. "Maybe…I ought to slice…your balls off…first."

"I think I'll be needing those," Helena voiced, and Gale watched the blurred, double images of Hopkin's head explode off his shoulders, the rest of his body flopping to the floor, suddenly a harmless sack of meat. Two superimposed images of Helena stepped into his sight, and for an instant they merged into one, then his stone heavy eyelids closed against his will.

When Gale's eyes fluttered open, he was laying down in his isolation room. The lights were dim, but he was able to see Tammara standing at the foot of the bed. She left the room as he blinked his eyes into focus, and a few moments later, she returned with Helena and Kurt. None of them were dressed in bio-suits, and Kurt's arm was in a sling with a small device clamped to his shoulder. Smiling, Helena sat on the edge of the bed, wasting no time in leaning down and pressing her lips to his. It startled him, and Gale realized that he too was just in his Omni jumper. She pulled away from him, her brown eyes sparkling.

"What's happening? What's…" he burst, his head clearing in a rush. Helena pressed a finger to his lips, cutting him off. "Relax. Everything's under control." She glanced at the others as she sat back. "The particles have dissipated, and the zombies still on their feet are moving around like flies in winter. We've all been inoculated with the antidote, which, according to a small computer journal, is the real deal, developed from the same World Government lab that developed Carnage." Gale blinked, puzzled. Helena continued. "Carnage: the World Government's classified name for the bug. Tammara discovered it in the colony research lab files."

Gale pushed his way up to his elbows, the pain present but not as sharp as he anticipated. His insides were in flux---relieved for the moment that the danger seemed to have passed, yet feeling the crushing weight of the grief from the loss of close friends… As a soldier, he had been trained to separate personal feelings from the results of any assignment to minimize problems. But as his mind began scanning through mental images of Jones and Gii and Pace and Julie, then he could only let all the emotions inside have their way.

By the time he'd regained control, he was alone.

173

PHASE V

Jefferson Gale sat in the Merlin command chair, his eyes staring a hole into the large view screen, a small part of his mind registering the fact they were drawing closer and closer to Earth. Everyone was on the bridge dressed in their bio-suits as they drew within audio/visual range. But most of Gale's attention was focused within, his mind still digesting the aftermath of the mission.

In the days that followed what they referred to as the Resurrection, they were still having problems getting some of the ship-wide systems on-line, which included the internal sensors. Kurt had volunteered to search for their missing crewmates, but Gale had insisted on going. Tammara gave them both a booster, and he and Kurt had set out in their bio-suits, the so-called vaccine circulating through their blood, but they weren't taking any chances. Normal lighting had been restored throughout the ship when they were able to online the life support, so they picked their way through the hold with a hand held scanner set to pick up the base materials of the biohazard suits.

After drawing a blank in the hold, he and Kurt had found Torbeck and T.T. lying side by side in the corridor not far outside it. Jones had been in particularly gruesome shape, and both men had to find something to focus on as they bagged the bodies. It was some time later when they located Pace and Julie, the remains enough to force Gale to turn away. Kurt folded to a knee, a steadying hand on his face shield.

Pace and Julie were in a Maze cube, locked in a grotesque, yet heart wrenching final embrace, Julie pulled tightly into her husband's chest. Neither man had the urge to touch either of them, much less separate them, so they simply covered their bodies with the bags and silently returned to medical.

Gale sat in the Merlin command chair, mulling over how this assignment was really going to end. His mind drifted over the murderous web he himself had unwittingly created with his suicidal grand stand on Mali Pri. He had played a vital role in both the first and second deaths of the Merlin's commander, Captain Hopkins, who himself led the murderous horde that had butchered his brother. Gale had also contributed to the death of Whittington's grandson, which had eventually led to Christopher's ship being assigned to Avaric. If Hopkins hadn't got to him, the virus would have surely taken his life. But even with all that, Gale still thirsted for revenge on Whittington. Even if Christopher hadn't been involved, Gale could not let Whittington get away with the deaths of thousands of people under the guise of weapons testing and revenge. The killing needed to end, but Whittington had to be stopped. But whether the solution meant taking Representative's life had Gale thinking long and hard. He was an ex-soldier, not an assassin.

At least not yet.

As the Merlin neared direct communication range, Gale moved from his chair to the cube. He glanced to Maggie.

"When we're in range, patch directly through to Whittington and connect him to medical." When the others heard Whittington's name, all attention turned to him. "Kurt, bring us to a dead stop once we're in range of the lab, and wait for my orders. Be ready to take us away at max thrust at a moment's notice."

Kurt shrugged at the last statement, smiling grimly. "We only have secondary engine power, but I'll be ready to limp us away." Gale nodded, then left the bridge.

The call wasn't long in coming, and Gale was ready. Maggie soon had Whittington on the line, and after a couple of moments, Whittington appeared on the view screen. He looked tired; his eyes glassy, his wispy, white hair sticking in every direction. Suddenly Gale realized---it was almost 4am Los Angeles time. Whittington forced a smile onto his face, his voice gravelly from sleep.

"Well, welcome back, Mr. Gale. I speak for the entire world when I convey praise for a job well done." Gale wore a cold, blank expression, and he let his shark eyes bore through the politician. Seconds passed, and Whittington's smile faltered when Gale didn't respond, but he continued on with his prepared speech. "I must admit that you had us all concerned when we received word on the various, uh, incidents that forced your late arrival, but the citizens of Earth are delighted to have you all home." Gale could imagine the piped in crowd cheers, and it disgusted and angered him. He didn't reply for a long time.

"I want to talk to you on your private line. Now."

The older man's face wavered and he swallowed nervously. His voice was hushed, but there was an underlining strain when he answered. "There isn't a problem, is there?"

Gale's face remained flat, and he didn't respond. Whittington stared into the screen for a few seconds, finally mumbling, "One moment." The screen went black for nearly a minute before the connection was re-established. Gale guessed the old man went to the bathroom and dropped a stinky load. Whittington was certainly wide awake now, his expression a simmering mix of anger and fear. "What the hell is going on, Mr. Gale?"

The Omni commander took his time answering. "We ran into a few difficulties during the mission that dictated the use of some extreme measures. I lost four of my team on this assignment; four good people that happened to also be good friends." Whittington's face turned ashen, and his angry mask cracked.

"So, what the two of us are going to do is start re-negotiating a few points of our contract. Right now."

Whittington balked, struggling for his composure. He tried to pump some dignity into his voice. "Now see here, Gale, this is not the time..."

Gale cut him off, using the same low monotone. His shark eyes never left the Representative's. "Whittington, our ship will have dozens of world capital news stations waiting to talk to me and the crew about the mission. If you and I can't come to an understanding, I will use the world press to gain the leverage I need to get what we deserve and crucify you in the process." Gale inched his face closer to the screen. "You want to play God? After I'm done with you, I'd love to see your greasy ass political career rise up after three fuckin' days!"

Whittington's face quivered, infuriated from being bullied, but his survival instinct kept his mouth closed. He stayed quiet, waiting for Gale to tip his hand. The Omni commander sat back, the tiniest of evil smiles tugging at the edge of his mouth. "I know all about you and the World Government's involvement with Carnage and Avaric."

A sheen of sweat appeared like magic on the Representative's forehead. He spoke softly, his tone guarded. "What exactly are you talking about?"

Gale knew he had the man by the short and curlies, but he couldn't resist squeezing the old man's balls a little harder.

"I have a disk given to me by Roth; you know, the head councilman on Avaric. You know---the one you bought and paid for." Whittington sat quiet, and seemed to have forgotten how to breathe. He flinched, not once, but twice, and the flesh of his face flushed pink, then seemed to sag in defeat. Neither said a word for nearly a half minute, and then Gale drove the final nail into his coffin, his voice a threatening growl. "I know about your grandson, everything." Whittington's face turned bright red, nostrils flaring, his hands balling into tight fists. The facade was gone, and he yelled into Gale's screen face.

"All right! All right, you murderous son of a bitch! What do you want?"

Gale wanted to say the lives of his four friends and the thousands that suffered and died on Avaric and the Merlin. There was a desperate cowardice showing itself in Whittington's eyes, and Gale prayed the general public would see it before the election. Gale spoke slowly and steadily, not letting his emotions get the better of him.

"I want your personal guarantee that me and the remainder of my crew will be allowed the leave the ship as our contract states, with no delays whatsoever at the lab. I want the bodies of my deceased crew, and of my brother to leave with us. We also have taken on a test subject that I want clearance on, including a change of identity, complete with background history." Whittington's eyes widened but he didn't speak. "I want your guarantee that we will receive our full shares within 48 hours of our return. And lastly, I want my ship replaced ASAP with a new one, nothing better, nothing worse." Gale paused, not able to read beyond the hatred. When Whittington didn't reply, Gale said, "You do still want to be President, don't you?" Whittington's expression slowly melted into that of a condemned man, but with the practiced control of a master politician, Whittington smiled the fake smile of a man on the election circuit. He cleared his voice before speaking, the venom all but dripping from his lips.

"You have my word that all your requests will be met. I have some reservations on how you intend on smuggling the test subject past security, but I'm sure you have a plan. Proceed with your docking at the lab, and I'll have my people begin working on delivering your contract shares." Whittington paused, his eyes flickering as if checking to be sure he was alone. "And about that disk you mentioned...?" Gale shook his head.

"Don't you trust me?" Gale's tone and expression turned ice cold. "It stays with me. Insurance. And I warn you---this mission has made me more paranoid than normal. I see suspicious men hanging around or any of my team thinks they're being followed, the info gets leaked and you'll get what you deserve. Do we understand each other?" Whittington seemed to think a moment, then nodded once. It was obvious the old man didn't want to say the words, but he had to and Gale loved it.

"Yes, we have an understanding."

The two stared at each other, and finally Gale had to ask the question that had been burning inside him since the truth had come out. "If you wanted me dead, why didn't you just hire a hitter? Why kill all those people?" Whittington's face revealed nothing. "What's the real bottom line here? Revenge or credits?" The Representative didn't respond right away, finally leaning closer to the screen as if reluctantly sharing a secret. His voice was a practiced whisper.

"There are two separate topics, Mr. Gale. The first is I loved my grandson. He was all the family I had. Your arrogance and bravado took him from me forever. For that I will not truly smile again until you are cold in ground." His jaw clenched when he said the last sentence. "The Carnage project is merely a product of government research that can be used as trade. The alien government interested in the development of this viral weapon is set to trade us medical technology that could lead to the cure and prevention of cancer. Sometimes sacrifices have to be made for the greater good." He paused for a moment. "The field test was supposed to be contained within the lab facility. The plan was never to directly involve the colony, and certainly not the crew of the Merlin."

Whittington tilted his head just a little. "As much as I'd like to see you dead, even you aren't worth thousands of lives---hero or no. Even you should understand that." Gale stared hard into the view screen, suddenly furious at the casualness of his statement.

"You're a fucking horrible liar for a politician," Gale shot back. "Captain Hopkins told me exactly how many lives it was worth to you to see me dead. In wartime, soldiers are supposed to die, but what happened on Avaric and the Merlin makes you a murderer, no matter how much paperwork you cover your ass with." Gale wanted so badly to spit in the man's face, then beat him bloody. 'I strongly suggest that you and your researchers discover the antidote for Carnage and share it with the world, then call off the warships and the quarantine. No more innocent people are going to die to cover your ass, you twisted fuck. I'll make sure of that." Gale felt like a hawk bearing down on a field mouse. "You know what? Screw you, Whittington. Don't even think about running for World President. The people of earth deserve an actual human being to lead their government. Retire gracefully, or the world discovers the truth behind the Avaric plague, and then you'll have a whole lot of people looking to see you dead. Or worse." Whittington stared flatly from the view screen, looking like a deer caught in headlights. He slowly nodded his head, aging years in just a few seconds. His anger turned into sullen resignation. He broke off the connection. Gale stared at the dark, empty screen, a weary half smile spreading on his face. This ordeal was almost over.

As part of their plan, the Omni crew was escorted off the ship wearing their bio-suits, Star Corp soldiers carrying off the five body bags containing the deceased Omni team members and Gale's brother. When they reached the de-contamination chambers, they were allowed to strip off the suits, tolerating the various forms of physical reentry. It wasn't until they were through that they were able to dress and get to Tammara, who had been carried off the Merlin in one of the body bags. Gale had come up with the idea when they decided to put Pace and Julie in the same bag. Gale and the others all thought that Pace and Julie would have approved of the simple deception. Tammara went into the bag wearing a bio-suit with over 24 hours worth of air.

The Omni crew was allowed to visit with the bodies of their deceased friends, and were granted as much time as they needed. They smuggled in a lab coat and nametag for Tammara, and they all walked out together, Tammara now in the guise of a nurse on the lab station. Because of the haste that the lab was set up and staffed, her new face easily blended in with all the others. Because of her medical background and knowledge of the plague, she fit right in. Then of course when they were all transported back to Earth, she was transferred off the station and back to a major Los Angeles university hospital.

A typical hero's welcome awaited the Omni crew: televised parade and ceremonies. Gale staged one massive press conference and fielded all the questions to ensure no slip-ups. Whittington had their shares credited to their accounts within 24 hours, with Pace and Julie's, Gii's and Jones' all going to immediate families.

The funerals were held as soon as possible, and after their friends were placed in the ground, the remaining crew, with the exception of Helena, took some time off and traveled, leaving Gale to continue to handle the press. And as with all big worldwide events, the hoopla eventually died down, and the world forgot about the Avaric plague and the mission there. The whole ordeal was finally over.

Midnight had come and gone, and the light sweat from their lovemaking had cooled. Helena had drifted to sleep, partially covered by a sheet. Gale had laid awake, watching her at peace, muscular chest and abdominal muscles in a steady rise and fall. She stayed curled against him, Gale admiring the way the thin cover clung to the smooth curve of her hip. An action movie was on the tele-viewer when suddenly a 'SPECIAL BULLENTIN' appeared on the screen. Gale blinked himself more awake as he glanced at his bedside clock. It was just minutes from 1 a.m.

The anchorwoman looked surprisingly crisp and awake, and she spoke in a tone that spelled disaster, even before the blank, light gray backdrop behind her changed to say Murder & Mayhem in the Southland. Of course, there were never special bulletins in the middle of the night alerting the public of good news...

"Good evening. Two stories have sent the Southland into both mourning and panic. The first story involves the tragic assassination of former World Presidential contender and recently retired Representative Conrad Whittington during a speech at a fundraiser at the Getty Museum." The screen behind the anchor changed to footage of the shooting, gunshots scattering a crowded ballroom, an attractive woman wielding a handgun being tackled by heavily armed government agents. Then the screen changed to a photo of the same woman standing side by side with a high-ranking Star Corp officer. Gale blinked at the picture; the man looked familiar... "The assailant has been identified as none other than Danielle Kathryn Teech-Hopkins, widow of Captain Lance Hopkins, commanding officer of the ill-fated Star Corp cruiser

Merlin, whose entire crew perished during the Avaric plague. Even before she was taken into custody, she was yelling information regarding both Whittington's and the government's involvement in the Avaric incident, citing both illegal bio-chemical experimentation and a massive government cover-up. Government officials are calling for an immediate investigation." Gale nudged Helena, but she just murmured and rolled over.

The anchorperson continued her broadcast. "Which leads directly into a breaking story developing at the UCLA university medical facility." The background behind her changed to an aerial overhead shot of the hospital where helicopters, searchlights, and armed local law enforcement were scrambling all over the area. "It has been confirmed at this hour there have been seventeen documented cases of a mysterious viral outbreak whose symptoms match the Avaric plague. At the center of this medical nightmare is Susan Winter, a nurse recently hired at the facility." Gale's mouth dropped open as the background changed again, this time displaying a picture of Tammara, straitjacket bound, stumbling around in a padded cell, eyes bloodshot, drool flying from her mouth as she charged toward the camera spying on her from the small observation window in the door. "Authorities are checking her background as speculation of her and any possible connection to the Avaric colony are explored. It is known that she had been assigned briefly to the orbiting research lab established for study of the Avaric plague, but that she was not on the roster of documented research personnel. Government and local agencies are following up all leads, and the hospital has been completely quarantined until further notice."

His first thought was the vaccine. Had it just been experimental? Had it been thoroughly tested, or had it been tested but the serum had proved less than 100% effective? Or maybe the stuff labeled vaccine was never meant to work...Gale blinked slowly, stopping in mid-breath. It wouldn't have been much of a field test with the antidote so readily available...Cursing, Gale shoved hard against Helena's butt, almost pushing her off the king size bed. He quickly swung his feet to the floor. As Helena questioned what was going on, Gale could hear the distant crash of metal on metal as something big and fast crashed through the iron gate of his home's winding driveway, and he knew there wasn't much time...He heard himself yell at Helena to get dressed right away, knowing that every second was vital. They both heard the downstairs front door rammed off its hinges, and in seconds Gale could hear countless heavy boots marching double time up the stone stairs and Gale knew that it was too late to get away, too late for the both of them... He started to move for the gun under his side of the bed, but didn't bother as a strong voice shouted from outside his bedroom door.

"Jefferson Gale, this is the World Government Armed Forces..." In the next split second, Gale dove for his gun, and his last few seconds passed in vivid snapshots...

The bedroom door exploded...several bio-suited soldiers burst into the room...a soldier stepped forward with tanks strapped to his back...a flash, and a long wide tongue of white and blue flame reaching toward him... Helena's scream...and the sizzle of his own flesh filling his ears...

He woke up screaming, jerking to a sitting position, staring blindly into the coffin darkness of his bedchamber, his flesh still melting off his bones in his nightmare shrouded mind. Despite the efforts of Helena to calm him, Jefferson Gale screamed for a long, long time.

This book is dedicated to my dad James & my sister Faye, both of whom are sharing in this from heaven.

Printed in the United States
102933LV00003BA/179/A